Who Ya Wit':
The Finale

Who Ya Wit':
The Finale

Brenda Hampton

www.urbanbooks.net

Urban Books, LLC
97 N18th Street
Wyandanch, NY 11798

Who Ya Wit': The Finale Copyright © 2013 Brenda Hampton

ISBN 13: 978-1-60162-386-7
ISBN 10: 1-60162-386-0

First Trade Paperback Printing October 2013
Printed in the United States of America

10 9 8 7 6 5 4 3 2 1

This is a work of fiction. Any references or similarities to actual events, real people, living or dead, or to real locales are intended to give the novel a sense of reality. Any similarity in other names, characters, places, and incidents is entirely coincidental.

Distributed by Kensington Publishing Corp.
Submit Wholesale Orders to:
Kensington Publishing Corp.
C/O Penguin Group (USA) Inc.
Attention: Order Processing
405 Murray Hill Parkway
East Rutherford, NJ 07073-2316
Phone: 1-800-526-0275
Fax: 1-800-227-9604

Who Ya Wit':
The Finale

Brenda Hampton

Thanks to all for the continuous support!

Let the struggle to keep *Black Love* alive begin . . .

Chapter 1
Desa Rae

I mean, just where do I begin? Never thought I would be revisiting the whole marriage thing again, but there I was planning every single detail in my head.

At almost forty-five, I didn't want an extravagant wedding. A nice, simple wedding with minimal family and friends would suit me just fine. I was more than thrilled about finding a man who I intended to spend the rest of my life with. Roc was a little over fifteen years younger than I was, but what I had learned over the years was that age was just a number. Roc had way more sense than my ex-husband, Reggie, had. Time and time again, Roc stepped up to the plate to show me just how much he loved me. We, no doubt, had our struggles, but what couple didn't?

After years of trying to fight my issues with him being younger, I finally looked in the mirror, deciding that life was too short to let a decent man pass me by. It wasn't worth it being so angry all the time and I couldn't make the people in my life be the way I wanted them to be. There were certain things about Roc that I was willing to accept. Minor things, like him smoking marijuana, using profanities, referring to his friends as niggas, and hanging with friends who I viewed as bad influences. The way I looked at it was, my love for him had to be strong enough to push those issues aside. I decided to save those concerns for another lifetime. In this lifetime, I would be Mrs. Rocky Dawson and nothing or no one was about to change that.

For the past two and a half months, Roc had been away from me and our four-year-old daughter, Chassidy. He'd been invited to be a participant in a reality show called *Hell House*. It revolved around the last person in the house winning some money, and I thought it would be a good idea for Roc to be a participant. Not specifically for the money, but I saw it as an opportunity for us to inject space into our relationship and for him to get away from some of those no-good friends of his. Roc didn't win the challenge, so he was now back at home. I was so glad about that, only because I had been going crazy without him. It upset me that while he was away, we weren't allowed to speak on a regular basis. But as soon as he came home, I was on a serious high. I'd been on a high ever since and only the Lord knew how much I missed my man.

While sitting in my office at work, I started to day-dream about the day Roc came home.

Chassidy and I just got done with dinner. Afterward, I tucked her in bed and read her a bedtime story. Almost right away, she fell asleep and I turned down the lights in her dolled-up room that was decked out in pink and white. I closed the door halfway, just so I could check on her before I went to sleep. On the way to my bedroom, I stopped in the family room to grab one of my favorite books from a bookshelf. I was in the mood to read it again, and on a Saturday night, I wasn't ready to call it a night. My best friend, Monica, was on a date with her man, and my son, Latrel, and his wife had their own lives. They definitely didn't want to be bothered with me.

With Roc being away, I did what I was accustomed to doing, which was chill at home and get cozy with a book. I got comfortable in my king-sized bed with my back against the headboard. My cotton pajama pants and top felt warm against my skin and my hair was full of curls that were cut into a stylish bob. Since my mouth was dry, I reached over to my nightstand to get a piece of Juicy Fruit gum. After popping the gum into my mouth, I got busy reading.

Nearly fifteen minutes in, I heard a noise that caused my body to stiffen. Every little noise alarmed me, especially since I had a bad encounter with a schoolmate who I invited into my home and trusted that he would do right. That didn't turn out so well, and he wound up being arrested for breaking into my home and assaulting me. The noise I heard sounded like a squeaking door. Since I forgot to set the alarm, I knew that sitting on my butt wasn't going to do any good.

I slowly moved the cover aside and tiptoed out of bed. My gun was tucked away in a shoebox in the closet, so I made my way over to it. I carefully removed the gun, and when I heard another noise that sounded like a floor creaking, my nerves started to rattle. My slippery palms could barely hold the gun that was shaking in my hands. All I could think about was Chassidy. I inched my way down the hallway, noticing that her bedroom door was still cracked how I left it. I glanced down the hallway, seeing a sliver of light coming from the kitchen. After a few more steps, I could see that the refrigerator door was wide open. I didn't know if I should scream or reach for the phone to call the police. I figured they wouldn't get here in time, so I took a deep breath as I moved forward to deal with my intruder.

The kitchen was partially dark and all I could see was his white tennis shoes.

"I have a gun aiming right at you. If you try anything stupid, I swear that I will shoot."

The man eased his hands in the air and slowly stood straight up. That was when I noticed it was Roc. "Now, why would you want to shoot me? All I was doin' was lookin' for some wine so we could celebrate daddy bein' home."

A sigh of relief came over me as Roc smiled, displaying those pearly white teeth and dimples that made my day. I hurried to place the gun on the counter and rushed right into his arms. His grip was tight around my waist as he squeezed me.

"No words can express how happy I am to see you," I said. I held the sides of his handsome face and wasted no time sticking my tongue into his mouth for a little dance.

"Mmmm," he moaned between sloppy, wet kisses. "Maybe I should stay gone this long all the time. I can't remember a time when you were ever this excited to see me."

We were still locked in a tight embrace. Neither of us was ready to let go. "No, I never want you to stay away for that long again. I was going nuts not hearing from you but I, at least, knew you were safe. I definitely want to hear about all of the action inside of Hell House, but tonight is about you and me."

"You're damn right it is and it will always be."

Roc leaned in for another kiss. That was when I pulled on his shirt, tearing it away from his chest that was built like a linebacker's. A few buttons hit the floor and I made a quick mental note to purchase him another shirt for Christmas.

"Ho . . . hold up, ma," he said, backing inches away from me. "I want this to be right. Let me go get out of the rest of my clothes, hit the shower, and then make love to you like I've been dyin' to do."

I ignored Roc. I had waited too long to feel him inside of me again. His hot shower had to be put on the backburner. He knew that we weren't going to follow his plan when I started to unzip his jeans. I also removed my pajamas, giving him a hint. All I had on was a pair of ocean blue silk panties, no bra.

"Shame on me for not being able to wait," I said. "To hell with your shower. I need you right now."

Filled with love and a whole lot of lust, Roc's hooded eyes searched me over. His smile was back again and I didn't have to remove his jeans because he did. He grabbed my waist and backed me up to the counter. After lifting me on top of it, he dropped his head to my breasts and brushed his tongue in between them.

"Have I told you how much I love you yet?" he said.

"No. Not yet. And I've been waiting to hear it, but you seemed more interested in what was in the fridge than coming to the bedroom where you knew I'd be."

"You can be sure that I was comin' there next. But I like it even better that you came to me."

Roc licked his tongue down my stomach and into my navel. I leaned back on my elbows then threw one of my legs over his shoulder. He touched up and down my leg, and then slipped his finger along the wet crotch of my moist panties.

"I can already taste what I'm about to get myself into. My dick aimin' for attention, but my mouth is thirsty for your pussy, too. Decisions . . . decisions."

It didn't matter to me either way where he ventured to first. But as soon as I thought about his tongue entering me, the phone rang in my office. My thoughts about our night together went straight out the window. I could still feel my coochie doing a number on me, so I crossed my legs and snatched up the phone.

"Desa Rae Jenkins. How may I help you?"

"You can help me by bein' on time for dinner tonight. How late are you workin'?" Roc asked.

I couldn't help but to smile. Almost every day that I left work, I had a caring, sexy, and good-looking man to go home to. Unfortunately, sometimes he stayed the night at his house, too. "I'm leaving on time today. I assume you're cooking dinner for us and I promise not to be late."

"Your assumption would be on point. I'm pickin' up Chassidy from school in about an hour, and then I'm takin' her to Monica's house for the weekend. When you get home, ma, you're all mine for the next three days."

"Is that so?" I teased. "I get to stay with you for the whole weekend? Please tell me what you're going to do for an entire weekend to keep me busy."

"I can show you better than I can tell you. I'll also say that you won't be disappointed."

"I have a feeling that I won't be either. Give Chassidy a big kiss for me and tell her I'll see her Sunday."

"Will do. Now, hurry home."

Roc ended the call. I looked at the round clock on the wall, seeing that it was almost three o'clock. I had two hours to waste, so I got busy looking over student information forms that needed to be filled out correctly.

Almost four months ago, several departments at St. Louis Community College downsized. Two executives cut their staffs and they were now in the same department with me and my boss, Mr. Anderson. There was so much for me to do that I was offered a promotion and was now the lead administrative assistant for our department. The other two ladies now reported to me. It was my responsibility to delegate work and assign certain duties that came from the executives. I loved how everything flowed well in our department. With the other ladies working just as hard as I was, I couldn't have asked for a better staff.

For the next hour or so, I worked on the student information sheets. I couldn't keep my mind off Roc, so I started thumbing through a Belize travel brochure. We talked about going there for our honeymoon, or to Hawaii. Nothing was confirmed yet, and I hadn't even set a wedding date. I was thinking more like late spring or early summer, possibly May. That was less than seven months away, so there was plenty of time to figure out honeymoon plans.

As I indulged in the brochures, there was a knock on my door. When I looked up, I saw Shawna peek her head inside.

"Do you mind if I take off?" she asked. "My work is done and I have a busy weekend ahead of me with my son's birthday party."

"Sure, Shawna. I'll see you Monday. Tell Devon I said happy birthday."

Shawna said that she would and left. Shortly thereafter, Paula came into my office and asked if she could leave too. I saw no reason why she couldn't, especially since Mr. Anderson, Mr. Lowe, and Mr. Gibson were already gone for the day. I, however, stayed around until five to make sure there were no issues in our department. There weren't, so I snatched up my purse and keys, and rushed home to my Roc. Unfortunately for me, when I got there, he was nowhere in sight.

Chapter 2

Roc

Talk about somebody who was glad to be back on my turf—I definitely was. *Hell House* was fun while it lasted, but I was ready to get the fuck out of there and back to reality.

Life with Desa Rae was peaceful. I'd been home for almost two weeks now, but only a few people knew I was here. Most of the time, I stayed at Desa Rae's house, but stayed at my crib a few nights to make sure my cousin, Andre, had been handling his business like he was supposed to. I let him chill at my place because he had no other place to go. Neither of his parents was around and I was tired of him always running to my grandmother for everything. It seemed like Dre and me were becoming what me and Ronnie used to be. Dre looked up to me, as I once did Ronnie. I undeniably had Dre's back and it was no secret that he needed some guidance.

After I dropped off Chassidy at Monica's house, I decided to make a quick stop at my crib, just to make sure everything was good. The music thumping through the speakers in my SUV was booming. I stopped at a red light on the corner of New Halls Ferry Road and Lindbergh. My head was bobbing to the beat of the lyrics, but when I heard a horn I turned my head to the side. Inside of the car beside me was a chick I knew from high school, Trinay. I lowered my window to holla.

"What's up, Rockster?" she said. "Looking good, with yo' fine self. I knew that was you over there."

"You lookin' good too, shorty. Stay up and I'll holla another time."

I hit her with deuces and accelerated so I wouldn't miss the light. Through my rearview mirror, I could see her following me. But, I would be the first to say that I was in no way interested in hooking up with nobody. I was with the woman I loved and the one I intended to spend the rest of my life with. Aside from the one unfortunate incident during my *Hell House* stay, I was done creeping on Desa Rae. I felt bad behind that shit, and over time, I realized just how fucked up my actions were. My mind had been flooded with the thoughts of what happened between me and a chick named Chase. What we had done was on my mind as I drove to my crib.

Chase didn't know how to get high, so I provided blow-by-blow details. She did exactly as I told her, and from there it was smooth sailing.

"There you go, ma. That's how you do that shit," I said with a slow nod.

She took another puff from the joint then another. I could see her eyelids getting heavy, but I was sure that the feel of my arms around her waist made her comfortable. She gave the joint back to me and watched as I finished it off.

"I feel lightheaded," Chase said, giggling.

"That's because it's workin'."

It was working for me too, so I got up to remove my wife beater. "It's hot as hell in here," I said. "That air conditioner ain't about nothin'."

Chase fanned herself with her hand. "Even if it was, I'd still be hot."

Following my lead, Chase stood to remove the yellow T-shirt she had on that was cut above her midriff. She also took off her jeans, leaving her in a nude-colored bra and panties. The room was partially dark, but I could definitely see her curves and gap that wanted to be filled. My eyes narrowed then I sat back on the couch, continuing to scan her curves.

"I wasn't talkin' about yo' kind of hot. Put your clothes back on before you start somethin' up in here," I said.

"Duh, that's what I want to do. And just so you know, our definitions of hot are different."

Chase straddled my lap to face me. Her arms fell on my broad shoulders, but knowing that Desa Rae wouldn't approve of this, I didn't want to touch Chase.

"I'm not mad at you for comin' up with your own definition, but we need to cool out with all these teasin' tactics," I said.

"How about you cool out and I go ahead and do me?"

My lips were clamped shut as Chase slithered down to the floor and got on her knees in front of me. She maneuvered her way in between my legs and tugged at the string on my sweatpants.

"Why you fuckin' with me, ma?" I said in a soft voice. "I already told you what was up."

"Yeah, you did. But don't be upset with me for trying to relax your mind and, for one day, relieve you of some of the overwhelming stress you've been under."

I didn't respond, so she assumed I was down for whatever. I watched as she carefully eased my dick out of my sweats, watching as it flung out long, thick, and hard as a piece of steel.

Chase secured my pipe with both hands then dropped her head into my lap to go to work. My muscle stretched her mouth wide. Deep throating me was near impossible, but she put forth every effort to bring me pleasure. Every inch of me was covered with her dripping saliva. I tried to fight it, but I couldn't keep still. I squeezed the back of her neck and pumped her mouth like it was a hot pussy.

"Daaaam," I said in a whisper. "Do that shit, girl."

Chase planned to do it, but not with my sweats on. She backed away from my goods to lower my sweats. I helped, and I also stood to remove my shoes. I even reached over to assist Chase with removing her bra and panties. And after we both were naked, I relaxed back on the couch, propping one leg on the table and stretching my other leg on the couch. With easier access, Chase got back on her knees and scooted in between my legs. This time, she added my balls to the mix, rolling them around in her mouth. Her slick hands massaged up and down my shaft, but most of the attention was given to my head.

"Mmmm," I moaned. "I'm about to turn loose on yo' ass if you keep that shit up."

Chase hurried to bring me to her justice, and when I let loose, she swallowed every last drop.

"Fuck," I shouted while squeezing my muscle. "This muthafucka feelin' hyped!"

It didn't take long for my goods to rise to the occasion again. Chase rolled a condom on my dick, but before she made another move, I positioned her in a sixty-nine position on top of me. She felt my cool breath blow on her pussy lips and giggled.

"My move." I dove right in with the tip of my tongue. I was flicking her clitoris so fast that she tried to jump away from me.

"Your move is working," she screamed out. "My clit is too sensitive right now, so you need to make another move. Please."

I ignored her. The only things that eased inside of her were my cold fingers that I circled and jabbed to bring down juices. Her insides were gushing because I lapped on her pussy juice like a thirsty dog. Her moans sounded like she wanted to cry, but the tears didn't come then. They came a few minutes later when I laid my warm body on top of hers and secured one of her legs around my back. With her other foot resting on the floor, I circled my chunky head around her hair-free slit then busted it wide open. Her body stiffened.

"Oh . . . my . . . God," she shouted and gasped to catch her breath. She could barely move with me inside of her, but I worked her over like a professional pussy eater and beater. She couldn't hang and got at me like an amateur.

"I want an apology," I said between each hard stroke. "Say you're sorry for treatin' me ill."

She didn't want to say it, but she had to, thinking I would ease up. "Sorry," she strained to say. "So sorry."

I kissed her cheek, but didn't let up. My strokes were backed up by a rhythm that kept tickling her insides. To calm her shakes, she took deep breaths and brushed up and down my muscular back with her fingertips. I continued to go hard, and as my pace picked up, she grabbed my ass and sunk her nails into it. That made me slow down a bit, but not for long. I removed her leg from around my back, and poured it over my shoulder. That made her more uncomfortable because she wiggled around.

"Thi . . . this really and truly hurts," she cried out.

I lowered my head to peck her lips. My lips smacked her cheek again; then they eased over to her ear where I licked around it. "I know it hurts, but if you work with me, this will feel so much better to you," I said.

Silence soaked the room for a while. I continued to fuck the shit out of Chase while watching her pretty breasts wobble around from my hard thrusts. She kept grunting, moaning, and groaning.

"Rooooc," she said softly. "You don't even have to go there with me like this, do you?

I gave her some relief when I lowered her leg from my shoulder then relieved her of my twelve inches. I could feel so much wetness on my shaft, but I ordered her to turn over. Pain or not, she seemed ready for more.

That day, I proved that I didn't have a gentle bone in my body when it came to Chase. I smacked her ass as she backed it up to me and spread her cheeks so I could enter her from the back. This time, with each thrust I pushed her forward. She tried to fight back, but her efforts had failed. I manhandled the hell out of her, and in less than five more minutes in, she was defeated. Her toes curled, her breathing increased and her next orgasm brought about one big creamy mess between her legs. She was spent after that, but to no surprise, I wasn't. I lifted her from the couch and sat her on the coffee table. She was still a sticky mess, but I sat in front of her and picked up a lighter.

"What's up with the lighter?" she asked, watching the flame flicker in front of me.

I didn't answer, but instead I picked up the joint and told her to rest back on her elbows.

She leaned back on her elbows and watched as I took two hits from the joint. I held the smoke in my mouth then leaned into her pussy and slowly released the smoke. Some of the smoke escaped in the room, but I could tell that the way I blew on her coochie felt good because her eyelids fluttered. I did it one more time, but the last time, I blew smoke inside of her. Then, with a long drag I sucked her wet pussy, as if I was sucking the smoke back in.

"Ain't nothin' better than weed and some good pussy, ma," I said. "Thanks for relaxin' me."

I damn near ate Chase alive, like only a thug like myself could do. And after the oral sex session had wrapped up, we were back to fucking again. This time, her legs were wrapped around my waist and I stood up, handling her with ease.

"Who in the fuck let you out of the house," she said, panting.

"Just hold on tight," I said in a calm voice. "Magic is about to happen."

After we came together, I took my ass to bed and hoped that none of that ever got back to Desa Rae. Hoping and praying that it wouldn't, I cranked up the music in my truck and headed to my house. As soon as I pulled up, all I saw outside was three young brothers who I didn't know. Dre had the hood to his car up and they all stood near him. One was smoking a cigarette and he flicked it into my grass. The other was cussing his ass off about something that happened and the other dude was ignoring everybody while texting. Dre just turned twenty-one and the fellas with him looked to be around the same age or younger.

I parked my truck on the street and tugged on my hanging jeans to pull them up. My gray tank shirt had my muscles on display, as well as the numerous tattoos that covered my arms. Like always, my coal black waves were flowing and my thin, sharply cut beard had been trimmed by one of the best barbers in St. Louis, Spanky.

"What's up, Dre?" I said, smooth walking up the driveway. I assumed the fellas with him had been in and out of my crib while I was away. But I told Dre that if anything ever came up missing, I was going after him.

Dre gave me dap. "Nothin' much," he said, wiping sweat from his forehead with the back of his hand. "Just tryin' to get my car to show me some love. I didn't know you were stoppin' by. Had I known, I would've cleaned the place up."

"You know I ain't no tidy nigga, but I hope you didn't mess up things too bad. If you did, all I'ma say is clean it up. Get these lazy partners of yours to help you."

I mean mugged his friends, and as I made my way to the door, I heard one of them ask Dre if I was talking about him, referring to my lazy comment.

"Yeah, fool, I was talking to you," I said, answering the question for Dre and boldly walking up to his friend. "You got a problem with what I said?"

His face twisted from anger. "I do have a problem, nigga. You don't know me, do you?"

I moved face to face with the youngster who had big balls. "I don't have to know you or know your name. What I do know is that you thumped your cigarette butt in my grass. That's some lazy shit right there, so since you want to open your mouth and beef about it, go get it up. If not, watch me stir my foot in yo' ass."

I was waiting for this chump to jump bad, but Dre had sense enough to pull his friend away from me.

"Nigga, you trippin'," Dre said, tugging at his arm. "Didn't I tell you about my cousin, Roc? I don't think you want to go there with him."

"Nope, especially not today," said another one of Dre's friends. "And just so you know, I don't have yo' back on this. You're on your own, if you do or say somethin' stupid."

Dre's friend snatched away from his grip and continued to glare at me behind his beady eyes. "I don't need any of y'all to have my back and I don't care who he is. If he wants respect he needs to give it."

I hated for people to talk shit, especially when they were on my turf. I was so sure that this fool had probably been in my house, drinking my water, sucking up air, and eating my food. There he was out here talking about respect.

He attempted to walk away, but I grabbed the back of his fat neck and squeezed it. My nails pinched his skin and I could tell it hurt because he was squeezing his watered-down eyes.

"Before you leave, get that cigarette out of my grass." I spoke through gritted teeth. "After that, don't bring yo' ass over here again."

This punk tried to elbow me in the stomach. I jumped back and quickly tripped him to the ground, where he fell to his knees. The other two brothers stood back, speechless. Dre, however, pleaded for me to let the dude go.

"Don't hurt him, Roc," he said, trying to get my attention by standing in front of me. He knew me all too well. "He don't know no better."

"People who don't know better need to be taught lessons."

I lifted my foot, kicking the youngster as hard as I could in his midsection. The hard blow caused him to gasp and double over to grab his stomach.

"Yo . . . you trippin'," he strained to say. "It's just a damn cigarette butt."

"Exactly. And it wasn't the cigarette as much as it was your slick mouth. Go get the cigarette out of my grass before I go inside to get my gun. When that touches my hand, I always have an urge to make use of it."

It didn't take long for big mouth to crawl in the grass and pick up the cigarette butt. After that, I made my way inside and I heard Dre ask his friends to jet.

"Holla at me tomorrow," he said. "I need to get at Roc."

You damn right he did, especially when I went inside and saw how messed up my crib was. The first time I stopped by it wasn't so bad. But this time it looked like somebody had thrown a party and forgot to clean up.

Dre came inside with his head hanging low. He was kind of on the chubby side, and with his clothes being extra big he looked slouchy. He wore a mini-afro, but always kept it trimmed. I sat on the arm of the couch with my arms folded while listening to his excuses.

"See, before you say anything, I was gon' straighten the place up as soon as I got my car started. But then I started thinking that you could call one of yo' boys from the shop and have them bring a tow truck to get my car. If they can handle that, then I can get started on cleanin' up yo' crib. I invited some fellas over to play cards and, as you can see, we had a good time."

My eyes shifted around the room at empty cooler bottles and smoked blunts in ashtrays. Several pieces of clothing were strewn over two chairs, and an empty box of Church's Chicken, along with paper plates with bones on them, were on the table.

"Looks like one hell of a card game went on, but at least you ain't out in the streets causin' trouble. As for yo' so-called friends, get rid of those niggas—they trouble. I know trouble when I see it and those fools don't have your back. I'll call Butch at the shop so he can come get your car. Meanwhile, clean my shit up."

Dre did as he was told. I called Butch to come get Dre's car, but Butch held me up on the phone.

"You back," he said. "When you get back? We sholl been missin' you around here and things been chaotic. We didn't know where you had gone to."

"Craig knew where I was and I left him in charge. I've spoken to him since I've been back and he told me everything was all good. If I find out he lied to me, it's gon' be some shit."

"I'll let him talk to you about that, but I'm on my way to get Dre's car. Will you be there when I get there?"

"No, I won't be. I'm tryin' to get out of here so I can get back to my woman. And as far as this conversation goes, it didn't happen. You haven't spoken to me and you don't know where I'm at. I'm still MIA. I do not want my phone ringin' anytime soon, and I'll be at the shop sometime next week."

"Cool," Butch said. "Tell Dre I'll be there soon."

I ended the call, but dialed out to call Craig. A part of me was worried that he hadn't told me the truth about what had been going on at the shop. He didn't answer, so I left a message for him to hit me back.

I went into the kitchen, where Dre was putting dishes in the dishwasher while listening to music on his headphones. He removed them when he saw me.

"I'm out," I said. "I'm spendin' the entire weekend with Desa Rae, so don't call me unless it's urgent. Tell no one that I'm back and be sure to put that yale you got in the bathroom in a safe place. If the police bust up in here, yo' ass goin' to jail, not me."

Dre nodded and cracked his knuckles. "I can handle that. And I appreciate you for makin' that call for me. Appreciate everything you've done for me, for real. I owe you for this."

"We family, so we don't owe each other nothin'. Just do like I tell you to do because the last thing I need is heat comin' my way."

I left the kitchen and looked down at my watch. It was after six o'clock and I was sure that Desa Rae had beat me to her house. So much for the dinner that was supposed to be on the table, ready for me to feed to her. That wasn't going to happen and I was sure she would let me know how I had disappointed her again.

Chapter 3
Desa Rae

I couldn't believe that when I got home Roc was nowhere to be found. The first thing I did was call Monica to be sure that Chassidy had made it there. She had made it, and Monica said that Roc dropped Chassidy off around 3:30 p.m. I spoke to Chassidy and after chatting with Monica for a while, I ended the call to contact Roc. He didn't answer his phone.

Normally, I'd get upset, but what I'd learned was that there was always an explanation for everything. I promised that I would always give Roc an opportunity to explain himself, legitimate or not, before tearing into him.

Around six forty-five, he rushed into the house, bringing an instant smile to my face. I was in the kitchen, but had just got done calling a Chinese restaurant to deliver food. I had also cut into one of my favorite cheesecakes that was on top of the counter. It was placed inside of a white box with a purple bow around it. I had already closed the box to make sure it didn't look tampered with.

"Sorry for bein' late," Roc said. "I stopped by my crib and got tied up with Dre and some of his partners. His car wouldn't start so I had to call Butch to come get it."

I nodded and tried to wash the cheesecake remnants down my throat. When Roc moved in for a kiss, all I did was peck his lips.

"I figured it was something," I said, hurrying to back away. "I called your phone, but you didn't answer."

Roc searched into my eyes then crossed his arms. "Please tell me that you didn't."

I played clueless. "Didn't what?"

"You did, didn't you?"

"Roc, I don't know what you're talking about. What is it that I did do, or was supposed to have done?"

He shook his head and moved me aside to get to the cheesecake box behind me.

"What's in there?" I asked, as he opened the box and saw a slice missing.

He let out a deep sigh. "Why did you ruin my surprise?

My mouth dropped open. "Now, that's a shame. You really need to take that back to where you bought it. How they gon' give you a cake with a slice missing?"

"A big slice, too. But the question is, how you gon' stand yo' fine-ass, sexy self right there, in my favorite navy blue suit that's huggin' all of yo' curves and lie about it? I should be mad at you for lyin' to me, but you're so damn sexy I can't be."

"I should be mad at you for not being here when I got here. But you always make me forget about how mad I am when I see you. So, I tell you what. Let's call it a truce and get ready to chow down on this Chinese food when it gets here."

Roc backed me up to the counter, grinding his goods against mine. "How long do we have until the food gets here? I say let's get naked now, so I can knock off this hard on I got. We can save the Chinese food for later."

"The delivery is pretty quick, so I don't think we have time. Besides, the food will get cold if we don't eat it right away and I'm starving."

Before Roc could respond, his cell phone rang. I hadn't heard it ring until today. He looked to see who it was.

"I need to get this," he said, backing away from me. He put the phone up to his ear. "Speak," he said, then paused to listen. "Naw, I just called to see if everything was good. I hollered at Butch today and he told me the opposite of what you said. Said that things were chaotic." Roc paused again then I could hear him interrupting the caller. "Look, Craig. None of that matters. I trust you and I expect for my shop to be in order when I get there. If you say it's already in order then we're good. If not, we gon' have a problem. See you on Wednesday and, until then, please don't call and bug me unless it's urgent."

Roc placed the phone on the counter then reached for my hand. We walked over to the table, and after he sat down in a chair, he put me on his lap.

"Is everything okay with the shop?" I asked while watching him remove my heels.

"I'm not concerned about the shop right now. I'm focused on my future wife." He dropped my shoes on the floor and started to undo my blouse.

"Oh, yeah, right. Her. The one who ate the cheese-cake," I said, teasing him. "It was so delicious, too, and thank you for being so kind to me."

"You're welcome. I'm always gon' be kind to you. And just wait until we get married. When you become Mrs. Roc Dawson, it's gon' be on."

"So, are you saying that I'm going to really get the special treatment then?"

"Yes. The extra special treatment and then some."

I stretched my arms in the air and playfully cheered. "Yaaay! I can't wait! I'm so excited and I hope to God that you don't get sick of me."

"Never," Roc said, squeezing my waist. He puckered for a kiss and we indulged ourselves for quite some time.

When the doorbell rang, I got up to get it. I paid the Chinese man for our food and carried it to the kitchen table. Roc had already started to get plates from the cabinet. He set the table and poured red wine in two glasses. After he washed his hands, he dimmed the lights and lit a candle, placing it in the middle of the table.

"Have a seat," he said, pulling my chair back for me. "Don't get used to me doin' all of this, but I had to make tonight special."

"You make every night special by being you. I think I'm in love with you for being just the way you are."

Roc insisted that I take a seat, so I did. He then put the Chinese food on our plates and sat in a chair close to me. He scooted in closer, then picked up his flute glass of wine. I lifted mine too.

"Let's drink to Black Love finally makin' a comeback. I got a feeling that it's here to stay and we gon' ride this shit to the end," he said.

"To eternity."

I clinked my glass with his. We got busy on eating dinner, but when the subject changed to Roc telling me about all that had happened while he was away, he really didn't want to discuss it. Actually, he hadn't said much about *Hell House* at all, except for bits and pieces that he would speak on every now and then. I just knew he'd rush home to give me more details.

"On a for-real tip, ma, I really don't want to talk about it," he said. "I almost won, but I didn't. And you know how I don't like to lose."

"I understand all of that, but when I spoke to you that one time, it sounded as if you were having fun."

Roc wiped his mouth with a napkin while chewing his food. "Fun was not exactly what was expressed in my voice when I called to speak to you."

"Then what was it? I thought you were happy to talk to me."

"I was, but I'm not gon' sugarcoat nothin'. Reggie answerin' your phone that day had me swoll. I didn't like it. I've been here for a little over two weeks now, and not once has he called. When I left here, there were eleven beers in the fridge. Now, there are only six. I know you or Chassidy don't drink beer."

My brow rose. I was surprised to hear Roc's concerns about Reggie being here while he was away. Reggie and I were a done deal and Roc had nothing whatsoever to worry about. The last time I hooked up with Reggie was at Latrel's basketball game. Roc and I were having some difficulties in our relationship, and after a few drinks, one thing led to another with Reggie. We both agreed that having sex was a big mistake. His recent visit was all about him being able to spend as much time as possible with our son, Latrel. He and his wife now lived in Texas, so they rarely visited.

"I'm stunned to hear how upset you are about Reggie being here. I wish you would've said something to me about your feelings because trust me when I say you have nothing to worry about. Reggie is all about my past. The future is here with you."

Roc continued to eat, ignoring my comment. Something was bothering him, and I wanted to see if his attitude only arose when I mentioned his time away.

"You never did tell me, were there any cute girls in the house?"

His eyes shot up and he looked in my direction. "Nah, not really. None as fine as you."

I played it off and laughed. "I'm sure they weren't, but I assume there had to be some decent-looking women there, right? And by the way, how many were there?"

Roc laid his fork down and chewed. He swallowed then sucked his teeth. "Three. Three women who worked my damn nerves. Fine or not, I wasn't interested."

Roc's demeanor and tone disturbed me, bothered me so much that I continued to push. "I'm sure you weren't interested, but what else happened in that house? What did everyone do to pass the time away, and did anybody hook up?"

This time, Roc cocked his neck from side to side, but he didn't look at me. "No. Nothing like that happened and all we did was play games, work out, eat, swim . . . you know, all that kind of stuff."

"I see. But did you—"

I couldn't believe when Roc cut me off. "Ma, listen. I really don't want to go into details about what happened while I was away. I met some people who I didn't necessarily get along with. You know that everybody ain't down with how I do things, so I found myself havin' plenty of confrontations. For now, I'm home and all I want you to concern yourself with is us. Nothin' else matters but you, me, Chassidy, and Li'l Roc."

I said nothing else and switched the subject to what Chassidy and his son, Li'l Roc, who was several years older than Chassidy, had been doing while Roc was away. Li'l Roc had a different mother, Vanessa. We barely got along, so I assumed that Roc didn't want to hear about my gripes with her either. I discontinued our conversation about his time away, but his reaction made me curious to find out more details.

Chapter 4

Roc

Desa Rae kept on bugging about what had happened while I was away, but I was glad that after dinner the other night she seemed to put it to rest. That was good news to me. Now, it was time for me to get back to the real business, which was my mechanic shop.

Desa Rae had taken a few days off from work. After we dropped Chassidy off at school, we headed to my shop to see what was up. Once upon a time, Desa Rae wouldn't be caught dead in my hood. She didn't even know that mechanic shop existed, but that all changed. She'd become more supportive of me and my career, and she got along better with my friends. She didn't necessarily approve of them, but just for me she was willing to put her ill feelings aside.

I parked my SUV down the street from my shop. There was nowhere else to park because so many cars were lined up to be serviced. Like always, a bunch of fellas were hanging around out front. Some talking, some laughing, some smoking, while others were cussing. I noticed Desa Rae take a deep breath as I reached for her hand. We then made our way across the street together.

"Wait up," she said, clacking her high heels on the ground. I was walking too fast because I was eager to get inside. With tight leather pants on that looked painted on her curvy hips, she looked spectacular. The royal blue sweater she wore matched her five-inch stilettos that gave her much height. I was happy to have such a beautiful full-figured woman by my side who would ultimately become my wife.

Some of the fellas nudged each other when they saw me coming. I often complained about so many niggas hanging around, only because the constant loitering had to be bad for business.

"What up, playa?" Junebug said, reaching out to slap his hand against mine. Several others were riding my nuts too.

"What you bring us back?" Lawrence asked. "I know you ain't come back here empty-handed."

"Do I look empty-handed to you?" I said, lifting up Desa Rae's hand with mine. "Y'all fools better acknowledge my woman before y'all say anything else to me."

They all spoke to Desa Rae. With a blushing smile on her face, she spoke back and we went inside. The first thing I saw was a crackhead-looking lady arguing with my boy, Troy, who was behind the counter.

Her dry lips were cracked and her goose-like neck was rolling. "All I'm sayin' is my car broke down on the highway one day after y'all told me the problem was fixed. Either give me my damn money back, or somebody up in here gon' buy me a new car."

"That ain't gon' happen," Troy said as a matter of fact. "And I told you that you gon' have to leave yo' car for a few hours so we can check it out and see what's wrong with it."

"I'm not leavin' my car nowhere. Get me the manager up in here so he can tell you to give me my money back."

I could tell that Troy just about had it with the woman, along with her ridiculous request and attitude. He looked over her shoulder at me. I loosened my hand from Desa Rae's and stepped up to the woman.

"What can I help you with?" I asked.

Her head snapped around and her bugged eyes searched me from head to toe. "Damn, yo' black ass is fine. Are you the manager, though?"

All I did was nod.

"Well, uh, I brought my car in here to be fixed and when I got on the highway it broke down. I want my money back, or somebody gon' have to buy me a new car."

"Unfortunately, I can't buy you a new car, but give me a chance to make it right for you. I'll put one of my best mechanics on it right away to see what's up."

She put her hand on her hip and expressed dissatisfaction with what I'd said.

"The problem is, I don't have all damn day. Y'all motherfuckers in here be playin' too much with people's cars. All I want is my money back."

My face twisted from the smell of her alcoholic breath and her tone rubbed me the wrong way. "I'm not givin' yo' money back, at least not until I've had a chance to see what's up with yo' car. Have a seat and I'll do my best to let you know the status of yo' car in ten to fifteen minutes."

The woman stomped away, mouthing and rolling her eyes. She plopped down in an orange chair and started talking smack to another woman next to her.

I held out my hand to Troy. "Let me see her invoice."

He handed it over to me. "She had almost three hundred dollars' worth of work done on her car. Craig worked on it. You may need to holla at him to see what he did."

"Where he at?"

"He should be in yo' office, or in the shop area."

I turned to Desa Rae. "Come on," I said.

She followed me as I made my way down the narrow hallway that was stacked with new tires and shining rims.

"Did she have to be so rude?" Desa Rae asked. "Some people are just out of control."

"All day. Every day. But I'm used to it."

There were several more people sitting in the back area, waiting for their cars to be serviced. When I looked inside of my office, I could see Craig through the squared glass windows. His feet were propped on my desk and the phone was pushed up to his ear.

I frowned and pushed on the door to let his ass have it.

"Get off my muthafuckin' phone and remove yo' funky feet from my goddamn desk."

Craig slammed the phone down and jumped to his feet. "I . . . I was on the phone with the parts manager at Car Quest. What's up, boss? Good seein' you."

"Save the bullshit. I got customers out there complainin' and lookin' irritated because they ain't gettin' in and out of here. What's with this?" I gave Craig the invoice in my hand. "Did you work on her car?"

He looked at the invoice and nodded. "Yeah, I did. What's the problem?"

"The problem is she out there complainin' and wants her money back. If I have to up one damn dime, that shit comin' out of yo' paycheck. Right now, you need to get yo' fat ass out of my office and go see about her car. If I find out all you've been doin' is sittin' up in here, we gon' have some problems."

"No, we won't, because I've been handlin' mine. Let me go check out her car and I'll be back."

Craig rushed out of my office, turning sideways to squeeze his potbelly by Desa Rae as she stood in the doorway. At least he had sense enough to speak.

"Come in and sit down," I said to Desa Rae while looking around at my junky office. My desk was cluttered with papers and the three chairs inside had newspapers and mechanic books on them. I removed them so Desa Rae could take a seat.

She sat down and crossed her legs. "Did you have to be so mean to Craig? You about scared that poor man to death."

"He knows how we get down. And in no way am I mean to these fools. They be gettin' over."

I looked out the glass windows where I could see into the shop area. Two of my mechanics, Gage and Romo, didn't look busy.

"Ma, chill for a minute," I said to Desa Rae. "I'll be right back. Can I get you anything?"

"Yeah, bring me a soda back. I'm thirsty."

I left my office and went into the shop area. Most of my boys were working and Craig had already pulled the irate woman's car into the garage.

"Listen up," I shouted in the noisy shop area where hip hop music was playing. "I need all of these cars to be cleared out of here in the next thirty minutes. If you're standin' around with nothin' to do, pitch the fuck in and help the next man get done. If these cars ain't out of here in thirty minutes, all of y'all niggas fired. Don't be no fool and try to call my bluff because you will be ass out."

Some laughed, some got busy.

"Welcome home, Roc," Gage said.

I gave him dap and hollered at some of the others who seemed glad to see me.

"You were gone for too long," Romo said. "We thought you had run off and gotten married."

"Or went in hidin'," Butch added.

"Why would I be in hidin'? I just needed a break from all this laziness around here."

"Then stop talkin' and let us get to work, before you fire us. Thirty minutes ain't a lot of time," Romo said.

I looked at my Movado watch. "Twenty-five minutes. Handle that."

I went over to where Dre's car was and talked to Butch about what was going on with it. He said it needed a new carburetor and spark plugs.

"Okay, then fix it," I said with a shrug. "Why ain't it fixed?"

Butch tucked his dirty work gloves in his back pocket and wiped sweat from his forehead. "Because I didn't want to order the parts without yo' permission. You said not to call you unless it was urgent so I figured I would wait."

"That's what's up, but Dre is family. Go ahead and handle that so he can get his car back. Call him, too, so he can come up here and help you work on it."

Butch nodded and walked away to call Dre and to order the parts. I went to check on Craig, who was looking underneath the hood of crack mama's car.

"What's the verdict?" I put my hands into the front pockets of my boot-cut jeans. "Her fault or ours?"

"To me, I'd say her fault. Looks like somebody's been tamperin' with these hoses and the brackets came loose. It's a minor fix, but I know damn well that I tightened these things. Besides, loose hoses won't cause her car to stop on the highway. She loosened that shit up before she came here."

Craig tightened the hoses and turned the ignition to start the car. He left it running for a while then turned it off. "She said it wasn't runnin', but I drove it around the block before bringin' it in here. Looks like somebody just want her three hundred dollars back so she can go get high."

I slapped my hand against Craig's. "Call that trick to the shop area so I can tell her what's up. Better yet, go get her."

Craig left the hood up and went to go get the complaining woman. I started the car again, just so she knew what it sounded like running.

A few minutes later, she came into the shop area, smacking on gum.

"What you find out?" she said.

"We found out that there ain't nothin' wrong with yo' car," I said. "It's runnin' right now and I just took it for a long spin to make sure everything was good."

"Well, it ain't good to me. It started shakin' and cut off on me twice. I don't know how you consider that good."

"Bottom line is I do. Ain't nothin' wrong with yo' car other than some loose hoses that were tightened. I don't mean to be blunt, but you need to jet. I got work to do and I'm not gon' stand around here repeatin' myself. Yo' keys are in the ignition. Craig gon' back it out of the shop area so you can make a move."

She put her hand up near my face. "Hold the fuck up, nigga, wait one doggone minute. This car is not . . ."

I ignored the woman and told Craig to back her car out of the shop area. She charged after me as I walked away. When she raised her hand at me, I backed away from it. By then, Romo and Gage had Glock 9s raised, aiming them at her.

"Back the fuck up," Gage said. "I'll drop a bitch in a minute and won't think twice."

"So, it's like that," the woman shouted with bugged eyes.

I snickered and walked away, thinking, *Yeah, it really is like that. My niggas always have my back.*

Before going back to my office, I stopped at the soda machine to get Desa Rae a Diet Pepsi. I told my other customers their cars would soon be ready and they seemed cool.

I saw Desa Rae moving around in my office, and when I got inside, she had cleaned it up for me. I couldn't believe how much she'd gotten done in such a short period of time.

"Damn, ma. You didn't have to do this," I said, looking at the glass on my desk that hadn't been visible in ages. She even removed the smudge marks from my huge widows with Windex.

"I know I didn't have to, but I did. Besides, I'm so proud of you for putting so much into your business. I want you to be comfortable in your office."

I sat my butt against the desk and reached out for Desa Rae, pulling her up from the chair. While holding her waist, I put her right in between my legs then gave her the soda.

"I like it when you stroke my ego, and if you want to decorate my office, have at it. It does need a makeover and I really could use a secretary around here, too."

"Really," she said, smiling. "I wouldn't mind working for you, but how much are you willing to pay? I don't come cheap."

"I'll pay whatever you want. Just name your price."

"Hmmm. If I work here, that means I'll have to quit my other job. So, for starters, I'll at least need about sixty thousand dollars a year."

"What?" I shouted and cocked my head back. "Sixty thousand my ass! That's too much for a secretarial position. You in here tryin' to rip me off like these other fools are."

"I told you I didn't come cheap. But since you put it like that, I'll work for free. Whatever you need for me to do, I'll do it."

Before I could respond, someone yelled over the intercom. "Roc, Craig said he sorry for slackin'. He got tears in his eyes and truth is, we all guilty."

I hit the intercom button to respond. "Truth is, y'all still fired. Includin' that lazy bum Craig and no apologies will be accepted." I could hear laugher and waited for a response. They said something, but my attention was directed elsewhere when I saw Dre walk in with his two friends. Unfortunately, he was with the one from the other day who I had to check for thumping a cigarette butt in my grass.

Dre came into my office with both friends trailing behind.

"Yo' friends ain't welcome in my office, so tell them to wait for you on the other side of the door. Afterward, close it."

It was no surprise that they didn't like what I'd said, but Dre did as he was told.

"In a minute," he said to them, then closed the door. "Butch called and said somethin' about my car."

"And?"

"And what?"

"And I know you'd better show my woman some respect and speak to her before you say anything else to me."

Dre smiled and looked at Desa Rae. "What's up, beautiful? How you doin'?"

"I'm doing fine, Dre, and I see that charm runs in the family. How are you?"

"Good. Just came to thank my cousin for takin' good care of me and for fixin' my car. How much do I owe you?"

"A whole lot. More than you can handle right now, but before you exit, your car ain't fixed yet. Butch waitin' on the parts. When they get here, you can help him get yo' car together."

Dre nodded and thanked me again before going to check on his ride. I kept my eyes on him and his friends. When my eyes connected with the one I had beef with, his eyes narrowed and he gave me a slow wink. In return, I gave that nigga a killer stare, then closed my blinds so me and Desa Rae could have some privacy.

Chapter 5
Desa Rae

Roc sure did have a lot going on at his shop. Talk about being busy—he was. I meant what I had said about being proud of him. I truly was. He'd made so many changes since I'd met him and the changes were positive changes that brought out the best in him.

We stayed at his shop until it was time to pick up Chassidy from school. I couldn't believe all of the fires he had to put out. My job was much easier than his and I couldn't even imagine that many people depending on me. At least I didn't have to be bothered by a bunch of people running in and out of my office. I could close the door and no one would ever see me. Roc, on the other hand, couldn't. But I thought he didn't mind, not one bit. His workers had a lot of love for him. That was so obvious, and as long as he was happy I was too.

The next day at work I couldn't help thinking about Roc and his crazy shop. I had been in a meeting with Shawna, Paula, and the executives. They complimented us on doing a great job and treated us to lunch. They also gave us tickets to go see *Wicked* at the Fox Theatre tonight. I hated to bug Monica about watching Chassidy again, but she was the only person I trusted. Before I called her, I called Roc to see if he wanted to go with me.

"Hold on, ma," he said. I could hear him talking to someone in the background before he returned to the phone. "Sorry about that. I swear these fools can't get it together. I'm never, ever, ever leavin' for that long again."

"Not even when we go on our honeymoon? You know that's going to be at least a week or two. So, you still have time to get everything in order before May rolls around."

"Only then will I make an exception. And I hope you'll make one too, referrin' to the weddin'. You know I got plenty of friends and family who want to come. A simple weddin' don't work for me, but I already told you that it didn't."

"I know, but I told you that we could have a big celebration, after we come back from our honeymoon. I really want to keep it simple. A church wedding with ten or twenty of our closest friends and family members will suit me fine."

"Have it your way, but as long as the weddin' takes place at the church my family attends. We can do the partyin' thing after we get back from Belize."

I bit into my nail. "I've been thinking more like Hawaii now, and having the wedding at New Northside Baptist is fine with me."

"Hawaii, huh?"

"Yes, but I'll let you see the new brochures I got. Then you can tell me what you're feeling."

"Sounds like a plan."

I could hear someone talking to Roc in the background, so I wasn't sure if he was really paying me any attention.

"I know you're busy, but I really called to see if you would like to go see *Wicked* tonight."

"*Wicked?* What the hell is that?"

"It's a Broadway musical that's supposed to be fabulous. It's at the Fox Theatre tonight and my boss gave me two tickets."

I could have sworn that I heard Roc sigh. "You know I'm not down with no bullshit like that but, if you want to go, I'll go."

"If you don't want to go, you don't have to. I can always ask Monica to go with me. You can babysit tonight."

"No, I'll go. But, if I fall asleep don't be mad at me."

"I won't. Promise. Pick me up around six and don't be late."

"I'll try. Now tell me what I'm supposed to wear to a musical?"

"Wear whatever you want. Just not sagging jeans." I laughed, knowing that Roc would probably wear them just to irritate me.

"I look dope in my saggin' jeans, don't I?"

"Sexy as ever, but not tonight."

"Cool. And since you're tellin' me what not to wear, let me tell you what not to wear. Leave the baby-doll dresses on the hanger. I hate to see women with that shit on, especially you."

My mouth dropped open. "What? My baby-doll dresses are perfect for the occasion. You just don't know class when you see it."

"Thing is, I don't want to see it tonight." Roc told me to hold; then he quickly got back to our call. "Listen, I need to go handle somethin' real quick. I'll see you at six-fifteen."

I could barely say good-bye before Roc ended the call, leaving me puzzled about what was going on and about what to wear. I looked just as good as Michelle Obama did in the baby-doll dress she wore at the

Democratic Convention. Like it or not, I was going to wear mine. Before going to lunch, I called Monica to ask if she would watch Chassidy.

"Of course I will. If you want me to pick her up from school, I can do that for you, too," she said.

"Thank you so much, Monica. You know you're the best friend ever. I don't know what I would do without you."

"For starters, don't go talking all that teary-eyed stuff. We've been friends for too long and this is what friends do. We take care of each other. Have a wonderful time with Roc and you can pick up Chassidy in the morning."

"Okay, girl. I'll check with y'all later and thanks again."

When Monica hung up, I kept thinking what a jewel she really was. She was the only real friend I had and I didn't have much family. My mother had passed away years ago and my father died of cancer. The only family I'd had since then was on Reggie's side of the family. But after our divorce, I became distant with most of them. That was why a big wedding wasn't important to me. I didn't have many people to invite and I certainly didn't want to waste money that could go toward Chassidy's education.

Shawna, Paula, and I went to lunch at Culpeppers in the Central West End. They had some fiery sweet and spicy wings that I loved. Trying to watch my weight, I was sure to order a slice of the low-carb cheesecake for dessert.

As we sat for the next hour or so eating, laughing, and talking, I couldn't help but to notice a woman at the bar who kept glancing at me. When I grinned at her, she smiled back. Maybe it was just me; after all, we were being pretty loud.

"I do think Mr. Anderson is handsome," Shawna said. "And I wouldn't mind sampling the goods."

"Mrs. Anderson would mind," I rushed to say. "That woman has been to hell and back with him, and all she needs is another woman trying to dig her claws into her husband."

"I know, but one night would suit me just fine. He could be all hers again after that."

I just shook my head and kept my mouth shut. Shawna was going places that I really didn't want to hear about. I looked over her shoulder, noticing again that the woman at the bar was looking at me. I started to feel uncomfortable. I guessed she could tell because she turned her head and sipped from her wine glass. I saw a man at the end of the bar vying for her attention. She ignored him. She combed her fingers through the long, thin braids that hung down her back. When she got up, I checked out her shapely figure that was well fitted into a winter white suit with round black buttons. A colorful scarf was tied around her neck and she looked rather tall in her high stilettos. After leaving a few dollars at the bar, she turned to look at me. I shifted my eyes to Paula, who had added her two cents about Mr. Anderson.

"He is fine," she said. "But I wouldn't want to have a relationship with my boss. That could get real ugly."

"Very," I said with a tease. "Now, can we please change the subject?"

Shawna and Paula laughed. I couldn't because I saw the hazel-eyed woman coming my way with a grin plastered on her face.

"I . . . I apologize for constantly looking at you, but do I know you from somewhere? Desa Rae, right?"

I widened my eyes, shocked that she knew my name. She looked familiar too, but I just couldn't put my finger on it. "Yes, my name is Desa Rae. And even though you look familiar, I can't think of where I know you from."

We both laughed.

"I'm sure it'll probably come to us a week or two from now," she said. "Until then, sorry for interrupting, and just in case you don't remember, my name is Chase."

"Okay, Chase. No bother at all. Have a good day."

"You have one too," she said, then threw her scarf around her neck and sashayed away.

I watched as she made her way out the door, and I thought what a classy and professional-looking woman she was. Afterward, I got back to my conversation with Paula and Shawna, who wouldn't let go of her thoughts about Mr. Anderson.

"I don't care what you say, I'm getting some of that," she said.

At this point, all I could do was shrug. At least she wasn't speaking of getting a piece of my man, so it was really none of my business.

Chapter 6
Roc

The fellas kept messing around and I was trying hard to get out of my office to go home and change clothes. I didn't leave until 4:30 p.m. and you better believe that I was speeding through traffic. I had run a few red lights, too, but that was because I didn't want to be late. Desa Rae had been real patient with me and things had been going well for us.

As soon as I got home, I took a ten-minute shower then changed into my sagging, wide-legged dark jeans that nearly covered my Kenneth Cole strap-on loafers. The jeans were perfect for the occasion, especially since I rocked them with a button-down silver silk shirt. A platinum cross with diamonds hung from my neck and diamonds glistened in my earlobes. The waves on my head flowed like an ocean, and my Movado watch added class to my entire fit. I looked around for my cologne, but couldn't find it. As a matter of fact, I couldn't find much of anything I had been looking for because Dre still had my crib looking a mess. I'd been slacking, too, and most of the junk was in my bedroom, in the kitchen, and in Dre's bedroom, where I eventually found my cologne.

I dashed out the front door at ten minutes to six. Desa Rae lived about thirty minutes from me, but I intended to cut that down to twenty minutes.

I breezed my SUV through traffic, taking every shortcut that I could. When my phone rang, I hit the talk button on the screen.

"You got me," I said, looking at a number that I didn't recognize. There was no reply and then someone hung up. Ten minutes later, Li'l Roc's mother, Vanessa, called. I hit the screen again.

"Why you playin' on the phone?" I asked.

"What? What are you talkin' about? This is my first time callin' you."

"So you say. What's up?"

"What's up is I haven't seen you since you've been back. Li'l Roc ain't seen you either, so what's up, dead-beat dad?"

"Did he tell you that he hasn't seen me? Or are you just assumin' that he hasn't?"

"If he had, he would've told me."

"Breakin' news, ma. He doesn't tell you everything. He was with me over the weekend, and your mother dropped him off at the shop yesterday. Get the facts before you start callin' me names that don't apply."

"It ain't my fault that y'all always leavin' me out of the loop. I talked to Li'l Roc today and he ain't said nothin' about seein' you."

"He don't have to tell you how much time we spend together. Your only concern should be how much time you're spendin' with him. From where I see it, not much. He's always at your mother's house."

"That's his choice, not mine."

"I wonder why."

Vanessa snapped, knowing exactly what I was getting at. "For your information, most of his friends live near my mother so he likes bein' over there. It has nothin' to do with him not wantin' to be around me."

"I wouldn't put any money on that, and the last time I checked, he's been spendin' more time with Desa Rae this year than he has with you. He considers her more of a mother than he does you."

"Roc, don't make me go off on you. You barkin' up the wrong tree and the only kids that bitch got are Chassidy and what's-his-face. Don't make me go there with you. If you don't have anything nice to say to me then keep your mouth shut."

With that tad bit of information, I kept my mouth shut and ended the call. I cranked up the music and it was loud enough to drown out Vanessa's calls, as she kept calling back.

I got to Desa Rae's house around 6:20 p.m. I saw her move the curtain aside and look outside. Before I could get out of the car, she was already on the porch, locking the front door.

Looking fly as ever, she had on a deep burgundy, baby-doll dress that was accessorized with gold. Her hair was in a curly bob with one side shorter than the other. Her makeup was on like a work of art, and her wide hips swished from side to side as she headed my way.

"G'on wit' yo' bad self. Work that baby-doll dress," I teased.

She blushed, but smirked at the same time while looking at my jeans. "I knew you would go there," she said, puckering for a kiss. We kissed; then she backed up. "You look spectacular, but you're late."

"I'm aware of the time, but we will get to the Fox Theatre before the musical starts. Now get yo' fine self in the car before I take you in the house and make my own music with you."

Desa Rae threw her hand back and walked to the passenger side of the truck. As soon as she got inside, she turned down the blasting hip hop music.

"How do you drive with all of that noise? I would get a headache."

"I'm used to it," I said, backing out of the driveway. I advised her to tighten her seat belt because time definitely wasn't on our side and I was in a rush.

While speeding through traffic, I listened to Desa Rae tell me to slow down.

"You're going to kill us driving like this. Slow down. We'll get there."

I knew we would, but I didn't want her to miss one minute of the show.

We talked most of the way there, until Vanessa's number interrupted us when it appeared on the screen.

Desa Rae winced. "What does she want?"

"Don't know. Just buggin' as always."

Desa Rae hit the talk button. "Hi, Vanessa. Roc is driving and he can't really talk right now."

"I know that lousy muthafucka is listenin', and if you are, the next time you disrespect me, I'ma hunt you down and put a hurtin' on you. And for the record, Desa Rae, I'm the only mother Li'l Roc has. Don't get it twisted and please don't overstep your boundaries."

Desa Rae sighed and shook her head. "Handle your business, Vanessa. Nobody is trying to replace you. If you have any further issues be sure to take them up with Roc."

I had to add my two cents. "I hope you got that madness off your chest. But when you get done talkin', step up yo' damn game before you get replaced. Don't call me with no more bullshit, or else I'll have to sick my dogs on you."

"I got dogs too, and when you bring your happy-go-lucky ass over here again, I'ma introduce you to them. Bye!"

She ended the call and all I could do was laugh to myself. I couldn't believe that I had spent so many years of my life messing with a chick like Vanessa. I felt blessed to have Desa Rae in my corner. The two of them were like night and day.

I made it to the Fox Theatre at five minutes to seven. There was a line outside the door, but it went by quickly. I held Desa Rae's hand as we made it to our seats and got ready for the show to start. The auditorium was packed with a bunch of white people, and a few uppity black folks were sprinkled throughout. I had never been to a Broadway musical. The last time I was at the Fox was to see a Tyler Perry play. It was pretty good and I had come with my ex-girlfriend, Raven. I hadn't seen or heard from her since that dreadful day at my shop when I had to break her down and tell her I was still in love with Desa Rae. Raven said that she understood and wouldn't interfere with my relationship. I had seriously broken her heart, but she had kept her word and let me do me.

The musical got on the way, and on a for-real tip, I kind of enjoyed it. The props and scenery were dope and the acting was on a level that I hadn't witnessed before. I was tuned in to what was about to happen next. Desa Rae was engaged too. She kept laughing, smiling, and applauding with the others. But before we knew it, it was time for intermission. Desa Rae and I left the auditorium to go get drinks.

"You go ahead and get our drinks," she said. "I'm going to wait in line to use the bathroom."

I nodded, and as I walked off I held my head down while checking a text message on my phone. The message was from Li'l Roc asking if I would pick him up tomorrow, and telling me that he loved me. I texted that I would pick him up and that I loved him too. Right before I hit the send button somebody bumped my shoulder, damn near knocking me off my feet. When I looked up and turned around, all I saw was the back of a woman squeezing through the crowd. I started to go after her, but I didn't want to start no shit. Instead, I got in line and waited to order our drinks.

Desa Rae still hadn't made it out of the bathroom, so I stood away from the entrance to the bathroom with two drinks in my hand. I sipped on mine, but damn near choked on it when I saw Desa Rae come out of the bathroom with Chase next to her. She was the woman who had bumped my shoulder. I didn't recognize her because she had a hat on. I sucked in a deep breath before swiftly walking away from my spot. I definitely didn't want Desa Rae and Chase to see me. I was in disbelief that they knew each other and to say this was fucked up would be putting it mildly. I could feel sweat beads forming on my forehead. My palms were so wet that the glasses were about to slip from my hands. My silk shirt was sticking to my chest, and I almost tripped as I rushed through the crowd to get back to my seat. By then, my heart was racing a mile a minute because I didn't know what the fuck was going on. I thought about Desa Rae bringing Chase over to introduce us. Then I started thinking if I should go ahead and tell her the truth about what had happened. That was just a thought. I spotted Desa Rae heading back to her seat, alone, and I was relieved. She excused herself for stepping over the people to my right.

"Where did you go?" she said. "I went to the bar and didn't see you."

"I swooped by the ladies bathroom, but you were taking too long. I didn't see you, so I came back to our seats. What was the holdup? I bet you were in there runnin' your mouth."

She laughed. "No, not really. I ran into a young woman who I saw earlier today. We laughed about seein' each other again and that was it."

"That's odd. Where did you see her at earlier?"

"I was at Culpeppers. She was at the bar and we thought we knew each other."

"So, you don't?"

"No. Not to my recollection."

This was not good news for me. Maybe it was all just a coincidence, but that was a far stretch. I gave Desa Rae her glass of wine and guzzled mine down in two swallows. I kept hoping for the auditorium to get dark again; that way Chase wouldn't see where we were sitting.

All I could say was, this was some uncomfortable shit. I could barely focus once the musical got started again. Desa Rae was back into it and I was glad that she didn't notice my sudden paranoia.

For the next hour or so, I felt as if I were sitting on pins and needles. The play had finally ended and, with the lights on, nearly everyone was on their feet applauding, with the exception of me. Desa Rae looked over to see why I hadn't stood up, but I pretended that I was looking at a text message on my phone.

"That was awesome," she said as everyone started to make their way out. With the place being so crowded it was hard to see who was there. There weren't too many dark-skinned brothers with waves, so I stuck out like a sore thumb. I did my best to hurry to the exit doors, and was relieved when we had finally made it back to my truck.

"You haven't said anything about the musical," Desa Rae said. "Did you like it?"

I removed what looked to be a brochure from my windshield. "I did. Didn't think I would, but the whole show was interestin'."

We got into the car. Almost immediately, I noticed something written on the back of the brochure. I read it and it said, "Small world, Roc. Good seeing you again. Sis-in-law, C.J."

My face scrunched. It took me a minute to realize who had written the note. It had to be Chase. I recall her saying that her last name was Jenkins and that was when something felt like it dropped to the pit of my stomach. Why in the fuck was she referring to herself as my sis-in-law? She and Desa Rae weren't related. She was just fucking with me and I didn't like that shit. This was messed up. I had the power to have that bitch erased from this earth. If she ever went to Desa Rae about what had happened, I was afraid it would have to go down like that.

"Are you going to start your truck so we can go home?" Desa Rae asked, interrupting my thoughts. "It's kind of chilly out here and I need some heat."

I tossed the brochure on the back seat and started my truck. I wanted to quiz Desa Rae about Chase, only because they did have some similar facial features. What if they were related? Damn, that would cause major damage to our relationship. Desa Rae would never forgive me and our relationship would be a wrap. The thought of it made me dizzy but, for now, I had to get my act together before she got suspicious.

"You enjoy yourself tonight?" I asked, forgetting that she had already told me that she had. "As for me, I didn't think a musical could move me like that."

"It was excellent. I didn't think it could move you like that either. I'm glad that you came with me."

I leaned over to give her a kiss. "Me too. Thanks for the invite."

"Anytime. So, what's the plan for tonight? I'm a little hungry, but I don't want anything heavy to eat. When the time comes for me to get into my wedding dress, you had better believe that I'm going to do it."

"I'm sure you will, so I'm gon' fix you a healthy chicken salad when we get home. You're right about it bein' too late to eat anything heavy. I'm not that hungry right now."

"Sounds fine to me, but you are going to put croutons in my salad, aren't you?"

"Whatever you want. You can have whatever you want."

Desa Rae smiled and touched my hand. I felt so horrible inside because we had come too far to let a fuck-up like this destroy our relationship. Maybe I was tripping too hard and was worried for nothing. I hoped so because I was hyped about Desa Rae being my wife. I knew that if she found out, the marriage thing would never happen.

Chapter 7
Desa Rae

I was highly energetic after the musical was over and wasn't ready to go home. Roc drove to Forest Park, where he parked his truck near an almost-frozen pond that was surrounded by beaming lights. From afar, we could see the art museum and the numerous stairs leading up to the front doors. No one else was parked on the same street as we were, but several cars kept driving by.

"I wasn't ready to go home either," Roc said. "This park is where I chill at when I have heavy shit on my mind."

I reached over to rub the back of his head. "What's on your mind? Are you okay?"

He paused for a moment, while looking down at his lap. "I'm good, ma. Actually, I couldn't be better, thanks to you. Seems like everything is on the right track in my life, and it's almost scary because it ain't like my life to be drama free."

"Well, when you do right, right will follow you. That's something my mother always told me and I truly believe that."

He scratched his head and looked to be in a daze as he stared straight ahead. "I feel you. It ain't often that I hear you talk about your parents, especially your father. Why don't you ever talk about him?"

I shrugged, realizing that I hadn't said much to Roc about him. "There's not much for me to say about him, other than he was nice to me when he was around. I told you before that he died when I was nineteen, or, at least, that's what my mother told me. I enjoyed the time he spent with me, and the last time I saw him was at my graduation. He told me how proud he was of me, took me to dinner and gave me three hundred dollars as a graduation present. After that, I didn't see him anymore. My mother told me he had died, but that was weeks later. I didn't even go to his funeral."

Roc tapped the steering wheel. "Sorry to hear that. You don't have to talk about this right now, if you don't want to."

"I know. It doesn't bother me to talk about it at all. But since you asked, it's one of the reasons why I don't want a big wedding. My family is really small and it's nowhere near as big as yours. There's no comparison, and when you throw in friends, I can forget it."

"I told you we'd do this thing however you want to do it. As long as you become my wife, that's all I care about. I can understand how you feel about your parents not bein' there to share that special day with you. I didn't even think about you not havin' any brothers or sisters. Did your daddy have any kids?"

"As far as I know, I'm the only child. There's no telling what my father was up to. If he did have any children, I'm sure that after all this time I would know about them."

Roc stared straight ahead again, pondering. "I wouldn't be so sure about that. Some men have kids out there that they don't even know about. Plenty of my boys don't know how many kids they got floatin' around and many of them don't even care."

"That's terrible. But I'm glad that Chassidy has you and Latrel has Reggie. Both of you are good fathers."

"Yeah, we are. And even though Latrel and me are close in age, I got his back, too. When is him and Angelique comin' back to visit? I haven't seen Latrel in a while."

"Not until Christmas."

"That's only a month away, so I guess that ain't too bad."

"No, it's not. But until then, it gives me all the time I want to have as much fun as I want to with you."

Roc let out a soft snicker then unzipped his jeans. "Right. We really don't have to wait until Christmas to have fun, do we?"

I looked down at his dick that was standing tall through his zipper. My mouth watered and I wet my lips. "No, we don't have to wait. And in a few minutes, you're going to see why I felt as if my baby-doll dress was appropriate for the occasion."

I lifted my butt from the seat and eased my silk panties down to my ankles. When I tossed them over to Roc, he sniffed and held them over his lips. His tongue flicked the crotch area and that was when I snatched my panties away from him.

"You're so nasty," I said. "Stop playing."

"You're the one who threw those spicy muthafuckers over here. But I'm the one who's nasty."

"Spicy, huh? I'll show you spicy."

Roc moved the seat back as far as it would go. He then laid it back, until the headrest touched the back seat. As I watched him lower his jeans to his ankles, that was when I hiked up my dress and straddled him. At first, I was up high. But as he held his muscle straight up, I lowered myself, inch by inch. With Roc being so big, I could never just take all of him in with one swoop. My wetness made it easier for me to glide up and down, and before I knew it, I was filled with all the goodness only he could deliver.

"Polish it good," he said with his eyes closed. "Yo' pussy poppin' mad juices on me."

He was only speaking the truth. My overflowing juices brought music to our ears. Roc's hands were giving my ass cheeks a magnificent massage and his steel was so far up in me that I could feel it in my gut. With each glide, his meat brushed against my clit, causing it to stiffen more. My legs were shaking and nothing in the world felt better than having this man who I loved so much thrusting inside of me. There were times when I wanted to cry from his lovemaking skills. He damn sure knew how to please me, and today was no exception.

As he started to lift himself and pump inside of me, I tightened my coochie lips to halt the intenseness of wanting to come. My folds were being sucked in from the force of his dick, and as Roc started turning his hips in rhythmic circles, he managed to bring pleasure to every inch of my walls. I couldn't restrain myself much longer and he knew it.

"Wet my lips," he said, pulling out of me. "Come forward and bring that pussy to me."

My whole body quivered. I was so ready to release all that was inside of me. I crawled up to Roc's face, and while on my knees, I put my wet coochie lips over his mouth.

Through looking out the back window, all I could see were headlights from a car coming. I paid the car no mind, as Roc secured my thighs with his strong arms and slightly lifted his head to taste my pussy. Two minutes in, tears formed in my eyes. His tongue-turning skills working my hole had me going crazy. All I could do was pull my hair and grind my hips to show my enthusiasm.

"You are soooo in trouble," I said, panting. "I don't want to give you all of this, but here it coooomes."

"Give it here," Roc mumbled and flicked his tongue faster. "All of it."

He didn't have to tell me twice. I cut up and nearly broke his neck as I bounced up and down on his face. Roc didn't mind. The only thing he wanted to do was catch my buildup of excitement. I surely couldn't leave him hanging, and since his muscle was still hard, I turned myself around to face the front windshield. I got on my knees and hunched over the steering wheel while holding it.

"I see you fixin' to drive the shit out of my ride, huh?"

"Your ride? No. You? Yes."

Before I could reach down to do it, Roc slipped his dick back into my wetness. I looked straight ahead while holding on to the steering wheel and did my best to drive Roc insane.

His hands roamed underneath my dress that provided him easy access. He ticked my nipples with his fingertips and playfully smacked and massaged my ass. My cheeks were spread far apart, making the gliding process much easier.

"We were made for each other," he softly said. "I love you, ma, and ain't nobody ever made me feel what I'm feelin' right now."

"Same here," was all I could say. Then I got busy grinding my hips and tightening my coochie on his meat. He always loved the feel of that, and minutes later it was all over with for him. He punched the roof of his truck and nearly knocked me off his lap, as he jumped from the seat.

"Umph," he shouted out. "Desa Rae Jenkins. Please tell me what in the hell am I gon' do with you?"

I had already made my way off his lap and back into my seat. "If you haven't figured it out yet, I don't know what to tell you."

Another set of headlights were coming our way. But this time, it was a police car that pulled right in front of us with shining lights that lit up Roc's whole truck. Roc hurried to pull up his jeans, but by that time, the officer was already standing by the driver's side window.

Roc lowered the window. I was so sure that the officer got a whiff of our steamy sex.

"Man, what you doing out here?" the black officer said to Roc. I was relieved that Roc knew him.

Roc stuck his hand out the window, slapping it against the officer's hand. "I'm out here chillin' with my woman. That's all."

The officer bent down, peering into the car. He spoke and I spoke back.

"Y'all got the right idea," the officer said, "but you're in the wrong place doing it. The park is closed. I don't want you to get in any trouble if another cop swings by here. So, pack it up and go home."

"All right, Lou," Roc said. "I'ma check out of here and thanks for the warnin'."

Lou told Roc to be safe and headed back to the police car.

"That was nice of him," I said as Roc started the engine.

"Nice my ass. I can't stand that punk muthafucka. He used to be on Ronnie's payroll. I'm glad ain't no more of that mess goin' down, 'cause we got tired of payin' his ass."

"So, that means you're not shaking and moving anymore . . . period? I pretty much suspected you were done with all of that mess, but I'm just asking to be sure."

"Washed my hands to that shit, right after that shit went down with Ronnie. But just so you know, there is still a substantial amount of money due to me. When niggas pay up, I do accept it. All you need to know is my hands are sparklin' clean."

I didn't elaborate, but "pay up" didn't come across the right way to me. The drug game made Roc a fortune, so I suspected that he was still someway or somehow getting paid. To what level, I didn't know. When I questioned it, he gave vague answers as he just did. Nonetheless, I wouldn't have agreed to marry him if I didn't think his hands were clean. So I took his word that they were, or at least they were as clean as he could get them.

Chapter 8
Roc

I had a feeling that things were about to turn ugly. I wasn't sure how I was going to clear up everything with this Chase situation, and I was seriously considering telling Dez what had happened between me and Chase. It was just sex. There was no ongoing relationship and I had no ties whatsoever with that trick. My excuse was I thought it was inappropriate for Reggie to come around when I was away. I somewhat trusted Dez, but then again, there was a side of me that was taught never to trust anyone. Being in the game made me that way, and even though Desa Rae was going to be my wife, she didn't have to know that, no matter what, there was nothing she could do to earn my complete trust. My feelings came with the territory, so maybe that was why it was hard for me to believe that she and Reggie hadn't gotten their sweat on while I was away.

For the past week or so, things had been cool. No more notes were on my windshield, Dez hadn't said anything about my time away, and we'd been spending much-needed quality time with the kids. They were at the shopping mall with Desa Rae today buying Christmas decorations and picking out my present. I had some catching up to do at the shop, so I spent most of the day on Saturday trying to get things in order.

I was in my office, getting ready to place an order for some parts I needed to fix several of the cars in the shop area. When I looked up, Troy was standing in the doorway.

"Speak," I said, looking down again at the ordering catalog in my lap.

"There's a fine-ass chick up front askin' for you. What should I tell her?"

"What does she want?"

"Don't know. She just asked for you."

"Get more details. It may be one of those chicks tryin' to holla at me about fixin' their car for free. If so, tell Craig to handle that for me and remind him not to do shit for free."

Troy nodded and left my office. I picked up the phone to call the car parts distributor. As I waited with the phone up to my ear, Troy was back, two minutes later.

"She wants to speak to you, no one else," he said.

Irritation was clearly visible on my face. "So? I want a hundred million dollars, but can't get it. There are gangs of people who want to speak to me. You need to find out what she wants before you interrupt me again."

"I'm not sure. All she keeps sayin' is she prefers to speak to you."

I slammed the phone down and jumped to my feet. "Is it that goddamn hard for you to ask a person what they want with me? If it is, I don't know why I got you runnin' the front counter."

Troy tried to explain himself as he followed me. When I reached the front waiting area, I turned to Troy.

"Which one is she?" I said, referring to the three unattractive women sitting and waiting for their cars to be serviced.

He looked around before answering. "She must've left. I told her I would be right back."

I cut my eyes at Troy and headed toward the back to return to my office. On the way there, I bumped into a chick who rushed out of the bathroom. Before the words "excuse me" left my mouth, I saw that the chick was Chase. My mouth was open, but I hadn't said anything.

"What's the matter, Roc?" she said with a smirk on her face. "Cat got your tongue? You look like you've seen a ghost."

"What the hell are you doin' here? I'm not down with this game you're playin', and playin' these games may get you seriously hurt."

Chase continued to lock a big grin on her face. "Don't be so violent. I thought you'd be happy to see me, especially after what the two of us shared during our *Hell House* adventure. I understand if you're not happy about how things ended. Neither was I, but what I want from you is very simple."

I crossed my arms in front of me. "What do you want? Money? If that's why you're here, you can forget that shit 'cause it ain't happenin'."

I walked away and Chase followed. After I entered my office, so did she. She also closed the door behind her.

"May I have a seat?" she asked.

I didn't bother to respond, so she took it upon herself to take one. I sat on the edge of my desk, prepared to listen to what she had to say.

She crossed her legs and reached for a Newport cigarette in her purse. She lit it, and after one puff, she whistled smoke into the air. "I'm not here to cause you any harm, Roc, but what I would like for you to do is tell Desa Rae what happened between us. She deserves to know. Is that so hard for you to do?"

"No, it's not. And when I get around to it, I will tell her on my time, not yours. Now, get out and take your smoke with you."

"Is my smoke bothering you? I would think not, especially since you be firing it up. I guess since you're back at home with Desa Rae she doesn't allow you to get high like you did during your *Hell House* stay."

I cleared my throat and did my best not to reveal how irritated I was. "Chase, it's unfortunate, ma, that you don't know who you messin' with. I could pick up that phone right now and have your life ended in the very chair you're sittin' in. You ain't in no position to come in here and make no demands of me. I'm bein' nice, but just so you know, that nice bullshit is about to wear off."

Chase chuckled and whistled more smoke into the air. "Save the tough talk for another day. I don't want to hear it, and besides that, I don't scare too easily. I told you what I wanted. Just tell Desa Rae what happened. After you tell her, you'll never hear another peep from me."

"I don't know what business it is of yours if I tell Dez or not. And, trust me, I'm prepared to do what I must not to hear another peep from you. Since you seem to think I'm all tough talk and a joke, don't move from that chair."

I pushed the intercom button. "Gage, to my office. In a flash," I said.

"It's my business, Roc, because I do care about Desa Rae. I don't want her hooking up with a man who is no good, and like I said, she deserves better. I'm not saying that you're not decent. You're just not the kind of man I would want my loving sister to marry. Plus, I'm a little pissed that my father gave her all of the attention. He did more for her than he did for any of his children, so there's a little bad taste in my mouth because of it."

"Cut the sister act, Chase. Desa Rae was an only child, so get your facts together before you start talkin' that bullshit."

Gage opened the door to my office. "What's up, boss?"

"Come inside and close the door," I said. "I need a favor."

Gage had a look of concern on his face. He glanced at Chase then looked at me. "What you need?" he asked.

"See that young pretty thang sittin' in that chair right there?"

Gage shrugged and looked at Chase again. "Yeah, I see her. She is pretty."

"Not when you get done with her. I need for you to quietly get this bitch out of my office and make sure I never see her again. You feel me on that?"

Gage's eyes roamed down Chase's shapely legs that could be seen with the short skirt she wore. I assumed she got the picture, because she stood and smashed her cigarette into an ashtray on my desk. "I'm not into dealing with boys from yo' hood, so you have one week to tell Desa Rae or I will tell her myself. If you think that killing her sister is going to do you any good, I think you'd better consider plan B."

Gage pointed to Chase with a twisted face. "Did . . . did she just threaten you?"

"She's been at it all day," I said, rubbing my chin. Maybe what she said about being Desa Rae's sister was correct; then again, maybe it wasn't. She was right about coming up with plan B, so I did. "Don't kill her. Just knock her the fuck out, throw her in the trunk of one of those cars, and get her off my property. Like always, you know I appreciate ya."

Chase kept a smirk on her face, but as she rushed for the door, Gage washed the smirk away. He dropped her with a clean right hook that sent her stumbling backward and crashing to the floor. She was out cold.

"Who dis?" Gage said, feeling the pockets on Chase's jacket. He removed her wallet and tossed it to me.

"Her name is Chase, and the bitch is causin' me trouble." I looked at Chase's address on her driver's license and gave it to Gage. "Get her keys out of her purse and tell Craig to drive her car to this address and park it. With her in the trunk of yo' car, follow him to that address and dump her ass nearby. If she snaps out of it by then, put her to sleep again. Don't hurt her too bad, though. Not until I find out what's really up."

Gage nodded. He carried the title of being my bodyguard, so he picked up Chase's limp body with no problem, and threw her over his shoulder.

"She got sick and passed out," he said just in case the customers who were looking had concerns about why he was taking her out the back door. Shortly after putting her in his trunk, he came back inside to give Craig my order. In less than ten minutes, they jetted. I dropped back in my chair, wondering what to do and thinking if I should tell Dez that there was a possibility I had fucked her sister.

Chapter 9
Desa Rae

Christmas was less than three weeks away and I was just now decorating a real tree that Roc purchased last week. The smell of pine lit up the whole house. Chassidy wanted pink decorations and Li'l Roc wanted blue and red. We went to Garden Ridge, and I bought all of the pink, red, and blue ornaments and decorations I could find. Afterward, we went to Applebee's. Then we headed to the mall so the kids could find something special for Roc. I didn't know what to get him, but Chassidy picked out a Nike sweat suit for him and Li'l Roc chose the tennis shoes. Roc and I had already been shopping for the kids. All of their gifts were hidden in my walk-in closet, waiting to be wrapped.

Li'l Roc and Chassidy were putting the finishing touches on the Christmas tree. Roc had worked his magic by decorating the top of it and he was looking for the star in the plastic Garden Ridge bags that were scattered on the floor.

"I know I bought at least two stars," I said, helping Roc look through the bags.

Chassidy was awfully quiet. I could tell that she knew what had happened to the stars.

"Do you have the stars?" I asked her.

She moved her head from side to side and pointed to Li'l Roc.

"Do you got the stars?" Roc asked Li'l Roc, but he didn't respond. Roc held out his hand. "Give them here. Right now."

Li'l Roc walked over to the trashcan and removed the stars from the trash. I figured Roc was about to let him have it, so I quickly intervened.

"Thank you for getting these out of the trashcan," I said, pulling him close to me. "But why did you throw them away?"

Li'l Roc scratched his head that was full of waves like Roc's was. "Because I didn't want a pink star at the top of the tree."

"Well, I do," Chassidy said, pouting and running over to Roc for comfort.

"Just put the pink one at the top and be done with it," he said. "Li'l Roc ain't have no business throwin' nothin' away because he couldn't have his way. Get a grip on yourself, son."

I stood and smiled. "I don't know what the big fuss is about. I bought a pink star and a blue one. We're going to put both stars at the top, so everybody should be happy about that, right?"

Li'l Roc nodded and so did Chassidy. I gave both stars to Roc so he could put them at the top.

"You be babyin' him too much for me." Roc removed the stars from my hand and placed them at the top of the tree. "Is everybody happy now?"

Li'l Roc nodded again, but Chassidy's face fell flat. I sighed because I already knew what her problem was.

"Li'l Roc's star is higher up than mine," she said, pointing to it. "I want my star even with his."

Roc just shook his head, but you better believe he made sure both stars were even.

"Is that better?" he asked.

Chassidy quickly nodded and that was when Roc snatched her up to tickle her. She was screaming at the top of her lungs so loudly that my eardrums popped. Li'l Roc and I shielded our ears. I looked at him and nudged my head toward the kitchen. He knew that meant our cookies in the oven were ready.

Li'l Roc helped me put the cookies on a plate while Chassidy and Roc cleaned up the family room. When the phone rang, I moved away from the kitchen table to answer it.

"Hello," I said. No one replied. All I heard was a click. I hung up and Roc asked who it was.

"I don't know. Maybe somebody with the wrong number, because not too many people have this number."

"Is that the first time that's happened?"

"Yes. Why?"

"Just wonderin'," he said, coming into the kitchen with Chassidy on his shoulders.

"Put her big self down. Besides, I need some help eating all of these cookies. You need to help me, too, or else come our wedding day, I'm screwed."

"Come our wedding day, you'll be left at the altar if you're wearin' cookies. So I'd better help you get yo' grub on."

I took Roc at his word and shared two dozen of chocolate chip cookies with everyone. I ate at least seven of them and was stuffed. The kids had eaten a lot too, and they had gotten restless. Nearly thirty minutes later we put them to bed. Roc and I cuddled on the couch while drinking wine and listening to soft music. I was lying between his legs, rubbing his feet with mine as the soft blanket covered us.

"If this is how our lives are going to be, I'm going to love being married to you. The kids and I had a good time today. Wait until you see what they got you."

Roc placed a gentle kiss on my forehead. "Not as much as I'm gon' love it. As for the kids, they could have gotten me a stick of gum and I'd be satisfied."

"I'm sure you would be. They get along well and it's not that often when they have issues with what the other one wants. I was surprised by the whole star thingy, but I'm glad it was resolved."

"Yeah, me too. But that's how siblings do it. You wouldn't know anything about that—being an only child, right?"

"No, I wouldn't know, but I liked being the only child. It didn't bother me not one bit. Maybe because my mother and I were so close. She made me feel special in every way possible. I swear I miss her. There are many times that my life feels so empty. If she were alive, I wonder how she would feel about you."

"She would love me to death, as my lame-ass parents would've loved you."

"Well, Ronnie didn't care much for me. If he did, he wouldn't have tried to do away with me. He was the closest person you had as a parent, wasn't he?"

Roc didn't respond. It didn't dawn on me that he was still affected by what he'd done to Ronnie. Having him killed because of his threats to harm me and Chassidy probably still haunted Roc. I was mad at myself for even speaking that man's name in my house, and I hurried to correct myself.

"Forgive me for going there," I said. "I know you don't wish to talk about Ronnie and me . . ."

"Don't worry about it, Dez. That's the past and we movin' in a new direction. Let it go."

No doubt we were, so I let it go.

"Tell me somethin'," Roc said after silence soaked the room for a while.

"What?"

"If I wanted to get married tomorrow, would you do it?"

I hesitated to answer, but spoke the truth. "Yes. But why are you asking me that? Do you want to do it sooner?"

"Possibly. I don't really see what we're waitin' for. May seems way off. Don't you think so?"

"Hmmmm, not really. It'll be here before you know it."

"I hope so."

Roc closed his eyes and within a few minutes he was out. I got up to turn the lights off and to change into something more comfortable. Before I made it back to the family room where Roc was still sleeping, I heard his phone vibrate on the counter. I picked it up and read a text message from one of his mechanics named Gage:

> That was one tough B. I had to put her 2 sleep twice. Doubt that U and Boss Lady will have any more problems from her. Done deal.

Some of the mechanics at the shop referred to me as boss lady. I sure wanted to know who the tough B was, so I asked Roc during breakfast the next morning. All he did was give me an intense stare from across the table. The kids were cutting into their pancakes, boasting about how delicious they were.

"Have you been goin' through my phone?" Roc asked.

"No, I haven't. It vibrated, so I picked it up to see if anyone important had called."

"The most important people in the world to me are sittin' right here at this table. Just do me a favor and don't touch my shit, if or whenever it rings or vibrates."

I was completely taken aback by Roc's tone and his strong request. Hell no, I wouldn't marry him today, especially if he thought his phone was off-limits.

"I don't know why you feel as though I shouldn't be able to touch your phone or look at your calls. But I'll say this to you, just so you know, as your future wife I'll expect access to everything you have and/or own. There will be no secrets kept in our marriage, so you got less than six months to make sure you lay your shit on the table. If I'm not allowed to touch your phone then I have no desire to carry your last name. The choice is yours, Roc, and I'm glad you now know where I stand."

"I do. But, as long as you know where I stand too."

"At the altar alone," I said, getting up from the table and walking away. I was so pissed at Roc. *How dare he speak to me like he speaks to Vanessa and those other hoochies from his past?* As far as I was concerned, I wasn't going to pick up another vacation brochure until he got his act together.

Chapter 10

Roc

I was wrong for getting at Desa Rae like I did, but sometimes she was too damn nosey. I wasn't sure if she had checked all of my messages or not, but I seriously didn't have nothing to hide. I was more upset with Gage for being too specific. Rule number one was to always text in codes so no one knew what the fuck we were talking about. That fool spelled it out for Desa Rae, but I was thankful that he didn't include Chase's name.

Even though I was mad at him, I had to thank him for handling that business for me. Hopefully, putting a li'l fear in Chase would shake her up a bit. Now, she realized that I wasn't playing with her. I was still puzzled by her claiming to be Desa Rae's sister. The more I pictured Chase's face in my mind, the more I saw features of the woman I loved and intended to spend the rest of my life with.

With Chase's driver's license back in my possession, I decided to go pay her a visit. I wanted to settle this thing once and for all. I came up with a possible solution on how to do it, so that was what brought me to the front door of her apartment.

"Who is it?" she said from the other side of the door.

"Roc."

There was no response for at least a minute. Shortly thereafter, Chase put a wide crack in the door. She wore a cotton robe, her braids were tied down with a scarf, and her eye was a bluish black. Gage had messed her up.

"What do you want?" she said.

"I came to get at you about a few things and to make sure my boy didn't hurt you too bad. Can I come in?"

She hesitated but pulled the door open. I walked inside and looked around at the nicely decorated apartment that was neat as a pin. A burnt orange sofa was against one wall and two off-white chairs sat across from the sofa. Striped pillows were on the couch and the colors in the pillows matched an oval-shaped rug that covered the hardwood floors. Her kitchen was adjacent to the living room area and two barstools were in front of the granite-topped counter.

"Have a seat," she said in a calm tone.

Dressed in Levi's and a cream cashmere sweater, I took a seat in the chair. Chase sat on the couch, giving me her attention as I rubbed my hands together.

"I know you didn't have to let me in here, but we need to find a way to settle this issue between us. Why you keep sweatin' me, ma? Is my relationship with Desa Rae that important to you? I'm confused like hell. I thought I made myself clear when we parted ways in *Hell House*. I specifically said you go your way, I go mine. I don't know what you don't understand about that and your actions are troublin' to me."

"I'm sorry to hear that, but would you like to know what's troubling to me? Men like you are. You think you can go around screwing anybody you wish to, then turn around and claim to be in a committed relationship. Y'all always talking about how much love you got for your women, but these are the same women you wind up hurting the most. You played the love game when we met, and I didn't appreciate how you kept flirting with me and toying with my feelings. It wasn't right away when I found out that Desa Rae was my oldest sister, but the truth of the matter is, she is. Now, I'm sorry that you've found yourself in this unfortunate situation, but this is what can happen when you play with fire."

Every time Chase mentioned that Desa Rae was her sister, I swallowed hard. "Regardless, I made a mistake. And if what you're sayin' turns out to be correct, I made a big one. My question to you is what must I do to make this go away? I don't want Desa Rae to find out about this; and whether you know this or not, I do love her with all that I own and have."

Chase pursed her lips. "You'll have to convince her, not me. I told you what I wanted and I don't know how many times you want me to repeat it."

"How much money, Chase? Tell me now."

She scooted to the edge of the couch and darted her finger at me. "I'm going to say this to you one more time and I hope it finally sinks in. I don't want one damn dime of your money. There is nothing that you can give to satisfy me, not even your dick, which turned out to be pretty darn good. What I want is for you to tell Desa Rae. If the love is so strong then it will prevail. I will only be satisfied when she is provided the truth and can make a clear choice about the future of y'all's relationship."

"Twenty thousand dollars."

"Shove it up your ass."

"Thirty."

"You don't have enough to buy me."

"Fifty."

"No. A hundred won't do, but your honesty will."

Chase got up and left me alone in the living room. I wasn't sure what she was doing, but it wasn't like I didn't have my gun tucked down inside my jeans. I thought about ending this my way, but I didn't know what Chase had in her possession that involved me.

A few minutes later, Chase came from another room with several items in her hand. She stood next to me and handed me some pictures.

"This is our lowlife-ass father," she said, pointing to the man in the picture who looked a lot like Dez. I bit into my lip, as reality was starting to kick in. "He had Desa Rae years before he gave birth to me and she was his little angel. She was a spoiled brat, but all Daddy ever did for me was molest me. It started when I was five years old, and night after night he made me have sex with him. His abuse went on for several years. When I told my mother, she did nothing about it. Her love for him was more than her love for me. So, for me, this is personal, Roc. It has taken me years to get over what he did to me and I still feel as if I'm not over it. I have suffered by the actions of men too many times, and when I stand up for myself, I'm viewed as a stalker or a crazy bitch who done lost her mind. Either way, Desa Rae needs to be told about this. Maybe it's time for her to feel some of the pain that I have. If she does or doesn't, she still deserves to be with a decent man. You need to step up your game or step out. It starts with telling her the truth and there is no amount of money in the world that you can pay me to keep my mouth shut about this."

Chase laid a flash drive in my lap and went back over to the couch to take a seat. As I sat speechless, she picked up a cigarette from an ashtray and lit it. "On the flash drive is a video of us having sex. Heated sex that no woman wants to see her man indulged in, especially if the other woman just happens to be her sister. I don't want to go to her with that flash drive, but I will. Do the right thing, Roc, and please do it soon."

This was the first time that I really couldn't say shit. I was caught between a rock and a hard place, trying to figure out a way to wiggle myself out of this. Usually, money could buy anything. But this time it wouldn't save me. I hoped like hell that Dez's father hadn't molested her, and maybe that was why she never talked much about him. The thought of what he may have done to her made me want to hurt somebody. It was a good thing he was dead. She had endured a lot, and now she had to deal with my bullshit. This wasn't a good feeling, but I fished for more details about their father, just in case Chase was wrong.

"Desa Rae said her father died when she was—"

"She was lied to. He remarried and died less than two years ago. The bastard died of cancer and he's buried in Jefferson Barracks because he served time in the army. His name is Walter Jenkins. If you don't believe me go check. He has one more daughter still alive and she lives in California. His other son lives here in St. Louis, but he lives on the south side and he's a crackhead. My father had another son who died in a car accident almost five years ago, too. Desa Rae's mother, Leslie Coleman-Jenkins was his 'sweetheart' but he divorced her and married my mother. After dumping her, he moved on to the next then the next and all of his kids got left behind. I'm sure you didn't come here for me to break down our family history to you, but I want to make sure that you don't doubt me."

I didn't doubt Chase anymore, but I had to let her know I was on her side. "I'm sure you've been through a lot, but why would you want to ruin things for your sister? You know what this will do to her, and I can't bring that kind of hurt to her. You've got to keep this shit under wraps. I'm down with you gettin' to know your sister and maybe that's what you need to help you chill out with all that bitterness. Desa Rae is all good, ma, and from what she told me, her relationship with her father was just all right. It sounds like you're hypin' it up to be somethin' that it really wasn't, and you're takin' this out on Desa Rae, when it ain't got nothin' to do with her."

"Roc, this is where we differ. You can spin this how you wish, but she needs to know what's up. I'd rather she be hurt now than hurt later."

I was wasting my time with Chase. I couldn't even speak anymore, so I stood up and reached out to give the flash drive and pictures back to her.

"No, thank you. I have plenty more of those flash drives, so keep that one. As for the pictures, feel free to take one of Walter. Compare it to some of the pictures Desa Rae may have around the house. Then do what you have to do and tell her the truth. I gave you one week to do it, but since you let that maniac manhandle me, I'm thinking less than that. Your move, Roc, you're running out of time."

It was my move and I intended to make it. It was time to do what I didn't want to and that was tell Desa Rae the truth.

I left Chase's apartment with my mind all over the place. I didn't want to go to her house just yet, so I drove to my house to see what was up. When I got there, Dre was gone and the house was real quiet. I did something that I hadn't done in a long time: prayed. No matter what anybody thought, I did love Desa Rae. She had breathed life into the life of a man like me who had been seriously fucked up for years. I had my issues, no doubt, and there were some things that I just couldn't change with the snap of my finger.

Wondering what exactly was on the flash drive, I sat at a computer desk and stuck the drive into the computer. Almost immediately, a damaging video popped up of me having sex with Chase. While watching it, there was no doubt that I was the aggressive one. I couldn't even say that Chase had enticed me. Even though she had, it sure as hell didn't look like it. There was no question that if Desa Rae got wind of this, I would be out of her life for good. She would do her best to keep Chassidy away from me, and the people I cared about the most would be gone. Just like my parents. Just like with Ronnie. Now this. I removed the flash drive from the computer and crushed it with my feet. I wished it were that easy to wash this situation away, but it wasn't. With that in mind, today, I had to come clean. I couldn't find it in my heart to sit on the information with Chase being Dez's sister and me having sex with her. I wasn't a selfish man, and if I had to lose, so be it.

I pulled my cell phone from my pocket to call Desa Rae. Almost immediately, she answered.

"What you doin'?" I asked.

"I'm wrapping the kids' presents. I thought you were coming to help me. I'm almost done now, but there sure were a lot of gifts to wrap."

"No doubt. Save some for me to wrap. I'm on my way."

"Okay. The kids are playing video games in the family room. I don't feel like cooking, so do you mind stopping to get something?"

"What you got a taste for?"

"I'm not sure. I'm tired of chicken and Chinese, so what about some fish or something?"

"Sounds good to me. I'll stop to get some."

"Okay. Hurry. I love you."

"Not like I do."

We ended the call on that note. I left to go get fish for dinner, but on my way out the door, Dre parked his car in the driveway. To no surprise he had the same lame-ass friends with him and two girls.

"Where you headed?" he asked, slapping his hand with mine. "Or do I have to ask?"

"You don't need to ask 'cause you already know. When you get time, though, we need to holla man to man, all right?"

Dre nodded, already knowing what the conversation would be about. Some of his boys spoke to me, some didn't, including the no-good one who was starting to make my flesh crawl every time I saw him. I didn't have time to trip off that nigga, only because I had a bigger fish to fry. I got in my truck and jetted.

I arrived at Desa Rae's house nearly an hour later. My swag was gone, because I knew what I was about to go inside to do. My stomach was rumbling. It felt like I was walking in a fog, as I was so deep in thought.

Already having a key, I entered the house and could see the kids playing around in the family room. They rushed up to me, asking what was in the bags.

"Fish and French fries," I said. "Go wash y'all hands and let's get ready for dinner. Where's Dez?"

"She's in her room," Li'l Roc said in a whisper. "We've been peeking and we think she's wrapping our presents."

I couldn't do nothing but laugh. I put the food on the kitchen table and put some plates on the table, too. Letting Desa Rae know I was there, I headed to her bedroom. The door was closed, but when I opened it, that was when I saw her sitting on the bed in tears. The phone was pushed up to her ear and my heart instantly dropped to my stomach. I figured Chase had already gotten to her, so I rushed up to her, trying to explain myself as best as I could.

"I'm so sorry," I said, sitting on the bed in front of her. All she did was stare at me then told the caller that she'd call them back.

She wiped her dripping nose with Kleenex and wiped away her tears. "Sorry? Sorry for what?" she asked me.

"For not tellin' you what—"

Desa Rae threw her hand back at me and continued to wipe her tears. "I'm over what happened during breakfast the other morning. You still haven't cleared all of that up for me, but I hope you will soon. I was on the phone with Latrel. Angelique is pregnant and I'm goin' to be a grandmother!"

Desa Rae threw her arms around me. I sighed from relief and could've damn near cried myself. "Tha . . . that's what's up, ma. That's real good news. I'm happy for Latrel and Angelique. Give me the phone so I can call him back to congratulate them."

Desa Rae gave me the phone and she went into the bathroom to splash water on her face. I called Latrel and he answered the phone with much enthusiasm.

"Yes, Mama," he said with a sigh.

"It's Roc. Just wanted to say congrats on the baby. I know you and Angelique must be feelin' real good right about now."

"Man, we most certainly are. And to get this news before Christmas is the best present I could've gotten. I'm near speechless, but you know I had to call my mother to let her know what was up. She got so emotional. Started screaming for joy, but I wouldn't expect anything less from her."

"I'm screamin' too, but you just can't hear me. Good news . . . real good news."

Latrel laughed. "Yes, it is. We're thinking about coming there for Christmas, but I'm just not sure yet. Don't tell my mother, though, because I don't want to get her hopes up if we can't make it. Hope to see you then and I appreciate you calling."

"No problem, Latrel. Take care."

I ended the call, knowing damn well that I wasn't going to spoil Desa Rae's good news with my bad news. Timing was everything. This was not the right time. I went to the bathroom to check on her and she was still overwhelmed with joy.

"Boy or girl?" I asked her.

She turned around from looking in the mirror.

I was standing in the doorway.

"I honestly do not know. I'm thinking more like a girl, but then boys are much easier."

"Says who? Boys can be a pain in the ass and they get into a lot of trouble."

"Yeah, but girls are too expensive. They have this thing where it's all about them and their mouths are so sassy."

"You're right about that, but, see, sometimes, boys wind up hangin' with the wrong crowds and are often influenced by the wrong people. They lack compassion for others, never want to admit fault, and all they give a care about is video games."

"Oh, don't I know it. But girls can be influenced by the wrong people too. They're so emotional and always get tangled up in chaotic relationships. They want everybody to like them, and are highly offended when one person says anything negative about them. Boys just keep it moving."

"Sounds like you want them to have a boy then, right?"

Dez stood silent for a while then spoke up. "A girl. I'm thinking more like a girl, but after dinner I'm sure I'll change my mind."

"I'm sure you will too."

I hugged her again. Shortly after, she backed away, shouting, "I have got to call Monica! I wonder how Reggie feels about this, so I must call him, too."

I didn't like that idea and who gave a damn about what Reggie thought? I didn't want to show my hatred for that nigga, but I suggested to Desa Rae that she called them both after dinner.

"You know darn well that once you get on the phone with Monica your food is gon' be ice cold. Call after dinner. Let's go eat. The kids are waitin', and I'm hungry too."

Deciding not to prolong dinner, we headed to the kitchen to eat. When we got there, it was a mess. Chassidy and Li'l Roc tried to set the table by putting food on the table, instead of on the plates. The fish was crumbled up everywhere and mountains of tartar sauce were on top of several pieces. Coleslaw was on one plate and red Kool-Aid had missed several of the glasses and was dripping on the floor.

"Go get me a rag," I said to Li'l Roc. I understood how Chassidy could do something like this, but Li'l Roc was old enough to know better.

He shrugged his shoulder and pouted as he stomped away to get a rag. "I didn't even do nothing."

I looked at Desa Rae. "Didn't I just tell you how boys won't take responsibility? Now you see what I'm talkin' about." I snatched the rag from his hand.

"Chassidy is to blame too," Desa Rae said. "She had her hand in this mess as well."

Desa Rae ordered Chassidy and Li'l Rock to clean up the mess. I had to drive back to the fish joint to get more food, and immediately after dinner, the kids were sent to bed. Dez and me stayed in her room, where I finished wrapping the gifts that she didn't wrap.

"You never said what you wanted me to get you for Christmas," I said to her while sitting on the bed with my shirt off and briefs on.

Desa Rae put the Scotch tape down and kneeled behind me. She rubbed her hands over my shoulders and down to my buffed chest, massaging it. Her lips pecked the side of my neck and she took soft bites on it.

"I don't want to wait until Christmas to get my Christmas present from you. I was thinking that you could maybe *shoot* your present to me a li'l sooner."

I tilted my head as she continued to put bite marks on my neck. Her hands roamed my chest and also my package, which was already hard. "So, in other words, you want to get your fuck on tonight. Is that what you're sayin'?"

"Your words were a bit more creative and blunt than I would've come up with, but, yes, I'm ready for us to get our fuck on. Besides, I've been wrapping these presents all day. I don't want to see any more wrapping paper for the next few days."

Desa Rae came from behind me and pushed the remaining boxes and wrapping paper on the floor. She held thick red ribbon in her hand and pushed on my chest for me to lie back. I cooperated with her move, especially when she released my steel from my briefs. She tied a neat bow around it and held it up straight with her hand.

"Tell me," she said, observing my well-wrapped package, "how does a man get this big? Is there something special that you have to do or is being this big hereditary?"

"I played with myself a lot when I was a kid, so that may have helped some. But for some reason, it has a way of showin' up and showin' out when it comes to you."

"Obviously," Desa Rae said, lowering her head to take care of me.

I shut my eyes, thinking hard about my situation. Ending all of this would devastate me. I didn't know when our last time together would come to an end, so I cherished each and every second. Wondering if this would be our last time making love, I flipped Desa Rae over and pulled her nightgown over her head. Her wobbly breasts were so meaty and sexy that I covered one with my mouth and lightly massaged the other. My dick was already brushing against the entrance of her moist hole, and it wasn't long before she invited me in.

Like always, our bodies rocked together in sync. Desa Rae's legs were wrapped around my back, and for whatever reason, her warm pussy felt better than it had ever felt before. I felt high off of it and my mind was racing a mile a minute. As we passionately kissed, I could feel her heart pounding against mine. I could taste her sweetness, as I lowered myself and sucked her squirting juices that exploded from an orgasm. The sexy words that escaped from her mouth were always on point and this day was no different.

"I love it when you fuck me like this," she said. "Put it back in me, Roc. I want more."

I wanted to give her more. I wanted to give her everything that she deserved. But I had failed to do so. My failures were eating me alive, and after today, my selfishness that lingered somewhere within me kicked in. I was a coward and I couldn't tell Desa Rae the truth. It was too hard for me to do. Too damn hard and she definitely wouldn't hear about my wrongdoings from me.

Chapter 11
Desa Rae

Roc had put it on me for five days straight and I could barely walk. It had been awhile since we had indulged ourselves in such a way, but in no way was I complaining. We needed that quality time because Li'l Roc and Chassidy had been driving us nuts. Li'l Roc was back with his grandmother and Chassidy had been invited to a slumber party at Monica's house with her niece, Brea, who was friends with Chassidy. But before then, Monica and I met for lunch. We sat at the Cheesecake Factory in Chesterfield, cracking up.

"I thought I saw you walking crooked when you came in here," Monica said. "I was like, look at her. She must've just gotten her some."

"Not today, but Roc has been on a roll. My legs have never been this sore and every muscle in my body hurts. I feel like I did one of those Insanity workouts or like I've been in Zumba class all day. I'm exhausted, but I don't want Roc to think this old woman can't hang when I can."

Monica shook her head. "Roc doesn't know what he's getting himself into with marrying you. Does that poor man have any idea?"

"Oh, he knows. He knows that a wonderful future awaits him, and even he said that he didn't want to wait until May. I'm thinking that we may do it sooner, but not until we get a few kinks ironed out pertaining to his phone."

"I know. That was crazy. Have you thought more about what the text message was referring to?"

"I have, but Roc's friends be talking off the wall. They're always calling women bitches and hoes, and I'm pretty sure it probably had something to do with Vanessa."

"Speaking of Vanessa, how has she been acting these days? I don't hear much about her anymore."

"That's because she has a new man keeping her busy. She don't have time for her son, and he spends a lot of time with us. I don't mind at all. I'm just happy that she's backed off Roc."

The waitress came to our table with the food. She placed our plates in front of us and asked if we wanted anything else.

"You can bring me some more water," Monica said. "And I'll be ordering some dessert when I get done with this."

The waitress stared at Monica and smiled. "I'm sorry for staring, but has anyone ever told you that you look like—"

"Vivica Fox," we said in unison.

"Yes," Monica said. "All the time, but I am soooo much more gorgeous than her. The only thing she has on me is 50 Cent and I'm still working on getting him in my corner."

The waitress laughed and walked away.

"You mean in your bedroom more like it," I said. "I don't know how that will work, especially since Shawn is always there. Are you and him getting serious?"

"It depends on what you mean by serious. Marriage is out for me. I doubt that I'm going that route again. I like Shawn, enjoy his company very much. We take trips together, have sex and talk on the phone quite often. I'm perfectly fine with our relationship as is."

"That's great, but never say never. I thought I'd never consider marriage again, but look at me. And then with a young man like Roc. I'm seriously happy, though, and that's what matters. This has been the best year yet. Got my grandbaby on the way and I have a man who has finally gotten his act together."

"It took him long enough," Monica teased. "But don't you start jumping up in your seat because it took you even longer to get your act together."

"I know. We both were so bad, but I think we finally came to the conclusion that we have to accept certain things about each other, we have to compromise and we have to be honest about our feelings and everything else."

"I agree and I'm so happy for the two of you. Now, what did Reggie say when you talked to him about y'alls' new grandbaby?"

"Girl, he was just as happy as I was. That man talked me to death and you know he wants Angelique to have a boy."

"That figures. It's good to hear that you and him are getting along much better, too. I guess that sexual encounter you had with him in Columbia helped."

I almost spit water from my mouth. "How in the world did you know I had sex with Reggie in Columbia? I know that I didn't tell you."

"No, you didn't, best friend. But Latrel told me. You know he's always calling me and griping about what you did and he told me about you threatening a girl at his school. He wanted me to talk some sense into you, and then he told me that you and Reggie hooked up."

I pursed my lips and got down on my pasta before responding to Monica.

"Latrel needs to stop spreading my business. As for me and Reggie, it was nothing. We had a few drinks and one thing led to another."

"Really," Monica said with an inquisitive look in her eyes. "One thing never leads to another, and that statement is so lame. I'm just wondering if it will ever happen again, especially since you were so sure you were done with Reggie."

I rolled my eyes, because Monica was moving in the wrong direction. "Are you serious? I can't believe you asked me that. Reggie and I are done. I have no sexual desires whatsoever for that man. Like I said, the only reason we went there was because I was intoxicated."

"People do what they really want to do when they're intoxicated. Something led you to the bedroom and made you crack your legs open. You say alcohol, but I say feelings."

Monica was so wrong, but I wasn't about to spend our whole lunch disputing what she had said. "The only person I have feelings for is Roc. Let's be done with this because talk of Reggie always works my nerves."

At my request, Monica changed the subject. We ate, talked, and laughed through the next hour or so then left.

"I will pick up Chassidy from school and bring her home late Sunday," Monica said, opening the door to her Lexus. "Be good this weekend and no more sex for you, Miss Hottie."

"None. At least not for another two days. Roc is out of town for two days. He won't be back until Sunday. So, looks like I have a date with my books."

Monica shook her head and got in the car. I watched as she drove off; then I noticed the same woman I had seen at Culpeppers and at the Fox Theatre come out of the Cheesecake Factory. Now, I believed in coincidences, but these were too many. She never looked my way though. I saw her get into a car, and shortly thereafter, she drove off. I did too. I followed her to the stoplight, just to see if she would pull over and say something to me. She didn't. And, by the time we reached the highway, she went in one direction and I went in the other. Seeing her so many times felt strange to me, real strange, but if she was following me I was sure she would've said why.

As soon as I got back to work, Shawna ran up to me. "Mr. Anderson was looking for you and he's very upset. He already left, but please call him on his cell phone."

I went into my office to call Mr. Anderson. I already told him I would be taking an extended lunch, so I wasn't sure what his concerns were.

"Mr. Anderson, this is Desa Rae. Shawna told me to call you."

"I was looking for the notes taken during our last meeting. I know you typed them up, but I couldn't find them. I had Dean Lewis on the phone and I needed to clarify a few things for him. I found the notes, so don't worry about it."

"Shawna said you seemed upset. I wanted to make sure that you remembered I requested an extended lunch."

"I did remember, but you know how I get when I can't find things. Thanks for calling and I'll see you when I get back to the office on Tuesday. Enjoy your weekend."

I told Mr. Anderson to do the same. I started to call Shawna to my office and speak to her about blowing this incident out of proportion, but I decided against it. I only had three hours left at work and was ready to get out of there. I wouldn't be spending the weekend with Roc and I was already missing him. It seemed like I had been doing that a lot lately. I was so ready for us to live in one house and be done with it. He'd already said that he wanted to move in with me, but we agreed to take advantage of the time we now had on our own.

When five o'clock rolled around, I turned off the lights in my office and left. I stopped by Ashley Stewart to see what they had new and wound up leaving there with $300 worth of merchandise. Since the holidays were coming, I wanted something nice to wear. Our Christmas party was next Friday, so I purchased a fitted red dress that crisscrossed at the chest. It sure was sexy and I couldn't wait to wear it. I hadn't told Roc about the Christmas party yet, but I reminded myself to tell him about it when I talked to him later.

It didn't take long for me to get home and relax. I called Monica to check on Chassidy, called Latrel to see what he and Angelique were up to, and I called Roc but he didn't answer. I left a message telling him to call back and I also told him about the Christmas party.

Since I'd eaten a heavy lunch, I made a fruit salad and poured a glass of wine. After that, I changed into my pajamas and stood in front of my wide bookshelf in the family room, looking at hundreds of books.

"I hope somebody gives me a Kindle for Christmas," I said out loud.

Even if they did, I'd still be reading from my paperback books. I reached for a book from one of my favorite authors and tucked it underneath my arm. Still sipping from the glass of wine, I turned down the lights, grabbed the whole bottle of wine, and headed to my bedroom. At first, I sat in the sitting area in my bedroom, reading the book. I was interrupted by the phone ringing, so I got up to answer it and sat on the bed. I could see that the call was from Roc.

"What's up, ma?" he said in a higher tone, due to the noise in the background. "I just saw that you called, but I didn't hear my phone ringin' from all the noise."

"Where are you?" I asked, then poured more wine into the glass.

"Still in Michigan. I'm at a car show and I know you can hear those white boys revvin' up their trucks right now. Once we leave here, I'm goin' to pick up those car parts I told you about. After that, we gon' swing through Connecticut to load up some tires and rims. I may be back soon, if we don't make a run to Florida."

"Sounds like a lot of driving. Be careful and be sure to get some rest before you get on the road. Don't drive straight through, Roc, okay?"

"I won't. I'm a li'l tired right now, especially since you done wore my ass out. My energy is gone," he joked.

"That's what you get for trying to hang with grown women. Seems like you're the one who needs to be taking your One A Day vitamins, not me."

"Don't flatter yourself, please. And what's this about your Christmas party on Friday?"

"Yes, I forgot to tell you. Will you be able to go with me?"

"I should be. And I hope you'll be comin' with me to Craig's Christmas-slash-birthday party, too. It's on Saturday."

"I'm down if you are. Now, get some rest and let me get back to my book. Call me later."

"All right, ma. Holla back."

I hung up the phone and read a few more chapters of the book before getting tired. My eyelids got heavy, thanks to the wine that had me a bit tipsy. I couldn't stop yawning. I placed the book on the nightstand and pulled the soft blankets up to my shoulders. As I started to fade, I heard a car door shut. My body was too tired to see who was outside, and most likely, it was my noisy neighbors. That was what I thought until I turned in bed and saw my motion light in the backyard come on. Still a bit sluggish, I sat up and rubbed my achy forehead. I wanted to go see why my motion light came on, but decided not to get up. Sometimes, a stray dog or cat would make the light come on. That was possible too, so I lay back down. A few minutes later, I heard another noise. I wasn't sure what it was, but this time, I figured I would get up. Since I was at home alone, I went to the closet and got my gun again. I always feared that my classmate would come back to harm me, and that was the first thing on my mind whenever I heard a noise. I did feel safe, because my burglar alarm was on.

I put on my robe and tightened the belt around my waist. My gun led the way as I held it out in front of me. I stopped in the living room, just to double-check the alarm. It was still on, so I headed toward the kitchen so I could get a closer look in the backyard. I reached for the light switch to the patio to turn it on. But when I flipped the switch, the light didn't come on. Obviously, it had burned out. I squinted while peeking through the kitchen curtains that covered the window on the door. I could see the motion light still on, but only a sliver of that light was coming from the side of the house. The rest of the yard was almost pitch black. I double-checked the back door, making sure it was locked. I then looked out the curtain again, seeing no one. I turned around, and seconds later, I heard another noise. I snapped my head to the side, and that was when I saw a shadow appear at the door. I could tell it was a man by how large the shadow was. The knob turned, and fearing for my life, I aimed the gun and pulled the trigger. The pop was so loud that it rang my ears. The glass shattered, causing the house alarm to go off and make a loud blaring sound that could wake the neighbors. Realizing what I'd done, I covered my mouth and dropped the gun that trembled in my hand. The phone was ringing, so I hastily ran to the other side of the room to answer it. I could barely keep the phone in my jittery, sweat-covered hands.

"I . . . I just shot an intruder who tried to enter my house. Please send the police," I shouted in a panic. My jaw trembled as I spoke and tears flooded my eyes.

The operator continued to question me, but I was so scared that the man would get up and come after me. I slammed the phone down and skidded on the floor in my slippery socks, rushing to my bedroom. I grabbed the cordless phone from the nightstand and ran into the bathroom, locking the door behind me. My fingers were trembling so bad that I could barely punch in Roc's number. After two rings, he answered. I was glad to hear his voice.

"Roc!" I screamed out. "I . . . I just shot a man who tried to come in here on me! I'm so scared and don't know what I've done. I . . . I think I killed him! I need you! Please!"

"Call the muthafuckin' police! Ma, I will get there as soon as I can! I'm on my way."

I knew it would be hours before Roc got here and I felt helpless. I didn't know if the man outside was dead. Sweat and tears were rolling down my face and the knot in my stomach was pulling in every direction. Feeling queasy, I crawled over to the toilet to release the vomit that crept up my throat. While holding my stomach, I staggered over to the towel rack to get a towel and wet it. That was when I heard police sirens. I was still afraid to move. In tears, I slid my back against the bathroom door, easing to the floor. I covered my wet face with my hands and screamed out, "God help me!"

A few minutes later, I heard an officer's walkie-talkie. He knocked on the bathroom door, asking if anyone was inside. I reached back and turned the knob to open the door. Two officers rushed in to help me. I could hear more sirens, so I predicted it was probably an ambulance.

I spoke to the officers through staggering breaths. "I . . . I had to shoot him because he was trying to come in on me. I did . . . didn't mean to hurt anybody, I swear. Is he hurt?"

The officers looked at each other as they held me up. They walked me to the family room and sat me down on the couch.

"I'll be right back," one of the officers said and walked away.

The other one stayed with me. I could hear a lot going on outside, but the last thing I wanted to see was the man's dead body. I had a vision of him in my mind and I now regretted having the gun.

"Can I get you anything to drink?" the officer said. "Or have you already had one too many?"

My eyes widened, only because I assumed my breath must have smelled like an alcoholic's from the wine I'd been drinking. But why did he go there with me? Wasn't he supposed to be asking me questions about how the intruder got shot in the first place? Not knowing if I would need a lawyer, all I did was sit tight, shut my mouth, and shake my head. Apparently, the man I shot was white.

For the next thirty minutes, I sat in silence. The phone was ringing off the hook, and I suspected that it was Roc. I was numb. Too numb to answer it, too numb to talk, and in complete, utter shock that all of this was going on at my house. The officer finally asked me what had happened. I told him exactly what went down, and even admitted to having several glasses of wine. When the other officer came back inside, I noticed him taking a deep sigh. I was afraid to ask, but I had to.

"Is . . . is he dead? Did I kill him?"

"It was a she, not a he. She's not dead, but we need to get her to a hospital soon."

My heart dropped somewhere below my stomach. The first person I thought of was Monica. I rushed up from the couch and ran to the back door so I could see the woman I had shot. I staggered sideways, as I saw the young woman, Chase, tightened on a gurney. Her eyes were closed and her blood had stained the white sheets. I covered my mouth, confused as ever as to why this woman would be at my back door. The officer interrupted my thoughts.

"I'm sorry, but it looks like this was an accident. Was she a relative?"

I was speechless. My heart was beating fast. I felt as if I were losing my mind. "No . . . no, I don't even know her. Who is she?"

"Her name is Chase Jenkins. I thought with her last name being the same as yours, the two of you were related. Are you sure that you don't know her?"

I slowly walked away from the door, squeezing my aching forehead. Why was this woman who had my last name following me? Why was she at my house and why did I feel a connection with her? From the moment I saw her, I thought she looked familiar. Who in the hell was she and what in the hell was going on? The officers must have viewed me as unstable. At that moment, yes, I was. I didn't understand any of this. I was glad that she wasn't dead. Hopefully, she'd be able to explain some of this to me.

"I do not know her, but over the past month or so I've seen her at least three times. I think she was following me, but I don't know why. Do you think she will live?"

"We don't know yet. But what we need right now is for you to put on some clothes and come down to the station with us. We need to ask you some more questions about what happened here."

I swallowed the oversized lump in my throat. "Am I being arrested? I . . . I didn't want to hurt anybody, but I was afraid because of an incident that happened last year. I didn't know who she was and I thought she was a man."

The officers tried to calm me. They could tell I was severely troubled by this and assured me that all they wanted to do was talk.

"Do I need an attorney?"

"That's totally up to you. For now, just get your clothes on so we can go."

With the phone blaring in the background, I ignored it and changed clothes. I didn't know if the officers were going to cuff me. Thankfully they didn't. Most of my neighbors were outside and I heard my neighbor Judy ask if I was okay. I couldn't even respond as I got into the back of the police car, looking disheveled and confused as it drove away.

Chapter 12
Desa Rae

This was torture. I had been at the police station for hours, trying to explain myself. It wasn't that they didn't believe me, but they, too, were curious about why Chase Jenkins had shown up at my house. I advised them to ask her and to please let me know why. I was so ready to leave, but one officer after the next kept coming into the tiny interrogation room, questioning me. To them, I must have seemed like a gun-happy drunk woman who lost control. First there was the situation with me shooting Darrell, now this. I really didn't know how to explain myself, but all I could say was that the gun was there for my protection. I didn't know what was going to happen to me, but I guessed the officers were only trying to do their jobs. As the one I had been speaking to stood up, I asked how much longer I would be.

"Not too much longer. We just want to make sure that we have a detailed account of what you said happened. Sit tight, okay?"

"I'm trying," I said, clearing my watery eyes again. "Do you mind if I make a phone call? I really need to call someone."

The officer was nice enough to give me his cell phone. He stood close by, watching as I dialed Roc's phone number. He quickly answered.

"Roc," I said softly.

"Where in the fuck are you?" he shouted. "I've been callin'—"

"I'm at the O'Fallon police station. They brought me in for questioning."

"Damn, ma. I'm less than an hour away. I'm tearin' this highway up, and if I can get there sooner I will."

"Hurry," was the only other thing I said.

I gave the phone back to the officer and thanked him. He left the room, and I didn't think I had ever been this nervous in my life. I assumed that what had happened was already being presented to the prosecutor. Maybe he would make the call on if I should be allowed to go home, or if a bond would be set. I was sure it would be a high one—one that I couldn't afford. I thought about my children and my grandbaby on the way. What if I went to jail and had to do time for attempted murder? How did I find myself in this mess? I didn't know. Yesterday I was the happiest woman ever. Today, I could find myself behind bars with no way out. Every thought possible roamed in my head. More than anything, who was Chase Jenkins?

Three officers came into the room. I was waiting for them to read me my rights, but they didn't.

"You can sit out here while we type up some paperwork with your statement on it, Ms. Jenkins. After that, you're free to go."

I heard what the officer said, but then again, everything was such a blur. Did I hear him clearly? Was I really free to go? I questioned the officers, and the one who spoke up first repeated himself, saying that I was free to go. I asked no further questions and sat outside of the interrogation room. Nearly fifteen minutes later, I looked up and saw Roc coming down the narrow hallway. He had on a long black trench coat that blew open as he walked smoothly down the hallway, looking for me. I stood and rushed into his arms. He held me tight while rocking my body with his.

"I'm so scared," I cried out. "Tha . . . thank God you're here. Don't leave me again. Promise me that you'll never leave me again."

"I promise. Never again, but I hope you killed that muthafucker for tryin' to come in on you."

Just then, the officer called my name and asked me to sign some papers.

"Right here," he said, pointing to the signature line on the paper he placed on the counter.

"Hold up," Roc said, looking down at the paper. "Explain what it is that she's signin'."

"It's her statement. Exactly what she told us happened."

"Do you mind if I read it before she signs it?" Roc asked.

I knew why Roc was so skeptical of the police, but the officer told him that if I didn't mind, he could read it. He picked up the paper and started to read it. He shook his head and then his forehead became lined with wrinkles.

"Who was shot?" Roc said with confusion all over his face. "A woman?"

I nodded. "Her name was Chase Jenkins. I don't know what she was doing at my house, but I thought she was an intruder."

Roc's face turned to stone and his eyes were without a blink. He put the paper back on the counter. He then closed his eyes and rubbed down his face with his hand. "Go ahead and sign it," he said. "Meet me out by my truck."

Roc walked away and I signed the paper. He seemed out of it. I watched him until he left through the door. Something wasn't right.

The officer caught my attention as he started to talk to me. He gave me his card and told me not to leave town because they may need to question me again. I was also told, just in case, to consult with an attorney. I was nervous as ever, but I thanked the officer and left the police station to see what was up with Roc.

Roc stood outside of his truck, pacing the ground. Two of his friends were inside of the truck, and when I got closer, I could see that it was Craig and Troy, who had gone out of town with Roc. His face was flat as ever and there was no smile there whatsoever.

"What's going on?" I said, standing in front of him. I was afraid to question him about Chase, because it was starting to become apparent that he somehow knew her.

He nudged his head toward his truck. "Get in the truck. Let's go home."

My throat ached so badly. I could tell this was not going to be a good night. I opened the door to Roc's truck and got in the front seat. He got in on the driver's side and drove off. The ride was quiet—so quiet that you could hear a pin drop. When we got to my house, Roc turned to Craig.

"Take my truck and call Drake to tell him we can't make it. I'll holla later."

I opened the door to get out and Craig sat in the driver's seat when Roc got out. He followed me into the house, where I laid my purse on the table and turned to him in the foyer.

"Tell me," I said, biting my lip. "You know her, don't you?"

Roc stared into my eyes then blinked and walked away. He removed his trench coat and tossed it over a chair in the family room, where he sat on the couch.

I calmly walked into the family room and stood in front of him. "Who is she?"

He rubbed his hands together and looked up at me. "She's your sister."

What he'd said shook me to the core. I squinted and a serious frown covered my face. "My sister?" I questioned. "She couldn't be my sister because I don't have any sisters."

Roc nodded his head. "Yes, you do. Chase is your sister and you have another sister who lives in California. You also have a brother who lives right here in St. Louis."

My lips quivered and my face became even more twisted. "Wha . . . what is this? Some kind of game that you're playing with me, Roc? Is it? If it is, you need to stop right now because this shit is not funny."

Roc dropped his head and looked down at the floor. When he lifted his head, I could have sworn that I saw tears in his eyes. A knot in his throat appeared and it moved in and out as he swallowed. "This is no game, ma. Your mother didn't tell you the truth. They are your father's children, and I'm sorry that after all this time you didn't know anything about them."

I squeezed my forehead again and took several deep breaths. "Are you telling me that I shot and almost killed my sister? Is that what you're saying, Roc. Did I?"

All he did was nod. Right then, I started to break down. I didn't want to believe him, but I did. Roc was known for investigating people, so that was probably how he found out about my family. But why hadn't he told me? Why? Did he not want to hurt me? My father had been all over the place and there was no doubt that Chase looked a lot like me. Was it possible that she had been reaching out to let me know who she was? The thoughts of what I did brought me to my knees. Roc reached out to grab me. He held me tight, so tight that I couldn't breathe.

"What is wrong with me?" I cried out. "What in the hell did I doooo?"

"You didn't know, ma," he said. "You had no idea who she was."

Roc lifted me from the floor and put me on the couch with him. I leaned into his chest, releasing cries that were long overdue. The betrayal of my father hit me. His abandonment of me and my mother was fresh in my head. Not even knowing that I had other siblings stung like hell, and I was weighed down with emotions. Roc did his best to console me. He kept saying that everything would be okay, but I wasn't so sure. What if Chase died? If she didn't, what would she think of me? I had a million and one questions, but the first thing I had to do was go apologize to her.

I pulled myself away from Roc's hold and wiped the tears from my face. "I need to go to the hospital to see her. I want to make sure she's going to be okay. What if she won't be, Roc? What am I going to do?"

I fell into his chest again. Roc kissed my forehead. "Everything will be okay. We'll call the hospital to see if—"

I quickly sat up. "No. I want to go now. Go with me. Don't make me go alone."

I hurried off the couch to go wash my face and quickly changed clothes. After grabbing my purse, I made my way toward the front door, but Roc was still on the couch.

"Are you going with me?" I asked, standing in the foyer. "Don't make me beg you."

Roc didn't budge. I walked into the family room to find out what was going on.

"Why are you still sitting there?"

Roc put his hands behind his head, narrowing his eyes as he looked at me. "Sit down, Dez. There are some other things that I need to tell you."

I mean, how much more of this can there be? I was feeling frustrated. "I'm not sitting down right now. I'm ready to go. You can tell me whatever else I need to know while we're in the car. And if you don't want to go, fine."

He didn't move, so I stomped away. That was when I heard him shout my name.

"What?" I shouted back and turned in my steps to see him slumped farther down on the couch.

"I don't want to go because your sister, Chase, came here to tell you that I had sex with her. She's also upset with you about some shit that went down with you and your father, and, unfortunately, her motive was to make your life miserable."

It felt like every ounce of air had been knocked out of me. I inched my way back into the family room, feeling my blood boiling. I didn't know where to start. Chase couldn't have been upset with me about our father because it wasn't like our relationship was all that. The situation with Roc left me stunned. "You what? Had sex with her? When? This . . . this had to be way before I met you, right?"

Roc sat up straight and moistened his dry lips with his tongue. "It was recent. Took place while I was, uh, in that house. I met her there and we had sex. I had no idea that she was your sister until much later. She wanted me to tell you, but I couldn't. I didn't want to lose you, ma, and I figured that you would never forgive me for this. I can't say anything to let you know how sorry I am. We had sex one time and I haven't been with nobody else but her. I was upset about Reggie bein' here and it caused me to do somethin' real stupid. Real stupid."

I probably looked like a mannequin as I stood and listened to Roc. After he was done, I cleared the clogged mucus from my throat and pointed to the door.

"Get out. Now," I said as calmly as I could.

"No. I'm not gettin' out. You need to hear me out on this."

"Roc, don't force me to hurt somebody else tonight. Just go. Please."

"If I go tonight, I'm comin' back tomorrow. I'll give you time to think about this, but please don't give up on us, Dez. I need you. You need me too. Don't you know that?"

I remained calm, even though I wanted to take my fist and bang it upside his fucking head. "What I need is for you to leave."

Slowly, Roc stood to his feet and walked over to the chair. He picked up his coat and placed it over his arm.

"Desa Rae, as you take time to think about this, please realize that I'm a human bein' who tripped, fell, and bumped my head because it wasn't on straight. If you find it in your heart to forgive me, I will never take us down this road again. You've got to know how much I love you, ma, don't you know?"

I turned my head, avoiding the pained look in his eyes. It meant nothing to me. The hurt he'd brought to me was unlike anything I could ever do to him. Just so I didn't have to subject myself to further conversation, I walked away. I went to my bedroom and closed the door. Minutes later, I heard Roc call for someone to come get him; then the front door closed.

My body shook from this horrific situation that delivered so much pain—pain that brought me to my knees again and left me releasing a deafening cry.

Chapter 13
Roc

I made my bed, but I damn sure wasn't about to lie in it. I had to fix this shit between me and Desa Rae and I knew it would take some time. There was no doubt that she needed some space, so I gave it to her. I wasn't going to call her to try to explain my actions. She knew what I'd done and so did I. Deep down, she also knew I loved her, too. That alone had to pull us through this, and even though it might take some time, I was willing to wait for her to come around.

My problem for now, though, was Chassidy and Li'l Roc. Yet again, they were caught in the middle. I changed my mind and waited for a few days before I contacted Desa Rae at work. I figured she wouldn't go off on me while she was there.

"I promise not to keep callin' you, but you know we need to talk about the deal with Chassidy and Li'l Roc. However you want to work this is fine with me. I just don't want to create distance, especially with Chassidy."

"Like always, I'm not going to keep Chassidy from you. I wouldn't do her like that. You are free to spend time with her. Just let me know and I'll make arrangements for you to pick her up at Monica's house."

Desa Rae hung up. When I called back, her phone went to voice mail. "Let me know if it's possible for me to pick her up on Christmas Eve. Her and Li'l Roc can spend the day with me at my house. I'll make sure they get back to you on Christmas; that's if Vanessa doesn't have any plans and Li'l Roc is okay with it. Holla later."

Five minutes later, Desa Rae sent me a text that said, OK.

After that, I didn't hear from her for the next two days. By Friday, I was feeling kind of down in the dumps. She had been on my mind twenty-four-seven and I was fighting my feelings like a muthafucka. I was getting in everybody's shit, from Dre's to all the fellas' at the shop. And you had better believe that they called me on it. Craig came into my office and stood by the door.

"Psst, where Roc at?" he said. "'Cause this mutha-fucka who been comin' here beefin' all week about to get shanked up in here. I had to stop Gage from comin' up in here with his piece."

"Say you did, huh?" I hit the intercom button. "Gage, bring yo' ass in here. Right now."

Some people in the waiting area looked shocked by my tone, but others laughed. They knew how we got down up in here.

Gage came into my office with a grin on his face.

"Nigga, what's this I'm hearin' about you wantin' to off me? After all that I do for you, it's goin' down like that."

Gage laughed wickedly and closed the door. "On a for-real tip, boss, you know you like a brotha to me. I would never do nothin' like that. Now, it don't mean that when you piss me off, I'm not gon' talk shit. And just so you know, I'm not no snitch or anything like that, but yo' boy Craig been talkin' mad shit too. We don't like this new nigga who been runnin' up in here for the past few days clownin' on us about every little thing. I mean, where my nigga Roc at? That's all I'm sayin'."

"Let's get real. Have I really been that bad where y'all talkin' about offin' me?"

"Not that bad, but you ain't been on the up and up either."

I placed my hands behind my head and leaned back in my chair. A smirk was on my face because I knew exactly where they were coming from. "I feel y'all, and I'ma get back to myself real soon. Y'all know I'm still swoll about what happened between me and Desa Rae, so give me a li'l time to get my shit together."

"I don't know why you just won't go see her," Craig said. "Women always play that game like they don't want to see you. Realistically, they can't wait for you to show up. Go take her some flowers, or chocolates, or somethin'. Buy her somethin' sexy to wear, or get her tickets to a play. That shit works every time. Trust me."

Gage sucked his teeth and disagreed with Craig. "Man, flowers and candies, all that bullshit you mentioned don't work with women these days. What you need to do is swing through that party she invited you to tonight. It ain't like she will clown on you around the people she works with, and you know she wants to showboat you around to her coworkers. No woman likes to party with their coworkers without a man. I think you should go and shock the hell out of her by showin' up."

I rubbed the minimal hair on my chin, thinking that Gage's idea wasn't a bad one. I had given Desa Rae enough space and I was dying to see her. After all, she did invite me to come. I knew the party was at the Renaissance near the airport and it started at seven.

"All right," I said to Gage and Craig. "Get the fuck out of here and get back to work. I got a party to go to so I'ma need y'all to get some of these customers out of here before I go."

Gage and Craig gave me dap and left my office. Almost an hour later, I left the shop and went home to change. Unfortunately for me, Dre was there with his friends. They were in my living room, smoking weed and playing cards. Any other time it might not have bothered me, but now that I had been spending more time at home, the last thing I wanted was a bunch of hating-ass young punks in my house.

"Close the piano and turn out the lights. Y'all mutha-fuckers need to get out of here tonight. I got some company comin' through and I need some privacy," I said.

Dre stood to stretch and the other brothers started gathering their things. I could feel that I was being stared down by the troublemaker, but yet, again, I didn't have time for his ass tonight. It was already 6:30 p.m., so I left the living room to go get ready.

An hour later, I was dressed in my gray tailored suit that fit my frame to a capital T. A burgundy silk shirt was underneath and I left several buttons at the top undone. My platinum chain and watch made me look like millions and the diamonds in my lobes glistened from afar. I looked in the mirror at the finest dark-skinned brother on this planet and winked at the mirror before walking away. Dre and his friends had already jetted. I was glad about that and I hoped they stayed gone. I snatched the keys to my truck from the table and hurried to get to the Renaissance.

When I got to the Renaissance, there were several other Christmas parties going on. I was told by a lady at the front desk that the party was on the top floor. One of my friends had a wedding on the top floor before, so I already knew how the room was laid out. I took the elevator going up and had finally reached my destination. The double doors to the ballroom were open. Several people were standing around, waiting to get inside. We had to check in at the door and I hoped that Desa Rae hadn't removed my name from the check-in list.

I smiled at the African American woman with high cheekbones.

"Your name?" she said, smiling back.

"Roc Dawson. I'm here with Desa Rae Jenkins."

"I know Desa Rae. Roc, I'm Shawna," she said, holding out her hand to shake mine. "I've heard some wonderful things about you. Nice to meet you."

"Same here," I said as she rubbed her fingers against the palm of my hand. Then she had the nerve to wink. I just kept it moving, hoping that Desa Rae didn't consider her a friend.

Elegance soaked the room. People were decked out in Christmas colors and the room was packed to capacity. Some people were sitting, many were standing. I had my work cut out for me looking for Desa Rae, but I eventually spotted her at a round table with three other women and two men. They sat right by curved glass windows that reviewed a good portion of mid-St. Louis and the airport. Desa Rae looked dope in her sexy red dress. She had straightened her hair and part of it swooped across her forehead. A silver necklace fell between her breasts and her overall appearance garnered much attention.

Before approaching the table, I straightened my suit jacket, licked my lips, and cleared my throat. I had no idea how she was going to react to my presence, but I was willing to take my chances on this. I stepped forward, hitting the floor in my sleek, dark gray leather shoes, and made my way up to the table. Obviously not knowing who I was, the other women looked up at me with lust locked in their eyes. Desa Rae appeared speechless, but to relieve everybody, I bent down and planted a kiss on her cheek.

"You look beautiful," I said.

I noticed a slight roll of her eyes before she said, "Thank you."

The other ladies looked envious, but that was when the introductions started. Desa Rae told everyone who I was; then she stood up from the table. She picked up her clutch purse, tucking it underneath her arm.

"Follow me," she said. "I need to go to the ladies' room."

I followed as she walked away, clacking her peep-toe, high-heeled pumps on the floor. Her curvy hips swished from side to side, causing the edges of her dress to swing with the sway of her voluptuous hips. There was no doubt that she was the best looking woman in the room. Her walk alone demanded attention and she damn sure got it.

While on her way out the doors, she was stopped by several people who introduced her to others. She hugged some people, sparked up brief conversations, and I waited until she was finished. After that, she left and went to the elevator, pushing the down button.

"I guess you want me to leave," I said, standing next to her. "I just thought we could have a good time tonight, that's all."

The elevator opened and we both got on it. I turned to her, but she looked straight ahead. "Ma, you gon' have to talk to me. We can't go on playin' the silent game with each other. I know I was wrong, and if you need to hear me say, damn it, I was wrong as hell. You deserved better and I know this." The elevator opened, but before Desa Rae stepped forward, I grabbed her arm.

She glared at me and the look in her eyes was filled with so much anger. "Don't touch me, Roc. If you want to talk, let's go talk."

I released her arm and she walked off. I followed her into another, empty ballroom that was less than half the size of the other one.

Desa Rae turned to me near the door. "Please don't force yourself on me. I think we both know that we just can't keep doing this. And, as much as this hurts me, I think it's time to put closure to this. I'm throwing in the towel." She dug in her purse and pulled out the ring I had given to her.

Right then, my heart fell to the ground and shattered into a thousand pieces. I figured she would be upset, but the reality of how she would handle this was now staring me in the face.

"I don't hate you, Roc. You continue to be the man you want to be, so be that man. I'm not going to spend the rest of my life trying to change a man who has no desires to get his act together. Life is too short for that. I have too many wonderful things to look forward to and I'm not going to spend another day arguing, cussing, and fussing with you."

With her French-manicured nails, she reached out to give me the ring back.

Sadness covered my face. I eased my hands into my pockets and shook my head. "No. I'm not taking that ring back. I won't do it. I'll give you more time to think this through, 'cause at the end of the day, we are still gon' get married. I can promise you that. I will do any and everything I have to do to make that happen."

"You can't fix this, Roc. I have so much hatred in my heart for you right now, and my love for you flew out the window that day. What you did cut deep and it will be a long time before the bleeding stops. On May nineteenth, which was supposed to be our wedding day, my hope is that, by then, you've moved on with your life and you allow me to have what I want, and that is peace. If you love me, like you say you do, then that's what you can offer me."

I stood, silent, then turned around so Desa Rae wouldn't see my hurt. I could feel myself about to lose it, but that was when I heard the door squeak open and I turned and saw her walk out. I rushed out of the room, watching as she tossed the ring in a nearby trashcan. I ran up from behind her and pulled at her waist. She turned but backed away from my hold.

"I have never begged anyone for anything," I said with pleading eyes. "But I'm beggin' for your forgiveness. If you believe in your heart that this is over, tell me now. But dig deep, Desa Rae, before you tell me that it is. Think hard about it and look back to all of the challenges that we overcame together in this relationship. We got through that shit, ma. We made it. We can get through this too and you have my word, the word of Roc Dawson, that the days ahead will be on the up and up. Do not let this end on this note. Please."

"It ends on this note. Your word isn't worth a damn, but I hope that mine sticks. I forgive you, Roc, but this is over."

Desa Rae walked off again, but this time I let her go. It pained me to do it, but I promised myself that whatever decision she made, I'd live with it. I looked at the trashcan, thinking about retrieving the ring. I decided not to, and with my head hanging low, I went back to my truck, leaving behind the only woman I had ever truly loved.

Chapter 14
Roc

The next day, I kicked it with the fellas at Craig's birthday/Christmas party at one of St. Louis's hottest new club scenes off Washington Avenue. It had three levels and was crammed with partygoers from top to bottom. Craig reserved half of the upper level and the other half was reserved by an up-and-coming rapper in St. Louis, G-low. Mixed with my crew, we had the upper level on fire. I was chilling in a booth with white circular seating, and a glass table filled with alcohol and wine bottles was in front of me. A chandelier hung over the gang of fellas sitting with me and classic drapes with ropes were pulled aside, giving the space we sat in the hook up. Hip hop music was spilling through the loud speakers and the DJ had many people on their feet. The vibe was sweet and so was the mega joint that I had squeezed between my lips. I had been smoking weed all day and was high as fuck. My eyes were narrowed and my head was spinning a little from working my third glass of Cîroc vodka.

"Slow dat shit down," Craig said, sitting next to me. He was just as gone as I was, but we were there to party. If he wasn't, I certainly was. I hadn't danced all night, and there were some fly-ass chicks up in there to dance with. Many had already been over to the table, but I had to uplift my spirits before making a move.

I stood and placed my empty glass on the table. My attire tonight was laidback because I wanted to be comfortable. I rocked a thin black leather jacket that had square pockets on both sides. The red V-neck fitted shirt underneath hugged my muscles and it meshed well with my dark chocolate skin. The bottom of my loose jeans poured over my Timberlands, and my diamonds always set me off.

"It's time for me to run away from you niggas and go get my party on," I said.

Troy was all about that cane, so after leaning forward and powdering his nose, he got up with me. Craig, Gage, Romo, and plenty of others stayed behind. I stood on the balcony, looking down at the hundreds of people dancing. A silver disco ball turned above them and flashing lights let me see who was who in St. Louis. For starters, my ex, Raven, was there and so was Vanessa. She was with her man, so that was a good thing. I saw a few other chicks who I had hooked up with back in the day, and then I saw Dre and his partners chilling at some tables. I wondered how he even got up in here. He wasn't old enough to be in no joint like this. I walked away to go see what was up, but stopped when I heard G-low's voice.

"You ain't leavin', Roc, are you?" G-low said with two white chicks hugged up next to him in the circular booth.

"Nah, man. I'ma go check out some things then show these fools how I really get down."

"I'm comin' with you." He scooted his fat self out of the booth. It was definitely a struggle. "Move, bitch. Can't you see I'm tryin' to get out of here?"

The white chick moved out of his way, and G-low pimped his way to the elevator with me and Troy. As soon as we got off at the first floor, it was on. Brothers had hater looks in their eyes and some of the females were acting real thirsty. One grabbed the back of my jacket so hard that it caused me to stumble. I snatched myself away from her and turned around.

"Damn, ma, what's up?"

"You, baby, you," she said, licking across her thick lips. Her friends all had smiles and they were gazing at me like I was a piece of fresh meat. All I did was toss my head back and kept it moving. We inched our way through the crowd, stopping after every two or three steps to holler at the ladies, or shoot the breeze with friends from the hood. G-low was signing autographs and one chick put a napkin and pen in front of me.

"No autograph, but a phone number would be nice," she said, batting her lashes.

"A dance would be better."

The pretty chick with curly tresses dangling in front of her seducing eyes displayed her dimples with a smile. She raised her hands in the air and danced her way to the dance floor. All she had on was a strapless, pink dress that stretched around her shapely curves. The dress was cut at her thighs and inched up as she worked her hips. To me, she looked like a stripper—one who was capable of making a whole lot of money.

I moved in close behind her, occasionally grinding her backside as we danced to the music. She kept bending over to touch her toes, and the moves that she made validated that a stripper pole had been in her past, or it would be in her future.

She turned around, leaving no breathing room in between us. "This may be a real dumb question, but has anybody ever told you how sexy you are?" she asked. "I would love to look into those hooded eyes with you on top of me. And don't let me talk about the body." She fanned herself with her hand. "Whew."

I appreciated her compliments, but after ten minutes of dancing, it was time for me to get another glass of alcohol so I could wash away my thoughts of Desa Rae. I didn't even respond to the chick, but when Vanessa rushed up on the floor, my thoughts directed elsewhere.

She grabbed my hand, pulling it toward her. "I don't give a shit who you talk to, but do not talk to that hoochie mama right there. She's a slut. I thought you didn't do sluts."

The chick I was dancing with rolled her eyes and pursed her lips. She said nothing to Vanessa, just stormed away as I started to dance with Vanessa. All we did was stand face to face and move side to side while talking.

"That was rude as hell," I said. "You tryin' to get yo' ass kicked up in here or what?"

"That trick ain't gon' touch me. Besides, I'ma always have my baby daddy to protect me."

"I don't know about all of that, but where is my son at? With my baby mama up in the club, I suspect you probably don't know."

"Your son is with his grandmother, where he prefers to be. But the real question is where is Desa Rae?"

"At home sick. She was supposed to come with me, but didn't feel like it."

"Sick my ass. You know damn well she ain't comin' to no club like this. We too damn ghetto for her, and this is not her cup of tea."

I kept quiet. I was trying not to think of Desa Rae, but all Vanessa wanted to do was talk about her.

"Where your man at?" I asked, trying to change the subject.

"His tired butt over there sittin' down. I told him I wanted to dance, but he drunk as all outdoors. He knows I'm up here dancin' with you."

"Not only does he know it, but he can also see it. He ain't gon' trip, is he? You know that fool don't like me."

"No, he don't, but he ain't got nothin' to worry about. I am sooo over your black tail, and the heartache you brought me I wouldn't wish on my worst enemy. Desa Rae can have you."

"Come on, ma. I'm not that bad. You actin' like bein' with me was so bad."

Vanessa stopped dancing. She washed the smile off her face and shot me a serious look. "Yes, you were. You were somethin' else, Roc, and that's why I can't stand to be around that li'l nappy-head son of yours who acts just like you. I love my son to death, but I hate you with a passion. I prefer to keep my distance."

"And you should," I said, walking off the dance floor and leaving Vanessa to dance with herself. Some people just don't know how good they have or have had it. Vanessa had no room to talk shit about me, especially when she had gotten away with so much mess when we were together. While I was in prison, what did she do? She ran to one of my boys and started fucking him. I bought her cars, paid her rent, and gave her thousands to purchase whatever the hell she wanted. And after all of that, she hated me. I did dip into a li'l something else from time to time, but Vanessa wasn't on the up and up with me. On the other hand, Desa Rae was and it bothered me.

I searched through the crowd for Dre. Passed by Raven, but she turned away and didn't say anything to me. Troy and G-low were standing by the bar near a crowd of people, and that was when I saw Dre coming out of the bathroom. I made my way over to him, but still couldn't get there without being pulled on by women.

"You wanna dance?" one said.

"Be my baby's daddy, would you?" another said.

"Damn, he fine."

"I love a dark-skinned brother. Yummy."

My head was starting to pound more and my vision was blurred from the thick smoke filling the air. By the time I reached the bathroom, Dre must have gotten lost in the crowd. I turned away from the bathroom and bumped into the chick I was dancing with earlier.

"Do you want to go outside to get some fresh air?" she asked.

Actually, I did. The club had gotten hot and stuffy, but I didn't want to remove my jacket because it went well with my fit. I agreed to go outside with the sexy stripper, but we found ourselves in the back seat of one of the Hummer limos I rode in earlier with Craig and my boys.

The chick was sitting back on the back seat with her legs wide open, inviting me to come inside and see what lurked beyond her hairless slit, which was clearly visible.

"You got condoms, don't you?" she asked.

I had one in my wallet, but my thoughts were all over the place. Pussy had already fucked me up and that was why I was in the situation that I was in. I didn't want pussy to have no power over me. I was better than this, or should I say, I had become better than this—all because of Desa Rae. A quickie from a trick like this wasn't going to satisfy me. I couldn't wash away the pain I felt inside and I wasn't about to waste my time.

While sitting across from the woman, I lifted myself from the seat and pulled out my wallet. I gave her a hundred dollar bill then nudged my head toward the door.

"Close your legs," I said. "It stinks in here. I'ma need for you to take that money and jet."

The chick seemed shocked by what I'd said, but she smelt that shit like I did. She snapped her legs shut and crumbled the hundred dollar bill in her hand. After throwing it at me, she rushed to get out of the car and slammed the door behind her. I tapped the window to holla at the driver.

"Bo, take me home, man. I'm ill," I said.

"You sure you don't want me to take you to the hospital? Are you hurt?"

"Terribly bad. But I'm goin' home."

I lay on my back while resting on the seat and looking at the neon lights on the ceiling. My eyelids got heavy and then I went into a deep sleep that was more than needed. Hopefully, Craig would forgive me for checking out so soon.

Chapter 15

Desa Rae

What else could I do but keep it moving? This whole thing with Roc was devastating, but we had definitely been here and done this before. This time, it was different. Chase was involved and the situation with her had drained me. I had to find the courage to go see her. I had spoken to one of the police officers who were on the scene that day and he told me that it looked as if Chase was going to pull through. The shot I fired went into her side and she was unconscious because she had lost a substantial amount of blood. I felt like a coward for not facing her, and I wasn't sure if she was still in the hospital. When I called, I was told that she was. The nice lady connected me to Chase's room, but I hung up.

Feeling horrible about ignoring her, I decided to go see Chase on Christmas Eve. Roc had picked up Chassidy from Monica's house, so she was spending the day with him. As for me, I hadn't seen or heard from him since the Christmas party last week. I had a good time, too, with the exception of facing him when he showed up. My coworkers couldn't stop talking about how handsome he was, but they had no idea that there was so much more to him being a handsome man. I kept my personal business to myself, and when they asked why he didn't return, I told them that his mother had fallen ill so he had to go.

I arrived at Barnes-Jewish Hospital in St. Peters around noon. I knew Chase was on the second floor, so I made my way to her room. For the most part, the hospital was quiet. There were a few nurses and doctors walking around, and each of them greeted me with a welcoming smile. By the time I reached Chase's door, I began to regret being there. I was so sure that she had information about my father that I didn't want to know, and if she shared that information with Roc, I was sure she hadn't told him everything. I wanted to find out if or why she was so upset with me about our father. What did I do to her? The only way I'd get those answers was to go inside, so forcing myself to move forward, I straightened my back and knocked on the door that was halfway shut.

"Come in," I heard a woman say.

I walked into the room and the smell of strong disinfect hit me. There was an empty bed on one side and a hanging white curtain separated the bed on the other side. I peeped around the curtain and could see Chase sitting up in bed with a tray of food in front of her. Her eyes bugged when she saw me and she stopped chewing the food in her mouth. She then laid the fork on a tray and picked up a napkin to wipe her mouth. It felt so awkward looking at her.

"How . . . how are you doing?" I hesitated as I spoke. "Are you feeling any better?"

She shrugged with a slight attitude. "A little better, but what brings you here?"

I figured she could see how nervous I was, and her tone didn't help. I had to grip my purse to stop myself from fidgeting. "I have so much going on in my head, but do you mind if I take a seat?"

"Go right ahead. I don't mind."

I sat in a chair by the window and placed my purse on my lap. Once I was comfortable, I looked at Chase, who appeared to be doing okay. "First, I want to sincerely apologize for shooting you. I had no idea who you were and I thought you were a stranger trying to get into my house. I had been very paranoid because of an incident that took place at my house last year. My hope is that you can find a place in your heart to forgive me. I'm not some kind of crazy woman who goes around shooting people."

"I figured it was an accident. When no one answered my knocks on your door, I went around back to see if I could see someone. I saw you standing in the kitchen and I turned the knob to get your attention. As for your apology, all I can do is take your word that you are sorry and go on from there."

"Thank you for that. Now tell me how you're doing. Are you going to be okay, and why are you still in the hospital?"

"I'll be okay. I lost a lot of blood and the lower part of my body was numb. The doctors thought I was paralyzed, but I'm starting to get some feeling back into my legs."

No words could express how horrible I felt right then. The fact that she was even talking to me made me feel a little better. "That's good news. I'm going to pray for you every day, in hopes that you get better."

"Please do."

There was silence between us until I cleared my throat and spoke again. "So, what brought you to my house, Chase? Do you mind telling me why you were there to begin with? I heard that you're upset with me about something pertaining to our father. Please share that with me, because I don't quite understand your ill feelings toward me."

She put a straw in her mouth and sipped from a carton of orange juice. "There were several reasons why I was at your house. One was I wanted to let you know that we were sisters. I recently found out that we were, and I had a desire to meet you and get a feel for what your life has been like compared to mine. Mine was a living hell. You were Daddy's angel and he always took care of you. He would always compare me to you and he'd tell me that he wished I turned out like you. I hated you, but not as much as I hated him. I also wanted to warn you about Roc because I think you deserve a much better man than him."

I was stunned by Chase's hatred for me. She was so wrong about our father and I had to let her know that. "Let me first say that I'm not here to discuss Roc. I know that he was intimate with you and nothing else needs to be said about him. How are you so sure that we're sisters? My father died when I was nineteen. And I was no angel to the man who jumped in and out of my life when he wanted to. He did some nice things for me, Chase, but I wouldn't say that he took care of me and showed love to a child who seriously needed more than what he gave me. Wherever you got your information from, it was incorrect. And when you say what your life has been like, what do you mean?"

"I got my information from my mother, who he treated like shit. According to her, the only people Daddy did anything for was you and your mother. That's why he didn't have time for us. I will tell you what my life has been like, but let me get something else off my chest first."

Chase raised the bed to sit up straight. She popped two pills in her mouth and then took another sip from the carton. Afterward, she continued. "I know you don't want to discuss Roc, but we have to. Putting all that other stuff aside, I do want you to be with a decent man. What I learned about Roc is he's not what I consider a dog or anything like that, but he wants to be boss and he likes to flirt. He's got some growing up to do, and just from talking to you, the two of you seem to be on very different levels. I pursued Roc in *Hell House* and he fought me off for a good li'l while. But then we got high together one day and he was willing and able to go where I wanted him to go. At that time, I didn't know you and I were related. I found out shortly thereafter that we were and I went to Roc, several times, to advise him to tell you. I knew y'all were getting married and I didn't want to see you hurt. I'm glad he found it in his heart to tell you what happened, and whatever decision you make from here is up to you."

Chase admitting that she pursued Roc didn't surprise me. He showed weakness when he wasn't able to shut that mess down and tell her he was engaged. If he had, I wouldn't have been sitting here with my own sister discussing how their intimate time together occurred.

"I know what kind of man I'm dealing with and I've made my decision. I appreciate your concern for me not getting hurt, because I have definitely been there before."

"Me too. Too many times, and I have so little respect for men. I don't even know why I still date them, but I'm just not into women. Pertaining to our father, I hated him, Desa Rae. You were lied to about him, as I was, and he just died a few years ago. He died of cancer. Sad to say, that day was one of the best days of my life."

It disheartened me to hear Chase speak about our father in such a way. What I did remember about him wasn't all that horrible, only that he never spent time with me. He did some disrespectful things to my mother, too, but she stood strong and moved on.

"Why did you hate him so much?" I asked Chase.

She began to tell me about him molesting her. I was on the edge of my seat, barely able to breathe. From what Chase told me, I began to hate him. I, too, was glad he was dead and from that moment on, I would never speak his name again.

Tears welled in Chase's eyes as she spoke. I saw the little girl who had been through so much, and the grown woman who was still affected by what he'd done. She was damaged. The men in her life who toyed with her emotions, betrayed her, and abused her, they reminded her of our father. She relived her childhood each and every time one of those men let her down. And for the next hour, she went on and on about relationships that left her bitter and plotting revenge.

"I've been in counseling. It has helped some, but, sometimes, I find myself going backward. Then I say I'll never love or date again, but I find myself hooking up with someone. It's been a true struggle for me and I have our father to thank for ruining my life."

"Chase, I'm so sorry for all that you've been through, and shame on me for praising the half-ass father I knew. I guess I'd been in denial. If I could tell you how to fix this I would. I'm no counselor or anything like that, but you have given our father too much power over your life. If when he died was the best day of your life then celebrate it every day. I know that's sad to say, but find it in your heart to forgive a sick, evil man who doesn't deserve to make you so bitter and steal your joy. You may think it's easy for me to say this because I wasn't abused by him, but my life has been affected by his absence too."

"I'm sure it has, and maybe that explains how you hooked up with Roc," she said, chuckling.

"I guess the same way you found yourself hooked up with him."

She paused before replying, then shrugged her shoulder. "You got a point. But I'm not going to be that hard on him. You have every right to be, but there is something about a man who is willing to pay a hundred thousand dollars to a woman for her silence. He didn't want you to know about us and he was willing to give me anything . . . any amount of money that I wanted."

I rolled my eyes. "How crazy is that? You should have taken the money and still told me."

"Now, you're sounding like me." Chase laughed. "I started to, and I know if I had asked for a million, he would've given it to me."

"Yeah, and I wonder how many people would have had to die for him to get that kind of money to you."

"Who knows, but he would have gotten it. Then again, he probably already sitting on it. That shop he has be booming. I witnessed that during the first fifteen minutes I was there. I was there to advise him to tell you the truth, but he wound up putting his pit bulls on me. That day didn't turn out pretty."

Chase began to tell me what Roc's friends had done to her. I had to stop her. "Please, tell me no more. It makes me so mad at myself for dealing with a man who is capable of ordering somebody to do something that horrible to a woman."

"Obviously, he is willing to do whatever to protect the ones he loves. Is that such a bad thing?"

Roc was a protector. He took the fall for his Uncle Ronnie and went to jail. Then he turned around and had Ronnie killed to protect me and Chassidy from being harmed. Now this. Lord knows what else I didn't know about, and Chase hadn't said anything to me that I didn't already know.

Our conversation continued for hours. Chase talked about our other siblings who she wanted to reach out to, but was skeptical. I was too, and sometimes it was wise to leave things alone. There was no telling what would happen if we opened up another can of worms, especially in connection with our father.

Chase yawned. She appeared to be getting restless so I told her I was getting ready to go.

"Has anyone else come to see you?" I asked her. Like me, she didn't have much family and friends were at a minimum.

"Some of my coworkers have visited. And one of my girlfriends has been coming up here to see about me. We're like sisters and she's really been there for me over the past few years."

"That's good. I have a friend named Monica who I feel the same way about. Maybe one day you'll get to meet her. I don't know where we go from here, but if you ever need anything, please call me. Call me anyway, just to let me know how you're doing. I want to know when you leave the hospital and if I can do anything . . . anything during your stay, call me."

"I will, but don't take offense to it if I don't call. I feel a certain way about this whole thing with Roc and it may be best that I stay as far away as possible."

I wrote my number on a piece of paper and gave it to Chase. "I'll let you decide, and I won't be offended if you decide not to call. It was good talking to you. I wish you all the best."

"You too," Chase said as I leaned in to embrace her. After that, I left and felt extremely good about our visit.

Chapter 16
Roc

Things were getting back to my kind of normal, without Desa Rae. I hadn't been bugging and I played by her rules when it came to Chassidy. Once she was done spending time at my crib, I dropped her off at home and drove off without going inside. Li'l Roc had been still making his weekly visits, too, and if I couldn't pick him up, Vanessa's mother would do it for me.

I'd been spending most of my time at the shop. During times like this, I always picked up my money game. Money was flowing through the shop. The fellas were working their asses off, especially since I was there around the clock. I even hired Dre to come in and do some work for me and he loved being on my payroll. Hell, everybody did, and this was definitely the place to be.

As I was in my office, flipping through a magazine with tires and rims, I heard my name being called over the intercom.

"Rockay," Craig shouted for a second time. "These fools in here passin' gas and stankin' up the shop area. All the gas gone 'cause some of these cars in here to blow up."

Everybody started cracking up. It felt good to have a laugh every now and then, but I ignored Craig. I wasn't about to touch the shop area, at least for the next thirty minutes or so.

Getting thirsty, I got up to get a soda. Romo came up to me while I was at the soda machine.

"Man, I need you to come take a look at this car. I ain't never seen this much rust on no car, and if Mr. Walls wants his car painted, he gon' have to up the dollars to have all this rust patched up first."

Dressed in my navy blue coveralls and black rubber boots, I followed Romo into the shop area. He pointed out the rust spots on Mr. Walls's 1956 Cadillac, which he wanted painted a shimmering gold.

"Look at this," Romo said, lightly kicking a big rust spot near his trunk. The car had more rust spots along the sides and some on the hood and front as well.

I rubbed my chin. "I mean, we can fix the rust spots, but I wouldn't put a lick of paint on that until those spots are taken care of. Redo his estimate and I'll call to let him know how much more this gon' hurt his pockets."

"That fool got it. He ain't hurtin' for no money, so hit 'em hard."

I walked away to where Gage was kneeling on the ground, looking for something underneath a car. "What you lookin' for?" I asked. "If you can't see, use the lift to raise it."

"I don't feel like foolin' with that right now. I'm just tryin' to see where this hissin' sound is comin' from."

I got on the ground and eased underneath the car. I didn't hear anything hissing, but I did see something big crawling on the exhaust pipe.

"What the fuck?" I shouted and quickly rolled from underneath the car, moving away from it. "I just saw something big and black crawlin' around in there."

I don't ever remember a time when I saw a bunch of black men move out quickly from one space. Then again, I had witnessed plenty of shootings that had everybody on the run. We all broke out of the garage and not one person stayed behind.

"What was it?" everybody kept asking. "How big?"

We couldn't help but to laugh, especially at the mechanics who had run all the way out in the street.

"I don't know what the fuck it was," I said, using my hands to show how big it was. "All I know is it was big, black, and ugly."

"That sounds like Craig's mama, but she too big to fit under there," Romo said.

We all cracked up again.

"Fuck you, you hot-breath funky, crusty-toe, black ape. Yo' mama be . . ."

Craig kept going off and Romo was firing back. It was all in good fun until we contemplated who was going to be the brave one to go back inside.

"Gage, go get the Glock and see what's up," I said, shoving him forward.

"No, thank you. It may be some kind of snake or somethin'. If that thing eats me, y'all asses will be standin' right there watchin'."

"It's winter time," Dre said. "Snakes are hibernatin'. Roc, g'on and see what's up so we can get back to work."

Romo sprayed an imaginary S on his chest and decided to be the brave one. He pulled his 9 mm from the back of his pants and charged inside. He pounded on the hood and growled like a madman, trying to scare whatever it was from underneath the car.

"Superman ain't packin' heat, and he don't be growlin' either," Dre shouted to Romo.

"Stop talkin' that mess and bring yo' happy ass in here."

Seconds later, a dirty squirrel ran from underneath the car. It stopped to look at us then jetted off toward the building next door.

All of the fellas turned to me, shaking their heads.

"Big, black, ugly creature, huh?" Craig said. "Have you lost your mind or what?"

"That couldn't have been what I saw. I know what I saw," I said.

"Stop smokin' all that weed," Gage said, patting my back. "You hallucinatin'."

"And then some," Dre said, hiking back up the long driveway.

A horn blew and we all turned around.

"Dre," one of his friends yelled. "Come holla."

Dre went to see what was up and I evil-eyed the brothers in the car. Yet again it was the same crew who were up to no good. I could hear them, trying to get Dre to leave with them. He wasn't with it and somebody called him a punk.

Romo could see how engaged I was and he stood next to me with his arms folded.

"I don't like those niggas," I said. "Do me a favor and keep your eyes on them, particularly the one with his hat on backward. Me and that fool ain't clickin' for some reason. Go up to the car and get familiar with their faces. Then tell Dre he's needed inside."

Romo went up to the car, speaking and slapping hands with everyone inside, as if it were all good. He shot the breeze for about ten minutes with them, before telling Dre he needed help inside. The car drove off and Dre and Romo came into the shop area. Without Dre seeing him, Romo brushed against my shoulder and whispered something that I already knew. "Trouble."

Later that day, I was at home chilling in my bed and watching TV. I had just gotten out of the shower and the only thing I had on was my cotton gray briefs.

White socks covered my feet because they were cold. I was at peace until I got a phone call from Latrel, who told me he was in town. The only reason it bothered me was because I was sure Desa Rae had told him what had happened. I figured Reggie would somehow manage to show up at her place again.

"I was calling to let you know we're in town for a few days. I had no idea that you and my mama weren't seeing each other anymore. I'm actually sorry to hear that."

"Not as sorry as I am, but she called this shit off and I got to live with it. I'm sure she told you what happened and I take full responsibility for what I done. That's not enough to make this situation right, but I'm hopin' that by May nineteenth she'll be singin' a new tune."

"I take it that was the planned wedding date, huh?"

"Yes."

"I'll see what I can do on my end, only because I do know how much you love my mother. She's a different person when you're around and all I want is for her to be happy. She has to admit that she's made some mistakes too and none of us are perfect. I've had my fuck-ups too, but haven't we all."

Something that Latrel said jumped out at me. The fact that he mentioned Desa Rae had made some mistakes was interpreted by me as she had made severe mistakes, as I had. I hated to question him, but I did.

"You know I'm down with anything you can do, but Desa Rae comes off as bein' perfect and it's hard to get through to a woman who thinks she is. Do you know somethin' about her so-called mistakes that I don't know?"

Latrel paused. I wasn't sure if it was because he realized what he'd said, or he was disturbed by what I had asked him.

"I . . . I said that as a general statement, not to say that she's done anything. If she has, she damn sure wouldn't tell me."

My gut didn't accept Latrel's answer. Something was up and somebody wasn't saying. I wasn't trying to pin anything on Desa Rae, but I wasn't going to let her come down hard on me, and she had skeletons that I didn't know about.

I changed the subject, pretending that everything was good as I continued my conversation with Latrel. He said they would be leaving in a few days and said if he had time, they would stop by to holla at me. Our conversation ended right there, but I was going to press Desa Rae whether she appreciated it or not.

When Monday rolled around, I headed to Desa Rae's workplace. No need to wonder why, only because I could always count on her to stay calm at work. I got off the elevator and walked up to the receptionist's desk.

"How may I help you?" the white chick with long blond hair asked.

"I'm here to see Desa Rae Jenkins."

"Who shall I say is here to see her?"

"Roc Dawson."

The receptionist picked up the phone to call Desa Rae's office. "Miss Jenkins, Roc Dawson is here to see you." The receptionist paused then repeated my name. "Okay," she said. "Thank you." She looked up at me. "Please have a seat. She'll be out shortly."

I stood close by the receptionist's desk, waiting for Desa Rae. Nearly five minutes later, she came into the lobby dressed in a money green pantsuit. The look in her eyes said that she didn't appreciate me being there, but she still invited me back to her office.

"Close the door," she said after walking inside and plopping down in her chair. I closed the door and watched as she opened the drawer to her desk and pulled out a stick of gum.

"You gon' offer me a piece, too?" I asked.

She folded her arms and shot me a devious look. "No. Now why are you here?"

I sat in a chair in front of her desk. "For starters, I'm here because I miss you, but I know that don't matter. Two, I've been thinkin' about some things, and I don't think you've been open with me about what you may have been doin' behind my back. Three, I wanted to find out how you celebrated the New Year; and, four, I just wanted to see you and tell you how much I still love you."

"One, you missing me doesn't matter; two, what I do or have done is not your business anymore; three, I spent New Year's with my best friend, our daughter, and my books; and four, now that you told me how you feel you can go. I'm real busy, Roc, and I don't appreciate you coming to my job to discuss our personal relationship."

"Ahhh, that's good news. At least we're still in a relationship, even though it doesn't feel like one. And I will always consider some of your business mine, especially if you got some skeletons like I think you do." I wanted to push Desa Rae on this, because I knew that if she got defensive there was something there.

"Skeletons? Is that the best thing you could come up with to justify your actions? I had a long talk with Chase and she told me everything. Everything, Roc, and you should be ashamed of yourself for running up in here talking about my skeletons. If I do have skeletons, I can assure you that the bones don't belong to any of your relatives."

I smirked, knowing that she wouldn't appreciate it. "That was a good one, but humor me some more and talk to me about your skeletons. If there are a lot, some may be related to me. Besides, it's a small world and that is a fact without all the fiction."

"No, I doubt that my skeletons would be related to you. I wouldn't make the same mistake twice, and one member of your family is more than I can handle."

"Could handle. You're not handlin' me anymore. But tell me who those skeleton bones belong to? Or are you gon' make me sit here and guess?"

Desa Rae didn't respond, so I started naming people. Reggie was at the tip of my tongue, but I decided to go elsewhere, just to see her reaction.

"Have you been seein' your coworker, Greg, again?"

No answer.

"The man at the grocery store who always bags your groceries?"

She didn't flinch.

"The white man who gave you a tight hug at the Christmas party?"

She pursed her lips.

"Your boss, Mr. Anderson?"

She rolled her eyes.

"I know. Reggie, right?"

"Reggie and I are over."

Bingo. Those skeletons belonged to Reggie. That was evident because she defended my mentioning of his name. "It's Reggie, ain't it? You've been fuckin' with him, haven't you? When I was away and called you, you had sex with him, didn't you? Don't lie, Dez. Lay your shit on the line."

"Let me repeat. Reggie and I are over, and I turn back the clock for no one."

I leaned forward and placed my elbows on her desk.
"I don't believe you. I can tell you're lyin' to me and
God help you if you are."

That statement rubbed her the wrong way. She
frowned and raised her voice by a notch. "Roc, get out
of my office. God help me? Really? No, God help you
for going around, beating up on a woman who wanted
to tell me the truth about you. Is that how you're doing
it these days? You'll do whatever to have it your way,
and how could you be so cruel?"

"Rule number one: when you know you're guilty,
change the subject. Come on, ma. Tell me what happened between you and Reggie. When did you give it
up? How many times?"

Desa Rae got up from her seat and walked over to
the door. She touched the knob. "If you don't leave, I'm
going to call security."

I slowly walked to the door and leaned in to Desa
Rae's ear. "I'm goin' to go see Reggie. I'm sure he'll tell
me the truth. You 'bout to get caught up in your lies,
and I got a feelin' that Miss Perfect won't be so perfect
after all."

Desa Rae was really steaming now. I could see steam
coming from her ears as she yanked the door open.
"Get out, Roc. And don't come back."

I left, feeling as if I was on to something. I wasn't trying to justify what I had done, and by all means, I knew
I was wrong. But Desa Rae wasn't going to play this
innocent, goody-two-shoes role with me. She wasn't
going to make me feel guilty when she was guilty
herself. I hoped like hell that I was wrong, because I
knew it was going to be fucked up if I found out she
had been getting it on with Reggie. She pretended like
she hated his guts. Told me time and time again that

he was the worst thing that ever happened to her. And
after all that motherfucker did to her, let me find out
she was still having sex with him.

I drove straight to Reggie's real estate office on West
Florissant Avenue. When I walked in, he came out
of his office. He must've seen me through the picture
windows that had the name of his business written on
them.

"May I help you?" he said with his hands in the pockets of his beige suit. I hated this baldheaded sucker, but
I tried to keep cool because I wanted to know the truth.

"Check this," I said, moving forward. "I need to ask
you a few things. I'm not here to start no trouble, and
all I need are some answers."

Reggie glared at me from behind his black-framed
glasses, looking unwilling to continue this conversation. "What you really need is to tone down that
attitude you always got on display and speak to me in
a different tone. I don't have to answer shit, and if this
has anything to do with Desa Rae, go talk to her."

"Tried that route, but I wound up at a dead end.
So now I'm here because the detour led me to your
doorstep."

I was almost positive that Desa Rae had called
him. But, as I did with speaking to her, I had a plan
to start off calm, cool, and collected, hit him with my
suspicions, and then make him mad.

Reggie walked into his office to take a seat and I
stood near the doorway. "What is it that you want to
know?" he asked with his hands clenched together.

"Did Desa Rae already call you?"

"That's not your business."

"That means that she did. Did she tell you why I was
comin' here?"

"As a matter of fact, she didn't."

"Of course she did. She called to save her ass, didn't she?"

Reggie chuckled and shook his head "Man, you are straight up a trip. Save her ass from what?"

"From me knockin' the shit out of her, if I find out she's had sex with you."

"Aww, so, you're abusing her now? And so what if she's had sex with me? She knows that I'm the only man really capable of satisfying her."

"That's not what she told me. And a man with a dick the size of my pinky finger ain't capable of satisfyin' her. I got that tad bit of information straight from the lady's mouth."

"I don't believe she told you that for one minute. Come again, Roc, you're starting to appear desperate."

"Maybe so. But, let me get this straight. You saw her when I was on vacation, right? She made you leave her house because seein' you made her sick to her stomach. Before then, you partied with her at Latrel's graduation, but she told you that your sex, for years, was lame and she was thankful for the divorce. Prior to that, you and her kicked it at one of Latrel's basketball games at Mizzou in Columbia. You tried to get at her that time, but she slammed the door to her hotel room in your face. And a few more months before that, you went to her friend Monica's house, beggin', cryin', hopin', and praying that Desa Rae would take you back. Bro, if you want to talk about desperate, I know a whole lot of things about you that makes you sound more desperate than me. Shall I continue?"

Reggie looked uncomfortable. He moved around in his chair and shrugged his shoulders. "I see somebody has been speaking ill about me, but you can continue all you want to. If I start telling you some things that she's said about you, it won't be pretty. I'm not going to stoop to your level, but I will say this. A woman doesn't stay married to a man for that many years and she isn't satisfied. And don't you believe for one minute that Desa Rae has ever slammed a door in my face. I may have asked for her to take me back, but I now know that had she done so, it would've been a big mistake."

Bingo, again. Reggie provided my answer without even knowing it. The only accusation that he gave an explanation for was when I mentioned the door being slammed in his face when they were at Latrel's basketball game. He defended that shit, because he knew something that I didn't. Slowly, but surely, the puzzle pieces were coming together. I knew I wasn't going to get much else out of him, so I quickly wrapped this up and was ready to go on to my next source.

"You're right, Reggie. We all make mistakes. When Desa Rae calls back, be sure to tell her that ass is cooked."

I walked out, and as soon as I got into my car, I called Latrel. He was the final piece of the puzzle.

"Hello," he said, answering his cell phone.

"Say, man, this is Roc. You got a minute?"

"Yeah, what's up?"

"I wanted to get at you about somethin' that took place while your parents were at your basketball game in Columbia. Desa Rae just told me somethin' that shocked the shit out of me. I seriously thought it was over between her and Reggie, but I found out that they hooked up that night. This shit got me feelin' ill. I'm at a point where I feel like completely givin' up, especially if she wants to make a move with Reggie again. I know he's your father, but Dez told me it was over and that she'd never go that route again."

"Aye, don't sweat it, Roc. My parents are done with each other. I know for a fact that love don't live in their hearts for each other anymore. I recall what happened between them the night of my basketball game, and I was mad because I felt my dad only went there because he had something to prove. My moms was upset with you about something, and when I caught them in the act, they tried to play me like I was stupid. I got into a heated argument with my mother that day because she was tripping. I'm glad she came clean about that day, and, now, maybe the two of you can squash the bull and move on."

Case closed. I hit the steering wheel with the palm of my hand, pissed about the lies I had been told and the secrets Desa Rae had kept from me. If I could recall, we were having some problems in our relationship then, but why did she have to have sex with Reggie of all people? How could she say that she hated him then go turn around and fuck him?

"I think we will be able to move on, Latrel. I'm not gon' sweat it, but I appreciate you for hearin' me out on this."

"No problem. Sorry we didn't get a chance to stop by when we were in St. Louis. Maybe you and my mother can come visit us soon."

"I'll let you know."

Our conversation ended on that note. I drove off and made my way to Desa Rae's house. She wasn't home from work yet, but I waited in the driveway for her to get there.

Chapter 17
Desa Rae

I could see Roc's truck parked in the driveway as I drove down the street. It was obvious that he was trying to upset me, but I wasn't going there with him today. It was ridiculous for him to run around trying to find something on me. I hoped Reggie didn't tell him anything. I called him to be sure that he mentioned not one word about our night together. Yes, we had sex, but Roc and I had separated. He was seeing Raven, so I didn't quite understand how he felt my night with Reggie was comparable to him having sex with my sister while engaged to me. I took a deep breath and promised myself that I would not allow him to anger me.

I pulled my car into the driveway beside Roc's truck and got out. Chassidy got out on the passenger's side and ran up to him.

"Daddy," she said, running into his arms.

He picked her up. "Hey, pretty girl. How was school today?"

"Good. But when I read from a book today and stumbled on a word, Nicolas laughed at me. He's always being mean to me and he refers to me as the chocolate monster in the classroom."

My heart felt heavy and what Chassidy said hurt me. I couldn't wait to go inside to call their teacher.

How dare he call her that? I told Chassidy to ignore stupidity.

Roc talked to her too. His face was already flat, but it turned even flatter. "You ain't no chocolate monster, and the next time he says that to you, punch him real hard in his fat, disrespectful mouth. What's his name again?"

"Nicolas," Chassidy said softly, then lowered her head.

"You tell Nicolas that I'm gon' beat his muthafuckin' white, racist, redneck ass if he—"

"Roc, stop it," I said, cutting him off. "Don't say that to her because she'll go repeat it and find herself in trouble."

"I don't give a damn. Tell him I'm gon' chop his ass up with a food processor, along with his ignorant-ass parents."

Chassidy quickly nodded. "I'm going to tell him just that, but what's a food processor?"

I'd heard enough and took Chassidy from Roc's arms. "You should know better, Roc. I'm sure with your way of handling this, Nicolas may be found somewhere dead in an alley. Chassidy, don't you go to school and repeat a word he just said. I mean it."

"You damn right he will and his parents' bodies might be somewhere stankin' too. If you don't like how I'm gon' handle it then you handle it yourself."

"I will. Trust me. I'm going inside to handle it right now."

"Hurry. Because I got some other shit I need to get off my chest. Are you gon' make me stand out here and put our business in the street, or are you goin' to invite me to come inside?"

I rolled my eyes. "Do whatever you wish, but you really need to tone that down in front of Chassidy."

He winked at me. "Whatever you say."

Chapter 18
Roc

I followed Desa Rae and Chassidy into the house. Desa Rae immediately got on the phone to call the school. I went into Chassidy's bedroom with her and closed the door. I then sat her on my lap.

"Check this out, pretty girl. Don't ever let nobody mistreat you. Always stand up for yourself and be tough. Let me see your tough look."

Chassidy grinned hard, showing every pearly white tooth she had.

"No, that's not a good look. I mean, it's a good look, but not a tough look. When Nicolas says and does mean things to you, you gotta look at him like this."

I narrowed my eyes, made my nose wince, and even held up my tightened fists and took swift punches at the air in front of me. "That's how you gotta do it, so let me see it."

Chassidy closed her eyes, wiggled her nose and mouth, and squeezed her fists together, leaving them by her sides. "Like this," she said.

"Not quite. Open your eyes a little and don't wiggle your nose so much. Don't move your mouth at all and your fists need to be up and swingin'."

Chassidy made a readjustment and I'd be damned if she wasn't on to something. "That's it, pretty girl. Do that every time Nicolas messes with you and I promise you that he'll stop."

Chassidy was all smiles as she swung wildly at the air. If Desa Rae's phone call or Chassidy's mean mug and blows didn't work, I'd deal with Nicolas myself. Or, should I say, have another kid deal with him. For now, though, it was time for me to deal with Desa Rae.

I told Chassidy to chill in her room for a while and that I would be right back. With Desa Rae's tone and attitude, mine too, I expected things to turn ugly. I went into the kitchen where she was. She had just hung up the phone.

"Done," she said. "Her teacher said she would talk to Nicolas and his parents tomorrow."

"Sometimes talkin' don't solve problems, but we'll see."

Desa Rae walked away from where the phone was and sat at the kitchen table. "What's on your mind, Roc? I know you just can't leave this alone and let this situation be, but no matter what you say, or how you say it, we're done."

I moved over to the kitchen table, but didn't take a seat. "You want to know what's on my mind? You. Your lies, Desa Rae. The way you pretend you're all that and you're not. How you hold me to a certain standard, but you think it's okay for you to fall short. How dare you make me feel guilty about what I did, but you were around here doin' the same thing? What sense does that make? Please help me understand why you think it's okay for you to go fuck Reggie, but when I fucked Chase it's a wrap."

Desa Rae just stared at me for a while. She then decided to speak up. "I don't know where you get this idea in your head that I had sex with Reggie. You have concocted this whole thing in your head, just to justify your actions. I—"

My heart was starting to beat faster from listening to her lies. I had to cut her off. "Don't play me like no sucker. I didn't want to come clean with you about my actions, but I did. Tell me why you decided to go all the way to Columbia and fuck the one man you claim you hate."

"Let me repeat myself, again. I did not have—"

"Yes, you did! And if you lie to me again, you gon' cause me to do somethin' that I don't want to do. I want the truth and I want to hear why it is okay for that muthafucka to walk out on you and your son, to be with another woman, tell you that he's fallen out of love with you, throw years of marriage away like it didn't mean shit to him, not pay his share of child support, flaunt his numerous hoes around you, leave you alone to pick up the pieces, yet you reward him by fucking him! What kind of shit is that?"

Desa Rae blinked tears from her eyes and shot up from her chair. Obviously, the realization of what I'd said shook her up.

"I'm done with this conversation," she said. "Get out. I don't have to explain myself to you anymore. This is ridiculous."

"I think it is too. It's ridiculous because when I say I love you, you try to convince me that I don't. You expect for me to be perfect and I'm not. You wait for me to fuck up just so you can say I'm just like him. Ma, you don't ever have to come clean to me about fuckin' Reggie, but in your heart, you know that shit happened. How many times, I don't know. Only you do."

"Never," she said, sticking to her lie. "N-e-v-e-r."

At this point, I was almost done with this. All I could do was shake my head. "Your son wouldn't lie on you and that is a fact. Then you want me to trust you. You tell me that all good relationships are based on trust,

but are they really? Especially, when you, yourself, have
failed to spill the truth. My gut told me that somethin'
happened between you and Reggie. Y'all got chummy
all of a sudden. The next thing I know, he's showin' up
while I'm not here. Instead of confrontin' you about
what I felt, I made a bad choice to lay my burdens
elsewhere. I was dead wrong and I admitted it. You,
on the other hand, are so full of shit. You need to take
that mask off you're wearin' and learn to keep it real."
I pointed to my chest. "As for me, I'm done kissin' yo'
ass, Desa Rae, and I'm done messin' wit' you. Ain't no
way in hell I'ma let you keep fuckin' that nigga behind
my back, and that's on a for-real tip right there."

I calmly walked to the door and left. The only thing
I regretted was not saying good-bye to my daughter.
Something inside told me that it would be awhile
before I ever saw her again.

When I left Desa Rae's house, I drove to Vanessa's
crib. I had some heavy shit on my mind and I was
confused about so many things. I knocked on the
door of her two-story house that was located in North
County. I had purchased this house for Vanessa years
ago, when drug money was flowing like water.

Vanessa opened the door in an orange sports bra
that had her breasts sitting up high. Her cotton shorts
barely covered her ass and she looked like she'd been
working out. When she invited me inside, I could hear
the workout music in the background.

She wiped sweat from her forehead then put her
hand on her hip. "What you doin' comin' over here?
You know my man won't approve of you showin' up
without callin' first."

I looked over Vanessa's shoulder. "Is he here?"

"No, but he will be."

I removed my jacket and tossed it on her couch.
"Good. Then we got time."

She cocked her head back. "Time for what?"

"Time for a little this," I said, easing my arm around her waist. My lips dropped to hers and Vanessa didn't hesitate to kiss me.

Afterward, she backed her head up. "What's goin' on, Roc? Tell me what all this is about."

"It's about me wantin' some pussy with no attachments. Can you handle that?"

"All I can do is try."

"Try hard," I said, backing her up to the couch and lifting her sports bra over her head. She sat back on the couch and rushed to remove her shorts. My eyes scanned down Vanessa's naked body, which displayed many tattoos. One in particular was a pretty butterfly that was tatted on her upper thigh, near the good stuff. I started to undo the buttons on my shirt, but before I could pull it off, Vanessa grabbed my hand and pulled me on top of her. She wrapped her arms around me, touching and squeezing every single muscle in my carved chest.

"This feels so guuud," she said. "I love the way your body feels against mine. It's been a long time, Roc."

"Love the body, but hate the man. That's what you said at the club, right? That you hated me."

"I said it, but let me be honest here for one minute. I love every single thing about you, Roc Dawson. From yo' swag, to yo' looks, yo' money, yo' father skills and even to that thing you about to put inside of me, I love it all. That, my dear, will never, ever change. I may form my mouth to say I hate you, but my actions will always speak the truth."

Women were some strange-ass creatures. Whenever I said that I hated somebody, I meant that shit. I guess Desa Rae felt the same about Reggie, and even though she spoke ill of him, she still was willing to give it up, as Vanessa was. I didn't hate Vanessa, but I made a decision a long time ago that I was done with her. Whenever I said something, it was wise to take my word for it. I jumped to my feet and leaned down to kiss her forehead.

"Put your clothes back on," I said, buttoning my shirt.

Her jaw dropped. "What?" she shouted. "Are you gon' play me like this?"

"I'm not playin' you, Vanessa. You should never be with a man you claim to hate. The problem is, when those words come from your mouth, they can sting. Your word is all you got, so use your mouth to speak the truth. That's all I'm sayin'. Now, I gotta go."

I turned to walk away, but Vanessa came after me. She pulled the back of my shirt, causing me to turn around to face her.

"You a dirty-ass nigga. Don't call me or come over here anymore. I am so done with you, and the truth be told, I do hate you. I hate your fuckin' guts."

I opened the door, knowing damn well that if I came back tomorrow, Vanessa would open her legs for me. For now, though, she had some explaining to do. Her man had pulled up in the driveway and the first thing he saw was me coming out of Vanessa's house and her standing in the doorway with no clothes on.

I held my hands in the air. "My hands are clean, bro. Ain't no parts of the pussy touch me."

His eyes narrowed, nose winced, and fists tightened. I moved out of the way as he stormed by me and charged inside, slamming the door behind him. With all the cussing and fussing going on, Vanessa definitely had some explaining to do.

Chapter 19
Desa Rae

Roc did his best to make me feel a certain kind of way for having sex with Reggie, and I would be lying if I said his words to me didn't hurt. What he said about Reggie was true. It made me realize how stupid it was for me to have sex with him while I was in Columbia.

Still, I felt, in no way did it compare to what he'd done. That was why I refused to tell him the truth. Whether he knew the truth or not—and obviously he did because Latrel confirmed it—I still didn't feel guilty about not spilling my guts.

Roc admitting to be done with this was like music to my ears. Of course I still loved the man, but enough was enough. I had reached that point and I must admit that knowing so left me on edge and moody. I'd been snapping all week at my coworkers, but when Chase called to let me know that she'd been doing well, I felt better. She was home from the hospital, and after several days of therapy, she was able to freely walk again. She wrapped up our conversation by saying that she would keep in touch. I wasn't sure if I believed her, but I was going to let her reach out to me whenever she wanted to. After that tad bit of good news, Shawna came into my office, thinking it was okay to tell me that she had been on a date with Mr. Anderson. I lost it.

"Please don't share that kind of information with me," I said, looking at her from across my desk. "What you do with him is your business. I just happen to think it's so damn tacky for women to throw themselves at married men. There are too many men out there, and you really need to find your own."

Her ignorant self had the audacity to defend her actions. "If he was taken, he wouldn't have agreed to have dinner-slash-sex with me. As for women like me being tacky, I don't think so. I see it as being ambitious and pursuing the things in life that you want. I suspect that if I play my position right, it may lead to a promotion—a promotion that may cause me to be sitting at your desk and you sitting at mine."

I wanted to yank that heifer by her weaved-in hair and toss her out of there. But I didn't have time for foolishness, especially when I had gotten a call from Chassidy's school. I asked her teacher to hold and ordered Shawna out of my office.

After she left, I put the phone up to my ear. "Hi, Ms. Morris. What's going on?"

"Well, we had an unfortunate incident today. Chassidy and Nicolas got into a little fistfight and she said some very disturbing things to him, too. I've already talked to both of them, but I would like for you to come pick up Chassidy and take her home for the day. She's very upset and I want things to calm down a little bit."

"I'm on my way," I rushed to say then hung up.

A fight? I thought as I drove like a bat out of hell to get to Chassidy's school. How dare this little boy put his hands on my daughter? I didn't understand why he kept messing with her, and the chocolate monster thing was already enough. The teacher told me that she had a talk with his parents. I was furious. I had no idea what disturbing things she said to Nicolas, but the teacher explained everything to me when I got there.

"She called him a white, racist fucker and told him that her father was going to beat his A. That's when the fight started and Chassidy balled up her fists and started wailing on him. Nicolas tends to bother some of the other kids too, but we just don't resolve issues in the classroom with bad words and violence."

I was furious with Roc and Chassidy both.

Embarrassed by her actions, she leaned her head against my arm while sitting in the chair next to me.

"Sit up straight," I said to her.

She did.

"Apologize to Ms. Morris for carrying on like this."

Chassidy poked out her trembling lip and started to cry. She leaned her head against my arm again and softly told Ms. Morris she was sorry.

"I appreciate that, Chassidy, but go home and get some rest. I'll see you tomorrow, and let's look forward to having a better day tomorrow."

I thanked Ms. Morris and left, holding hands with Chassidy. When we got to the car, she got into the back seat. I tightened her seat belt and let her have it as soon as I got into the car.

"You know better, Chassidy, don't you? I told you not to repeat any of that mess your daddy told you. I said you'd be in trouble if you did."

She didn't respond, but when I looked in the rear-view mirror, her eyes were narrowed. She was looking at the back of my head, wincing. When I snapped my head around, that was when I saw her fists tightened.

"Get that ugly look off your face," I shouted. "And let your hands go, now!"

Chassidy straightened up, but then she screamed back at me and covered her ears. "Stop yelling at me!"

I was in total shock. I'd never seen her behave this way before. I reached back and pulled her hands away from her ears. "Move your hands and stop this. Don't you ever raise your voice to me. Do you understand?"

Tears rolled down her face and she wiped them. "I was only trying to defend myself. Daddy said that I should defend myself and never let anybody punk me. He said that if I look like this"—she made that ugly face again—"that people would be afraid to mess with me. It worked because Nicolas is afraid of me now."

This was too much. No words could express how upset I was, and in no way did I want Chassidy traveling down a violent path. I appeared calm on the outside, but was fuming on the inside.

"Look," I said, reaching for some Kleenex and wiping her tears. "You're too pretty to have such an ugly look on your face, so never, ever, ever do that again. Violence is not the answer, sweetheart, and if or when anybody messes with you, please tell me first. If not, tell the teacher. It's better to deal with us than to try to handle these things on your own. All you'll do is get in trouble, and you don't want to get in trouble, do you?"

Chassidy moved her head from side to side, indicating no.

"Good. Now show me your pretty smile that I like to see."

She smiled and warmed my heart. I was definitely going to get into Roc's shit about this, and when I dropped off Chassidy at Monica's house to play with Brea, I was on my way to go see him.

"Are you sure you don't want me to go with you?" Monica said, standing in her doorway with a piece of chicken in her hand. "You already know Roc ain't gon' want to hear it."

"I know, but he needs to hear it."

"Good luck," Monica said with a grin, trying to make light of the situation. "Call me when you get home. I'll bring Chassidy home then."

I thanked her, got in my car, and left.

Unfortunately, when I got to Roc's shop there were gangs of people hanging outside. Just from looking through the window, I could see numerous people standing inside, too. Business was on the rise, but I definitely wasn't there to talk business. I put the strap of my purse on my shoulder and walked across the street in my high heels and magenta pantsuit. Numerous fellas outside spoke, but I kept it moving. Even when I got inside, I walked right by the counter where Troy was. He stopped me by putting his arm out in front of me.

"Boss lady, don't move so fast. I still need to let Roc know you're here before I allow you to go back there."

I lifted his arm, trying to move it out of my way. "He knew I was coming," I lied.

"Maybe so, but he didn't tell me, so you gon' have to chill right there."

I folded my arms and patted my feet on the ground. As soon as Troy walked away to buzz Roc's office, I walked off. He came after me, but didn't catch up with me until I was at Roc's door. Troy tightly grabbed my wrist, but I snatched it away and frowned.

"Don't put your grimy hands on me," I snapped.

Roc got up from his chair and looked at Troy. "What's goin' on?" he asked him.

"I told her that she couldn't come back here until I cleared it with you. She ignored me and rushed back here."

"No," I said, turning my attention to Roc. "What's going on is you and I need to talk about this whack mess you've been teaching our daughter. That's why I'm here."

"You could've called me on the phone for that," he said to me then looked at Troy. "Don't ever put your hands on her like that again. You feel me?"

Troy shrugged, but nodded; then he cut his eyes at me and made his way back to the front.

So many people were looking, trying to see what was going on, so I went into Roc's office. He closed the door, glaring at me like I had mess on my face. I pointed my finger at him.

"Thanks to you, your daughter got in trouble at school. Why would you tell her to go beat up on some-body and show her how to make that ugly-ass face? I'm not raising her as no thug. Tell me why any man in his right mind would encourage his daughter to pound people with her fists and resort to violence?"

Roc acted as if he hadn't heard a word I'd said. All he did was smile. "She kicked his ass, didn't she? My little girl put that muthafucka in his place and stood up for herself. Where is she so I can congratulate her?"

My mouth opened wide. I was in disbelief. Then again, I shouldn't have been. "She's in a safe place and far away from you. You have no idea what it felt like to go up to that school and hear the teacher talk about what Chassidy had done and what she said, like she was some kind of animal. She's making that face like it's cute, and what's with the tightened fists? I'm not happy about this, Roc, not one damn bit."

"Then go somewhere and punch a pillow to let out your frustrations. As you can see, I was gettin' my grub on. Now, if you don't mind, I got work to do."

Roc sat at his desk and bit into his Subway sandwich. He turned up the volume to a rap song—"Bitches Love Me" by Lil Wayne—and tuned me out by nodding his head. One of his hands was in the air and his eyes were closed as he started rapping the lyrics.

"'I'm on that good kush and alcohol, I got some down bitches I can call . . .'"

I was not only annoyed by him, but also with the song. My cell phone started to ring, but I ignored it.

"Would you turn that crap down? I don't care how many bitches love you, we need to talk. And as for punching a pillow, you're so lucky I'm not punching you, especially for being a lousy parent and for giving bad advice to your daughter."

I must have touched a nerve. The cold look in his now-opened eyes said so and he turned down the music. "You don't have to approve of my parentin' skills, but I will say this: nobody, especially no boys, no men, no girls, and no racist fool will be allowed to fuck with my daughter. I will always teach her to defend herself because there are some cruel assholes out there who will attempt to treat her as they wish. We both know that white boy is bothered by the color of Chassidy's chocolate skin. She's the only black kid in her classroom and he picks on her because of it. Talk is cheap and his parents couldn't care less about what he says and does to Chassidy because they teachin' him that shit at home. If Chassidy didn't do what she had to do, his ass would be runnin' up in there with whips and chains, tryin' to order Chassidy around. She may grow up to be what you consider a thug, but the last time I checked, ain't nothin' wrong with that."

Just then, Roc's cell phone rang. He looked at the number, saying that it was Monica.

"She's right here talkin' shit," he said to Monica then paused to listen to her. He then asked to speak to Chassidy.

"Pretty girl, I heard you got down on that bully today," he said. "That's what's up and I'm real proud of you for what you did. Tell that muthafucka I said more ass kickings will follow if he ever says anything else to you again."

I reached out, trying to snatch the phone from Roc, but he moved away from me. I was so mad at him for giving Chassidy bad advice that I lifted my hand and slapped the shit out of him. His cell phone crashed to the floor and slid across it. Roc shut his eyes and wiggled his jaw. He walked around me, then punched his finger on the intercom button.

"Gage, to my office," was all he said and said no more.

"I'm sorry for putting my hands on you," I said. "But why would you tell Chassidy you're proud of her for doing that mess?"

Gage opened the door. He could tell by the look on Roc's face that something was wrong.

"Please get her the fuck out of here," Roc said. "I don't care what kind of force you use, just make sure she is off this property and is never allowed to come back in here."

Gage pointed to me. "But, Roc, this boss lady. You may be mad right now, but—"

"Do it," he yelled. "Now, before I have you takin' her out of here in a body bag!"

"You'll be leaving out of here in a body bag before I do. If he touches me," I said, "I'm calling the police."

I apparently had the wrong answer. Mentioning the police up in there wasn't the right move and it angered both of them. Gage sure didn't like it. He pointed to the door, but I took my sweet little time exiting Roc's office, trying his patience. He ignored me and picked up the phone on his desk. He sat back in his chair and propped his feet on top of it.

"Sorry about that, pretty girl," he said. "But as I was sayin' before an interruption, always handle yo' business . . ."

I walked out pissed.

Chapter 20

Desa Rae

I was sitting on the couch at Monica's house, telling her what had happened. Seemed like everything was starting to fall apart and I didn't like this feeling that I had inside.

"Girl, you should have seen them. They treat Roc like he's a god or something and the second I walked in there they were on me like vultures. It amazes me how much control he has over the men who work for him."

"When you got money like that, people always find a way to respect you. I assume that Roc has had those friends for a long time, and they appear to have each other's backs. I'm glad the one named Gage didn't put his hands on you, as he did Chase. I still can't believe what he did with her, and when people say it's a small world, you'd better believe it."

Monica crossed her legs and sipped from the cup of tea she was drinking. I sipped from the cup she gave me, too.

"I know you'll be honest with me if I ask you this, and as my best friend, you don't always have to agree with me. But do you think I was wrong for not telling Roc about me and Reggie? Do you think I was wrong for ending our relationship, and what about this mess with Chassidy? Roc makes me feel like I'm wrong about everything and he always comes up with a weird way to make his point."

"I'm gon' always be your best friend, no matter what. But you and Roc relationship confuses the hell out of me. One minute y'all have me jumping for joy, rooting for y'all to stay together, then the next minute I be like run, Desa Rae, run. I guess it really doesn't matter what I think anymore. What matters is how you feel about all of it. As your friend, don't put me on the spot to answer questions for you, only because you may take offense to what I say. I don't want you to do that. Start with the first question you asked me. Do *you* think you were wrong for not telling Roc about Reggie? Dig deep before you answer."

"Flat out, yes, I do think I was wrong. But he was wrong too. Very—"

"Please don't go there. This isn't about him. This is about you. I'm talking to you right now, not him. And you just said you thought it was wrong not to tell him about Reggie."

"All right, Miss Iyanla Vanzant, go ahead and tell me like it is."

We laughed and I continued. "I felt bad about not telling him, especially when he asked for the truth. Maybe I should have told him when it initially happened. Or I could have said something after we got engaged, especially since I knew there was a possibility it would come up again, later on down the road. This is the second time I lied to him about not being with a man when realistically I was. You remember when I got busted with that Greg situation, don't you?"

"Yes, I remember now, and you're right. You did lie about that, so how can you continue to expect the truth from somebody else, yet keep your secrets? That's not fair, and as you feel as though you can't trust him for not telling the truth, why should he trust you?"

I sighed and didn't have an answer for Monica's question. "Okay, fine. But as for me ending it, I did what I had to do. I have no regrets and I will make no apologies for deciding to move on."

"You shouldn't apologize, but if you have no regrets, why do you keep talking about it? A woman who moves on doesn't second-guess herself like you are and she doesn't question for one minute her decision to move on. That's when she knows for a fact that she made the right call."

"You make me so sick," I teased. "After today, you will not hear me talk about this again."

"If you say so I believe you," Monica said sarcastically. "And do not even mention this thing with Chassidy, because you know I told both of my children to knock the hell out of anybody who continuously messed with them at school. Time and time again they went to those teachers and they didn't do anything. Roc did go overboard, but that's all I'm going to say about that."

"He threatened to hurt a child. That's a bit much, don't you think?"

"A child who called his daughter a chocolate monster. Think about how much those comments probably hurt her. Did they hurt you?"

"Of course they did. That's why I rushed to call the school about it. At the end of the day, words are just words. Hurtful or not, we can't go around beating up on or killing people who say inappropriate things to us. It's my job, as a parent, to make sure Chassidy knows she's not a chocolate monster. Telling her to fight someone over that is like telling her to believe she is a chocolate monster and defend it."

"That's your take on it. Roc has his take on it, as do I. As Chassidy's parents, y'all owe it to her to find common ground on situations like that because it will happen again."

"I agree. And when the dust settles, the conversation goes on."

"Don't expect for it to settle anytime soon. Not after that slap to his face. And speaking of that, you do know you were wrong, don't you?"

I threw my hand back and changed the subject, because he deserved it.

Chassidy and I stayed at Monica's house until eleven. We ate, watched television, and I told her about trifling Shawna at work. At least we were both on the same page about that issue.

The next day at work, I was surprised when Mr. Anderson called me into his office. I was even more shocked when he questioned my work relationship with Shawna.

"Our work relationship is fine," I said. "She gets things done and I can honestly say that I don't have any complaints about her work performance."

"That's good. Good to hear, because I've been thinking about moving her up, if not in this department then another one."

My brows heightened. "So, if she moves up in this department, where does that leave me?"

"In the same position. She can work hand in hand with you. You can teach her all that you know and that way she'll be prepared to move on when the time comes."

I swear, when it rained in my life, it always, somehow or someway, managed to pour. I tried to control my anger, but I knew it was visible on my face.

"I didn't think I needed anybody working hand in hand with me. I thought I handled my job very well. Am I missing something here or is it your ultimate goal to replace me with your side whore?"

Mr. Anderson's eyes grew wide and his head jerked back. "I'm not trying to replace you with anyone. You've been my employee for a long time. I'm just trying to give a young lady who deserves it a leg up. Is there something wrong with that? It wasn't when I promoted you, was it?"

I hated to go to this level with Mr. Anderson, but I was so overwhelmed with all this foolishness in my life. This situation with Shawna was a bit much.

"Mr. Anderson, do what you wish. You're running the show around here, but I must tell you that I am so sick and tired of people who lie in bed with others around here catching all the breaks and getting promoted. I earned my promotion the right way. By working hard and doing what was required of me, you had no choice because the other executives recommended it. If you want to give Shawna a leg up, please find time out of your busy schedule to show her the ropes. I don't have time."

I got up, only to hear Mr. Anderson threaten me.

"If you walk out that door, you're fired, Desa Rae."

I swung around and shot daggers at him with much fury in my eyes. "Good. At least I'll be able to collect my unemployment."

I stormed out of his office and went to mine to clear out my desk.

Chapter 21

Roc

These days, I had been living at the shop. I spent the night twice this week already and slept comfortably in my chair while watching the flat-screen television on the wall. I just didn't feel like going home, because every time I did I had to get in Dre's shit about something. There was no question that he was a decent young man, but I hated a person who didn't listen. He'd been running around, trying to sell dope and didn't even have to do it because I had given him a job. I warned him before that if the police ever came knocking at my doorstep, we'd have a problem. I didn't like problems, but I couldn't say nothing when two police officers, Officer Collect and Officer Collector, came to see me. They sat in my office like shit was all good.

"Roc, now you know since Ronnie was laid to rest we backed off. But things getting a li'l tight," Officer Collect said with a hardy chuckle. "Money raining up in yo' mechanic shop, but we're being left out of the pot. I see you're doing things on the up and up in here, but your cousin, Andre, hasn't been. Not only has he been in my neighborhood slanging dope, and stealing cars, but him and his friends have also been around here robbing folks. We're catching heat about this and we may have to make an arrest unless we can somehow *work* this out."

"Work it out?" I said with a shrug and holding out my hands. "Shit, arrest his ass. I'ma call him in here right now and y'all can put the cuffs on him."

I hit the intercom button, telling Dre to come to my office. Officer Collector added his two cents. "We . . . we really don't want to arrest him, Roc, because this whole thing can get ugly. We'll have to order a search warrant for your house, and if we find any illegal *stuff* up in there, or in here, it may fall back on you. It could fall back on some of the fellas here, too, who knows? I just think we need to play this whole thing safe. You tell Dre to chill, give us a li'l hush money, and nobody goes to jail."

Dre slowed his steps as he approached the door and saw the officers sitting inside. He opened the door and came in with a frightened look covering his face.

"Dre, these are Officers Collect and Collector. They came to take you to jail for robbery and distributin' illegal drugs. I told them that I didn't know nothin' about that, but what say you?"

Dre walked farther into the room, standing by me as I remained in my chair. "I say I'm innocent until proven guilty," he said.

"Innocent," Collector said, pulling out a notepad. "We got footage of you just last week driving a stolen car through the front window at a furniture rental store and running out with TVs. Then you fellas went into a convenience store and robbed the Arabian woman at the counter. After that, you stole some cars parked at the casino, and then you took some of that stolen merchandise back to Roc's place in North County. I'm positive that some of it is still there and I doubt that he knows about it."

Hell, no, I didn't know about it. This damn sure wasn't good. I looked at Dre, who had guilt written all over his face. He couldn't say shit. I hated a mother-fucker who couldn't answer for their shit. If my house wasn't involved in this, his ass would be going to jail.

"How much?" I asked the officers.

"All we want to do is settle this in a way—"

"Nigga, stop beatin' around the bush! How much do you want?"

"We want a hundred Gs apiece."

My face twisted with anger. "Get the fuck out of here. I don't have that kind of money to waste."

Dre held out his arms in front of him. "Shiiiit, I'm guilty without bein' charged. With that kind of money, just g'on and take me to jail. Fuck it."

Knowing that I would have to up a substantial amount of money, I stood up and landed a hard blow right at Dre's midsection. He grabbed his stomach and doubled over my desk in excruciating pain. I reached down and squeezed the back of his neck. Saliva dripped from his mouth and he kept coughing and gagging.

"Never, ever admit guilt, fool. Straighten yo' ass up and stay out of the streets. If you cause me to ever go to jail with you over yo' bullshit, jail is where you will die, family or no family. Got it?"

Dre nodded and I pushed his head. I then looked up at the officers. "One twenty-five, that's it. Split it or leave it."

The officers looked at each other and grinned. Without saying a word, I could tell they were pleased by my offer. I made arrangements to deliver the money tomorrow.

The night crept up on us. I was still at the shop, but had sent Gage and Romo to go withdraw some of the money at the bank for me. The rest I had at the shop.

I was swoll about what had happened. I told Dre that he'd have to work for me for the rest of his life to pay me back. He promised me that he wouldn't do no more stupid shit, and I had sent him to my house with Craig so they could wash through anything that didn't belong. They didn't get back until midnight and Craig told me everything was good. After such a long day, I was ready to pack it up and head out. So was everybody else. We rolled down the garages and locked them. Locked the front and back doors; then I sent Romo to go set the alarm. Dre, Gage, Troy, Craig, and me waited for Romo to come to my office so we could go, but it took him longer than usual. A few minutes later, he swooped around the corner with his hands locked behind his head. Two dudes with masks covering their faces were behind him and their guns were pushed against Romo's back.

"Everybody down on the floor," one dude shouted while waving another gun. They were double strapped with Glock 9s.

None of my boys, who I knew of, had easy access to their guns. We all eased down on the floor without saying a word. Eyes were roaming, ears were listening in, and fury rested in plenty of eyes.

"Y'all don't want to do this," Craig said on his knees. One of the dudes rushed up to him and put the gun on his temple.

"Down, nigga!" he shouted. "Now!"

I looked at Craig and lowered my head in a down motion, signaling for him to cooperate. He went down, just like everybody else did. The two dudes knew exactly what they were looking for, and one of them found it when he grabbed the briefcase filled with $125,000 underneath my desk.

"Got it," he said, lifting the briefcase so the other one would see it.

Over the intercom somebody said, "No, you don't got it, I do."

A bullet whistled through the window, hitting one of the dudes right in the chest, dropping him and splattering his blood. The other dude was so frightened that he tried to break out running. He didn't get too far, and was hit in the back five times by Romo's gun, which was smoking at the tip. Butch was the one who shot the other bullet. Thankfully, he had still been in the bathroom. He stepped over the dead dude's body, and as we all were now off the floor, our eyes roamed the room. We all knew this was a setup and every eye was locked on Dre. He was fidgety and his shirt was soaked with sweat.

"Glad that's over," he said. "Those fools were ruthless."

"Take the masks off their faces," I said, asking Dre to do it.

First, he removed the mask from the one dude who was close by my desk. When he saw the face of his friend, he cocked his head back.

"Hell, naw," he said as if he were surprised. "Naw, they assess didn't!" He then removed the mask from the one who was shot five times by the door. Another friend. "This fucked up. You told me those niggas weren't no friends. Now I know." Dre shook his head. His acting skills were bad.

In the eyes of my boys, who didn't like to do this kind of shit, I could see their need to get this over with. We were trying to do right, but there were always fools out there trying to take, take, take. It hurt more when the betrayal came from family, family who I tried to put before everybody else, people who I would give the shirt off my back to. But, there were some who took advantage of my kindness and all I did for them was never enough. I was sick to my motherfucking stomach, sick about my life traveling down this same path, with the same ol' hating, back-stabbing niggas who wanted something for free. I dropped back in my chair and closed my eyes as I rubbed down my face. Normally, family was up to me to deal with, with the exception of Ronnie. Gage handled him for me because he knew that shit was tough. This was tough too, but I reached for my gun that was secured underneath my desk and laid it on top of it.

"You fucked me bad, Dre. Real bad and there is no way out of this."

Dre stood close by the door, looking around the room at a row of angry brothers eager to kill him.

He pointed to his chest. "Who me? You think I had somethin' to do with this shit? Man, please. We family. I wouldn't do you like that, Roc, I swear I wouldn't."

I couldn't bear to listen to any more. I snatched my gun off the table and aimed. Dre took off, but by then, Gage pressed down on my gun, lowering it. In return he shot his and a bullet hit Dre in the back.

"I didn't want you to have that shit on your conscience," Gage said to me. "Sorry." He looked at the others. "Time to clean up."

I could see Dre moving. His legs were flopping around; he wasn't dead. I surely didn't want him to suffer, so I got up and stood over him. I fired two shots at the side of his head and watched him take his last breath.

I looked at Gage with rage and frustration in my eyes. "Don't worry about my conscience. Like I said, family is on me. Now, it's time to clean up."

As they all helped to remove the dead bodies, I returned to my desk. I lowered my head on it and returned to darkness when I shut my eyes. Sadness was upon me and I was hurting. Sure I had been brought up in the game, but my life didn't have to remain like this, did it?

All I wanted was Desa Rae back. She may have lied to me, but I knew I didn't have to worry about her ever putting a knife in my back. She loved me too much for that, vice versa. I wanted to see Chassidy and hold her in my arms. Li'l Roc, too. I wanted a peaceful life with my real family—the people who helped me leave this kind of shit behind. I wondered if I called Desa Rae, would she take me back? Would she forgive me, as I was ready to forgive her? She had to, because I couldn't go another day without her.

I lifted my head and wiped a tear that had slipped from the corner of my eye. When I picked up the phone, I heard someone call my name. I slowly turned my head and stared right into the eyes of Dre's friend I'd had beef with.

With a gun in his hand, all he said was, "You forgot one. The underground is waitin' for you."

I heard bullets whistling through the air; then I felt a burning sensation flowing through my neck. I squeezed the side of it, and through blurred vision I could see blood dripping through my trembling fingers. The sound of war rang loudly in my ears, as more bullets whistled through the air. I couldn't stay conscious so my limp body hit the floor and I returned to the darkness again.

Chapter 22
Desa Rae

I was disappointed about what had happened on my job. It upset me to walk out like that. Mr. Anderson had the nerve to call and offer my job back, but I told him that I needed time to think about it. He gave me two weeks off to decide if I would return.

At that point, I wasn't so sure. I didn't like how things had gone down, and Mr. Anderson's personal life was starting to affect me. I didn't appreciate knowing about his shenanigans, but it wasn't like he ever kept his affairs a secret. It was hard for me to work for a man who didn't seem to care. If I did return, I'd have to make him aware of my true thoughts. Maybe that would stop him from being so open but, then again, maybe not.

Either way, I was going to enjoy the next two weeks off. It wasn't like my money was tight, but I didn't want to take off and go on vacation. The money Roc and I had put aside for our honeymoon was still in my account. I'd been saving money from my paychecks, too. So, if Mr. Anderson thought I'd be over here struggling, he was sadly mistaken. I had learned my lesson last time. After Reggie left me high and dry, I vowed to never be without again.

By eleven o'clock in the morning, I had already dropped Chassidy off at school and had gone back home to clean up. After cleaning my bathroom, I sat on the couch in the living room and paged through a magazine that was on the table. I got bored with that, but I wasn't in the mood to read a book. Reading was what I preferred to do at nighttime, so I turned on the TV and picked up a book with crossword puzzles. I started filling in the words until I heard the news reporter mention a shooting that happened on the north side of St. Louis. Any time I would hear the north side mentioned I would always tune in. This time when I looked at the TV, I could see yellow police tape surrounding a building that looked to be Roc's shop. My heart was already racing as I scrambled to find the remote on the table to raise the volume.

"The police are citing an attempted robbery gone very bad. More details about the shooting will follow at noon," the reporter said.

I jumped up from the couch and rushed over to the phone. I dialed Roc's number, but it went straight to voicemail.

"Call me as soon as you can," I hollered into the phone. "Please."

I hung up, hoping to get a returned phone call while I changed clothes. I didn't have time for makeup, nor did I have time to curl my hair. Since it was chilly outside, I put on my heavy black coat and hurried to my car. The feeling I had inside wasn't good. Roc's shop was almost forty-five minutes away from my house, but afraid of what I was feeling, I rushed to get there sooner. I dialed out on my cell phone to call the shop, but no one answered. Called his home phone and got nothing. Tears started to well in my eyes. I kept thinking the worst possible thing, but kept closing my eyes to wash away my thoughts. With my mind racing, I failed to focus on a gray Saturn that was driving slowly in front of me. I was so close to it that I had to slam on the brakes to avoid hitting it.

The man in the Saturn moved over in another lane and he put up his middle finger as I drove by. I was so unstable, and by the time I reached the Kingshighway exit, getting closer to my destination, my sweaty palms could barely stay gripped on the steering wheel. More tears had fallen because Roc had yet to return my phone call. My throat ached. My head started hurting. My body felt numb and that was how I knew this wasn't going to be good.

No sooner than I turned the corner to where Roc's shop was, I could see the police tape securing the building. Numerous media outlets were outside, and even though there were some people hanging around, there were not nearly as many people there like it was on a regular business day. I rushed out of my car, leaving the door wide open.

"What happened here?" I said, running up to three officers who stood nearby.

"Ma'am, we're in the middle of an investigation. You need to step back."

I knew they wouldn't answer me, but I pushed harder. "Please," I begged. "The owner, Roc Dawson, is he in there? Is he okay?"

One of the officers backed me away from the yellow tape because I had gotten too close. He still didn't answer me. I looked around to see if there were any familiar faces. Not one. I even ran up to the news reporter who seemed to have some information, yanking on his arm.

"Who was it?" I asked him. "Who in there was hurt?"

"I'm sorry, but the police are not releasing any names right now."

I was about to have a panic attack. I squeezed my chest and slowly walked over to my car to close the door. I then continued to look around for someone

I knew. Finally, I saw Troy, who worked the front counter at Roc's shop. He appeared to be in a daze and had just gotten out of the car. I moved fast to catch up with him before he got away.

"Troy," I shouted, causing him to quickly turn around. "Where is Roc? Have you seen him? Please tell me that you have."

Troy's face was flat. His bottom lip trembled as he bit into it; then he swallowed hard. "Yeah, I've seen him. I just saw him."

I exhaled and sighed a bit from relief. "Whe . . . where is he? Tell me, please. I need to talk to him."

Troy hesitated to answer, but when he did, I swear I must have lost my hearing because his mouth was moving, but that was all. "What did you say?" I repeated for the third time.

"He's at the morgue. I'm sorry, Desa Rae. Roc was killed."

My whole body froze in that moment, at that time. I gasped and was unable to catch my breath. I then wrapped my arms around my waist, squeezing it. I could feel goose bumps forming on my arms, and as chills ran through my body, I rubbed all of it.

"Nooooo," I screamed. "God, please no! I don't believe you." I gritted my teeth and pulled on Troy's jacket. "This is a game and you know it! Stop playing. Tell him not to play with me like this! Please! If he's at the morgue, take me to him. I want to see him. Now!"

Troy embraced me, trying to console me. I was so weak that I could barely stand, as he held me up in his arms. "Please," I shouted out. "Take . . . me . . . to . . . him!"

The news reporters and their cameramen used this opportunity to get me on tape. Troy opened the door to his car and sat me inside of it. I bent over, rocking back and forth as I thought about our last conversation. The slap was fresh in my mind, and I had the nerve to say he'd be the one leaving here in a body bag. *Did I speak something like that into existence? Shame on me! Shame on me!* I thought while pulling at my wild hair. *Why did our conversation have to be so negative like that?*

Troy pulled out his cell phone, as he saw me falling apart. "Let me speak to Craig," he said to someone. "Where are you?" He paused for a few seconds then spoke up. "Hurry. Desa Rae is here. I . . . I can't hold her down, man, somebody else needs to do it."

Troy hit the end button and kneeled in front of me. "I want you to know that the niggas responsible for this have already been taken care of. Roc left specific—"

"No," I said, smacking away tears and shaking my head from side to side. I sat up straight, refusing to believe this mess. "No, he didn't leave anything. I . . . I want you to take me to him, Troy." I poked my finger into Troy's chest then pounded it. "Take me now! Stop lying to me. Please! How much is he paying you to lie to me?"

Troy stood up and spun around. He looked up and down the street, appearing to be searching for someone.

"He's coming, isn't he?" I said, gathering my composure again. "I'm staying right here until he comes, so you may as well tell him to stop this nonsense."

Troy got loud with me and shook my shoulder. "I wouldn't lie to you about nothin' like this! Craig should be here in a minute. If you want to go to the morgue then we'll go to the morgue. Damn!"

Hearing him say those words ate me alive. My fingers roamed through my messy hair; I knew that I looked like a madwoman. When Craig pulled up, he came up to the car. His eyes were fire red and he reached for my hand.

"I'm so sorry, ma. There was nothin' that we could do. We tried our damndest to save him, but it was too . . . too late."

I swallowed my spit and wiped the dripping snot from my nose. I stood up and straightened my coat that fitted slouchy off my shoulders. "No need to be sorry, Craig, because until you take me to him, I don't believe a word you say. Where is he?" I said again through gritted teeth. "Goddamn it where is he?"

He looked at Troy. "Help her to my car."

Troy reached for my hand, but I snatched it away. "Do . . . Please don't touch me. Just take me to where he is and everything will be good."

I stumbled my way to Craig's car. Troy held the door open for me and when I got inside he closed it. I sat on the passenger's side, feeling as if I were losing my mind. This had to be a dream. That was it . . . I was dreaming and in a minute I would wake up from all of this. Craig drove off, and when I realized I wasn't dreaming, I hugged my stomach again and squeezed it. I gagged and vomit rushed to my mouth. I couldn't hold it, so I threw up all over myself.

"Man, you need to take her to the hospital," Troy softly said. "Don't take her to the morgue."

I wiped my mouth with my hand and looked over at Craig, who had pulled over to help me. A glassy film covered my eyes and I shook my head. "Go. I don't want to go to the hospital. I want to see Roc."

Craig sighed and looked in the rearview mirror. He then drove off.

Twenty minutes later, he pulled up at the morgue. Reality was starting to set in and I couldn't even walk inside. My legs had weakened. I felt like I had run a twenty-mile marathon without a drop of water. My mouth was dry and my head was thumping so badly that I thought I would faint. Troy held me up on one side, Craig the other. He rang a doorbell, and when a suited-up man came to it, we followed him down a long hallway and into a basement surrounded by concrete walls. My feet dragged along the floor, and by now Craig and Troy had to carry me along.

"Wait right here," the suited-up man said as we stood outside of a white wooden door with a tiny window. A few minutes later, he opened the door wide and motioned his hand for us to go inside. From the hallway, I could see my Roc with a white sheet up to his shoulders. A chill came from the room and I stared at my handsome man without a blink. Tears poured from my eyes and dripped from my chin, causing a tiny puddle to form on the floor.

I tussled with Craig and Troy for them to let me go. "Get away from me," I said, pushing them away. As they backed up, I stood still to look at Roc again. I couldn't even move. My dry lips cracked apart and the sound of my soft voice pleaded with him. "Baby, please get up. I . . . I got so much that I want, I need to say to you, and . . ."

From the corner of my eye, I saw Craig walk away. Troy, however, held on to me so I wouldn't fall. I took two steps forward, but could go no farther.

"Whyyyyy?" I cried out to Roc. "Geeeet up! Why did you leave me like this? We . . . we were supposed to get married, you . . . you promised me that we would always be together, didn't you?" I gasped, trying to suck in every ounce of air that I could so I could breathe. "Wha . . . what am I going to do without . . ."

At that moment, I thought of Chassidy. I immediately ran away from the door and up the concrete steps, where I fell on my knees and had no strength to move. Craig and Troy carried me to the car, where I blamed them for all of this.

"Why couldn't you save him?" I questioned as I looked over at Craig. "You could have saved him, couldn't you? How could any of you in that shop let something like this happen? How couuuuld you?" I cried out.

Neither of them responded, but I snapped out of it when I heard my cell phone ringing. Maybe it was Roc calling me back. I rushed to grab the phone from my pocket and answered in a hurry.

"Dez, where are you?" Monica said. "The school just called and said you were late picking up Chassidy so I went to get her. I've been calling you—"

"Monicaaaaa," I whined. "Help meee, pleeeeease!"

"Dee? What wrong? Please don't scare me like this."

I dropped the phone in my lap and let my head rest on the passenger's side window. I looked straight ahead, staring without a blink. Roc's smile flashed before me. I saw those dimples. He was standing in the kitchen cooking me dinner. We were making love. I saw him picking up Chassidy and tossing her in the air. Him and Li'l Roc playing video games. At the carwash where I met him. Sitting at his desk at the shop. Laughing with his friends—all of it played right before my eyes.

Craig picked up my phone, as he could hear Monica yelling. "Meet us at Desa Rae's house in thirty minutes," he said. "I'm bringin' her home."

Thirty minutes later, Craig pulled in my driveway. Monica was already there, without Chassidy. She rushed out of her car and I ran up to her as I exited Craig's car. I threw my arms around my best friend, using her stable shoulder to cry on.

"He left me, Monica! Roc was killed."

Monica squeezed me tighter and she started to cry with me. "It's going to be okay. I promise you, girl, everything will be all right."

Unfortunately, without Roc, it wouldn't be.

Chapter 23
Desa Rae

Life was precious and it was so important to savor every moment of it. We just didn't know when things would one day come to an end, but what had happened to Roc had come too soon. The timing was bad. I was mad at God, upset with myself, and I didn't want to speak to anyone. Needless to say, I was out of it and it took at least a week and a half for me to gather myself and come out of my bedroom. Night after night, I cried. I got no sleep whatsoever, and when I did close my eyes, I could hear Roc speaking to me. I'd jump up and look for him in the room, but he wasn't there. He, simply, was not there.

Thank God, though, that Monica was. She had come to stay with me. She took care of Chassidy, cooked for me, and cleaned. I didn't have the guts to tell Chassidy what had happened, but she knew something was wrong because Daddy wasn't around anymore and I had been out of it. Li'l Roc hadn't been by and our whole lives were different. All I could tell Chassidy was that Roc had gone away and he wouldn't be back for quite some time. In a few more years, I'd tell her the truth. Today, I couldn't do it. I just could not do it.

Monica had been bringing breakfast to my room, but today I got up to join her in the kitchen. When she saw me strolling in with my housecoat and nightgown on, she walked up to me and gave me a hug.

"You feeling okay?" she asked.

"As good as I can get," I said, backing away from her. "It smells good in here." I moseyed over to the kitchen table and sat down. Monica went back over to the stove.

"You know how I do it. We got bacon, eggs, grits, and toast this morning. Do you want grape or strawberry jelly?"

"You don't even have to ask, do you?"

"You're right, I don't. Strawberry it is."

"And only one piece of bacon, Monica. I'm not that hungry."

"I'll give you two pieces. You haven't eaten much and it's time that you start eating before you get sick. I know you've lost some weight and I can see it in your face."

"I've lost some, but I don't know how much."

Monica brought our plates over to the table. She poured two glasses of orange juice and joined me at the table, where we held hands and said a quick prayer.

"Do you feel like talking about a few things?" Monica asked.

I picked at the eggs with my fork. "Talk about what? Do you have something you want to talk about?"

"I do. But first I want to let you know about some important phone calls."

"What about them?"

"Chassidy's teacher called to tell you that Chassidy and Nicolas are getting along much better. Chassidy also told her you were sick, so she wanted to check on you because she hadn't seen you at the school."

"That was nice of her. I'm glad to hear about Chassidy and Nicolas. That makes me feel good."

"Me too. Then Latrel called. Him and Angelique wanted to come here, but please don't be mad at me for telling them that I didn't think it would be a good idea.

I figured the last thing you wanted was company. I'm already enough."

"You're a blessing, that's what you are. And I agree with you. I don't want Latrel and Angelique to see me like this. He was hurt by the news and I have to call him back to apologize for hanging up on him."

"He understood. We talked and everything is okay. Just call him when you can because he's worried about you. Next, Craig called. He said that he needed to speak to you about something important, but only when you were ready to call him. I didn't pry, but he did say that Roc gave him some specific instructions about what to do if something ever happened to him. So, whenever you're ready, please call Craig."

My stomach started to hurt, so I laid the fork down. I hadn't eaten a thing, but I took a sip from the glass of orange juice. "I'll call him later today. But let me go call Latrel."

Monica reached over and touched my hand. "Fine. But, please eat something. Chassidy will be home at three. It would please her heart to see you up and moving around with a smile on your face. I know it still hurts. I know it takes time to heal, but you still have to carry on. Chassidy is counting on you and so are all of us, including Roc who will always be here in spirit."

I nodded and picked up a piece of the bacon. Monica put jelly on my toast and laid it back on my plate. We ate in silence. When the phone rang, Monica got up to get it. She whispered to me that it was Latrel. I nodded my head, signaling that it was okay for her to bring me the phone.

"Hi, Latrel," I said, trying to sound upbeat, but my tone was dry.

"Hello, Mama. How you feeling?"

"So-so. You?"

"I'm all right. Just worried about you, that's all. Angelique and I want to come and spend some time with you, if that's okay with you."

"I would love that, but just not right now. Give me some time. I'll let you know when I'm feeling better."

"Okay. But can I get you anything? I just feel helpless not being there. I want to do something. Wha . . . what about Chassidy? Is she okay? Maybe you should let her come stay with me for a while."

"No. She's fine, honey. I thank you, and the last thing I need is for you to feel helpless. Stay there and take care of Angelique. Life is so precious, and with the baby on the way, she needs you. Be there for her, always. I'll call you when I'm feeling better and, hopefully, that'll be soon. Just pray for me."

"Every day," Latrel said in a tearful voice. "I love you."

"Love you too."

Monica took the phone from my hand, replacing it with Kleenex. I blew my nose and got up to throw the Kleenex in the trashcan. Afterward, I washed my hands and stood by the sink, looking out the window at the first place Roc made love to me, which was on the swing set.

That day, I lay sideways on the swing set with my back facing Roc and his arms comforting my waistline. He intertwined his legs with mine and I felt quite at ease. I started to read my book, and at least twenty minutes into it, I could hear Roc's loud snores. He was tired and had just gotten done cutting my grass. Without a shirt on, his muscular chest slowly heaved in and out. When I turned my head slightly to the side, he looked so peaceful that I didn't want to wake him. I focused on finishing my book, but before I knew it, my eyes started to fade as well.

Roc's vibrating phone awakened me, but he remained in a deep sleep. I'd felt his phone vibrating several times, but was too tired to move. The sun had gone down and the night was definitely upon us. We'd been asleep for hours and I couldn't remember the last time I'd felt this good being cradled into someone's arms. I almost hated to wake up Roc, but it was getting late and the caller seemed anxious to reach him. I moved around a bit, causing the swing to slowly sway back and forth. Roc stretched, before opening his eyes to see where he was.

"Damn," he said, looking at the dark sky. "What time is it?"

"Late, but I'm not exactly sure about the time. You might want to check your phone to see."

He reached for his phone clipped to his jeans and pushed a button to check the callers. I saw his lips toot a bit, and when he dropped the phone by his side, obviously, he wasn't pleased about who the callers were.

"I can't believe time flew by like that," he said. "Why didn't you wake me? I thought you had somewhere to be."

I lay on my back and Roc kept his hand on my midsection. Our faces were extremely close and he looked down at me as I spoke. "I did have somewhere to be, but I changed my mind about going."

"Are you sure yo' man ain't gon' be mad at you for bein' a no-show?"

"Is that your way of asking me if I'm involved with someone?"

"Nope, I was just askin'. I didn't see no ring on yo' finger so I couldn't care less if you got a boyfriend."

"FYI, no, I don't. What about you? You got any girlfriends?"

"I shake, rattle, and roll sometimes, but you can believe that don't nobody excite me like you."

I didn't know what to say. It really didn't bother me that Roc admitted to having girlfriends, and at his age, what did I expect?

"You know what?" he said, looking at my lips. *"That sholl is a bangin'-ass dress you wearin'. I mean that mug—"*

"Cut with the foolishness, Roc." I smiled. *"You're only saying that because I backtracked on what I had planned for you. Sorry, you ruined it when you criticized my dress, and that should be a warning for you to keep your mouth shut while you're ahead."*

"Ha!" he shouted then lightly squeezed my stomach. *"Tell me . . . what did you have planned for me?"*

I shrugged my shoulders. *"I don't know. Whatever it was, I guess we'll have to miss out."*

"See, you playin' now. It's all good, though. I see how you gon' do me."

Roc's lips were already close and he seemed so surprised when I lifted my head and initiated a lengthy kiss. *"Mmmmm,"* he mumbled while indulging himself and circling his hand around on my hip. His hand went under my flimsy dress, and when he moved his body between my legs, I bent my knees. My legs fell farther apart and his hardness was right where I wanted it to be. My pussy was doing a happy dance and I felt juices trickling between my coochie lips. Roc's hand kept touching my hip, in search for my panties. When he didn't feel them, he halted our kiss.

"I knew there was a reason why I loved this dress so much. You ain't got on no panties, do you?"

I moved my head from side to side, indicating no. Roc quickly jumped up, dug in his pocket for a condom, and removed his jeans. I lay there in doubt, thinking if I should allow this to happen. He was too young, but maybe I could get an orgasm and call it quits. I needed some kind of action in my life, and if Roc was willing to give it to me, what the hell? He returned to his position on top of me, and slightly raised my dress for easy access. He lifted himself a bit, just to get a glance of my shaved pussy.

"Damn," he whispered while wetting his lips. "I wanna taste it, ma. Can we go inside? I need way more room than this."

I signaled no and reached down for Roc's hard meat that was poking me. Going inside of the house would waste time and it was not an option. "Work with what space you have," I suggested. "Be creative and don't keep me waiting."

Roc took heed and put it in motion. As soon as he separated my walls, my mouth grew wide. My walls stretched farther apart when he maneuvered all the way in, filling me to capacity. I inhaled a heap of fresh air. With every thrust, I sucked in more air, and released soft, pleasing moans. I kept telling myself that he was not a twenty-four-year-old man. His big dick was doing its best to prove it to me, too. Reggie is nowhere near this big, I thought.

"This shit feelin' so guuud," he whined. "I need to get at it, though. Why you won't let me go inside and get at this pussy like I want to?"

I basically ignored Roc's request. His package was delivering too much satisfaction for me to pack up and go inside. At this point, releasing my grip from him would've been a crime. Instead, I massaged his dark chocolate, muscular ass, and just as I'd imagined from the moment I'd met him, he put my legs on his shoulders, making every bit of my daydreams come true. I worked my body to the rhythm he'd chosen and *my insides tingled all over. When Roc pulled my dress over my head, and started in on my wobbling breasts, my body quivered even more. His lengthy steel dipping into my cream-filled pussy made me crazy as ever. No, I didn't want to come yet, but I had to. The rush was there and I let it be known.*

"Damn you!" I yelled with tightened fists. "I'm coming, baby. My pussy feels so good, but help it give you all it's got. Pleeese help it!"

Roc picked up the pace and used his two fingers to turn circles around my swollen clit. It was rock-solid hard and he loved it.

"Shit!" he said, taking deep breaths. "I love this feelin', ma. You . . . you workin' with somethin' and a nigga lovin' the hell out of this."

Enough said, enough done. Roc got tense, his ass felt like I was gripping stone, and he tightened up all over. He kept toying with my clit, forcing my juices to ooze out quickly. I felt relieved and my body went limp. Following suit, so did his body. He lay on top of me, while the swing squeaked and swayed back and forth. I gazed at the twinkling stars, thinking about how I couldn't wait to tell Monica about the new man in my life named Roc.

Today, that was only one memory of many that I was left with. Like a zombie, I walked away from the counter and went into the family room. Every place I went, the memories stirred in my head again. I lay on the couch and tucked my hands in between my legs. Monica came into the room and sat in a chair across from me.

A tear rolled from the corner of my eye. "When am I going to get over this?" I asked Monica. "I feel like I did when I lost my mother, but this is so hard because of how Roc was killed. He did everything for Dre.

Everything, Monica, and it was so wrong of him to set Roc up like that."

"Very wrong. It's some cold people in this world and what you do for them don't matter. I remember how you were when your mother died. You also remember how I was when I lost mine. But no matter how long it takes, I'll be here for you, as you've always been there for me too."

Monica's words gave me comfort. But, it would be at least another week before I was able to put on some clothes and leave the house.

I dropped Chassidy off at school the following morning and went to go see Craig. I had finally spoken to him yesterday, and we made arrangements to meet at the shop. I wasn't sure what this meeting between us would be about, but I gave Craig my word that I would be there by ten o'clock.

Doing nothing with my hair, it was brushed back into a curly ponytail. I had on jeans and a purple sweater with a belt tied around it. My boots had a high heel, but they were comfortable and easy to walk in. Not knowing what to expect when I got to Roc's shop, I was surprised to see it crowded. Not nearly as it was before, but business was still going strong.

I parked two vehicles away from the front door and got out of my car. I spoke to the fellas as I walked by and opened the door to go inside. Like on a normal day, Troy was at the counter, but he was staring up at a hanging flat screen on the wall. He smiled when he saw me then told me to wait one minute.

"You here to see Craig, right?" he asked.

I nodded. Troy called him to come up front and I stood with my arms folded and waited. Being here felt so strange. I didn't understand how everyone seemed able to carry on, but I guessed that was what you had to do when you lost loved ones.

As I waited for Craig to come up front, I looked at Roc's curvy painted name written in script on the huge picture window. Seeing his name and a little boy who was sitting on his mother's lap made me think of Li'l Roc. I hadn't spoken to him at all. I was surprised that he hadn't called my phone to speak to Chassidy, but I suspected that he'd been going through hell as well. I was sure the truth had been told to him, and I wondered about Vanessa's reaction, too. With Roc's request to be cremated, we didn't get a chance to come together and celebrate his life. I guessed we had to do so on our own time, but any kind of celebration for me wouldn't be soon.

Craig came up front and asked me to follow him. As I walked down the hallway, I was hoping that when I looked over at Roc's office that he would be there. He wasn't. The lights in his office were turned off, the door was shut, and no one was there. Craig took me to a tiny office that was connected to the shop area. It was a cramped space with a desk and two chairs. Before I went inside, several of the fellas walked up and offered their condolences.

"Hope you're feelin' better," Romo said, giving me a hug.

"I am," I said, then hugged several others who waited.

"If you need anything," Butch said, "let us know."

"All I want is Roc back. If anybody can make that happen, please do."

They all looked at each other. Some dropped their heads and others walked away. I then went into the office with Craig, where he asked me to sit and he closed the door.

He sat against the edge of the desk. "I gotta say this first, before I say anything else to you," Craig said. "I hope you ain't mad at us about what happened that night. That fool snuck up on Roc and we tried our best to save him. Shit happened so fast. We were all left caught off-guard. There ain't a brotha up in here who wouldn't trade his life for Roc's because we all had mad love for him."

"I know that, Craig. I . . . I'm just mad as hell that Dre was behind this. He was family. I don't understand what makes family, your own blood, do something like that. It seems like all this backstabbing stuff has gone on for a long time. I'm so hurt because I know Roc wanted better. He really and truly did."

Craig nodded. "Yes, he did. But there are a few things that you need to know about. It's all on paper and it's in this envelope. Look everything over and if anything don't jive with you, let me know."

Craig handed me the envelope and I opened it. The first thing that came out was keys that fell on my lap.

"Those keys are to his house. It's yours now, so you can do whatever you want to with it. The shop is Li'l Roc's, but I'll be helping him manage it. Most of the money made here goes to Li'l Roc and Chassidy."

I didn't say a word. I looked down at the papers that were trembling in my hands because on the very top was a letter written by Roc. As I started to read it, my tears dripped down and wet the paper.

What's up, ma. If you're reading this letter, it means that I didn't make it to continue my lifelong journey with you. I don't know how I got to the other side, but I'm here. Don't sweat it, even though I know you will. But just remember that what Black Love puts together, nothing can tear it apart. So, I'll be watching you. I'll be thinking of

you. I'll be loving you, still, like from the first day
I met you to the second I take my last breath. And
the only thing I want from you is simple. Take
care of yourself and take care of my children. I
don't want you running around fussing about
what you won't accept, but please accept any-
thing that I give because it comes straight from
the heart. I'ma end it on that note, because I don't
like writing this kind of shit. Peace, Mrs. Dawson.
I'll see you whenever you get to the other side.

I folded the letter and looked up at Craig to ask what
weighed heavily on my mind. "What happened to his
ashes?"

"They were spread over water."

"What water?"

"The Atlantic."

"Who put them there?"

"Me and Gage."

For whatever reason, none of this felt real to me.
I still couldn't accept the fact that Roc was gone. I
lowered my head and continued to look at the papers.
There were several bank accounts and trust funds. The
deed to his house in North County was there and there
were deeds to other properties, too.

"What are these . . ."

"He owns a lot of property in St. Louis. Like I said,
what you don't want to deal with, let me know."

I glared back at Craig. "Owns or owned?"

"Owned. Understand that it's hard for me to speak in
past tense."

"I'm sure it is."

I moved more papers aside, seeing titles to several
cars that I didn't know about. Roc was loaded, and
the most recent statement for his business account

at Bank of America showed a $9.8 million balance. I was stunned. I had no idea Roc had all this money, but probably because I never really inquired about his dealings. I put all the papers in the envelope and stood up.

My mood remained somber and my voice stayed calm. "Anything else, Craig?"

"Two," he said, leaning back and getting something out of his desk. "Two more things before you go."

Craig held a Tiffany & Co. bag in his hand and gave it to me. "When we were out of town, Roc picked that out to give to you on your birthday. I'm sure he would want you to have it."

My birthday was in another week. I had forgotten all about it because I had so much on my mind. I reached in the bag and when I opened the box, there was a beautiful butterfly pendant with pink diamonds. It was attached to a platinum chain designed like a key. I had never seen a piece of jewelry so beautiful, and it truly touched my heart.

Right after Craig gave me that, he gave me something else. It was a suede tiny black box with a diamond ring inside of it.

"He was goin' to propose to you again. He said you tossed your other ring, so he bought a new one."

All that did was bring back memories of how I'd treated him before he was killed. I wasn't proud of myself and it was hard for me to forgive myself for being so ugly.

"Thank you," I said, squeezing my forehead. "But I'm getting ready to go. I'll be in touch soon."

Craig opened the door and all eyes in the shop turned to me. I followed Craig back into the second waiting area, and when we passed by Roc's office again, I stopped.

"Craig, will you unlock the door for me?" I asked.

"I will, but you don't want to go in there."

"Why not?"

"Too many memories."

From what I was told, the chair was where Roc took his last breath. "There are good memories, too," I said, trying not to visualize what had happened that day. "Please unlock the door."

Craig unlocked the door for me and turned on the lights. Almost immediately, a whiff of Roc's cologne hit me. I could smell him all over the room and his presence was there. One of his leather jackets was still hanging on a coat hanger. It was my favorite, as he looked so handsome wearing it. I removed the jacket, holding it close to my chest. His scent was firing up my nostrils. It felt good to hold him again. I kept a tight hold on his jacket and moved over to his chair. I took a seat and looked at the messy papers on his desk. Some of the papers had dried bloodstains on them. The stains made me visualize how it all went down; being in his office put me right in the moment. Feeling it hurt so badly. I rubbed my fingers along the edges of his desk then lowered my head on top of it. I stretched out my arms and crumbled the papers on top of it with my hands, starting to cry.

Craig rushed over to rub my back. "Let it go," he said. "We just can't bring him back."

"I can't let go," I tearfully said. "I will never let go."

Craig allowed me time to get myself together. And fifteen minutes later, I walked out of Roc's place, not knowing if I would ever come back. I then did something that I didn't think I could do. I drove to his house and used my key to go inside. It was freezing cold. The heat was obviously off. The living room was spotless. When I looked around elsewhere, so was the rest of the house. I turned the light on in Roc's bedroom—a room where I had never spent one night. There was a king-sized bed inside that was dressed with navy and cream sheets. A dresser with mirrors was topped with numerous colognes, lotions, wave brushes, and spare change. A leather chair sat in front of an entertainment center with a flat screen mounted above it. The room wasn't fancy, but it was so fitting to Roc. I walked over to his nightstand where there was a picture of him at a barbershop. He appeared to be acting silly in the picture, but he looked fine as ever. I held the picture and sat back on his bed. It was comfortable and felt like a bed of clouds. Just for a moment, I lay sideways with his picture next to me.

"I'm sorry," I said in a soft whisper. "I'm sorry for not forgiving you. I apologize for not telling you the truth about me and Reggie, and I shouldn't have ever put my hands on you. If I could do it all over again, I swear I would do things differently. But it's too late, isn't it? Too late for me to try to make things right. How I wish I could."

I closed my eyes and faded until it was time for me to go pick up Chassidy.

Chapter 24

Desa Rae

I didn't do much at all for my birthday, which was in March. I still didn't feel up to a lot of company, but Monica and Brea stopped by with a cake.

"Happy birthday to you . . . Happy birthday to you," they sang out as we all stood in the kitchen. Once they were done, I blew the candles out and made a wish. Nobody had to wonder what it was.

"Yo' tail is getting old," Monica said. "How old are you again?"

"Forty-five in the mind, feeling great about the condition of my body and whatever I want to be in the soul."

"I heard that," Monica said. "Now cut the cake."

"Yes," Chassidy shouted with Brea.

I cut several slices of cake, and after the girls had their pieces, they went into Chassidy's room to play. Monica and I stayed in the kitchen. She started telling me about her breakup with Shawn.

"He just got too clingy, and the last thing I need in my life is a clingy man. Plus, he was jealous because I had been over here spending time with you. He accused me of cheating and that was it for me."

"I'm sorry to hear that, Monica. I really liked Shawn and I thought he would be the one for you."

"He was the one, on a temporary basis. I told you I wasn't going to get married again."

"You did, but I thought the two of you would be together forever."

"Uh, no," Monica said, laughing. She opened her purse and reached for something inside. After she pulled it out, she placed it in front of me. It was a Things Remembered bag and a card was inside. "Happy birthday," she said. "I hope you like it."

I smiled as I opened the touching card and read it. Afterward, I got up from my chair to go give Monica a hug.

"We should have been sisters," I said, returning to my seat. "Who did you say your father was again?"

Monica laughed and threw her hand back. "It wasn't yo' daddy, I can promise you that. But blood or not, we are sisters. It just don't get any better than this."

I agreed and opened a darling picture frame with a picture of us in it. At the bottom, the words FRIENDS FOREVER, MONICA & DEZ were written in script. The picture was from when we went on vacation, several years back, and about a year before I met Roc. I looked a bit chunky in the picture and the straw hat I had on didn't do me any justice. Monica and I were cheek to cheek while holding up margarita glasses.

"Now you know what," I said, still looking at the picture. "Out of all the pictures that we've taken, why this one? The only things that look good in that picture are those drinks."

Monica laughed and agreed. "But we had so much fun that week. Remember? We laughed and danced and ate, and you had sex with some white man, didn't you?"

I put my hand on my hip. "Monica, please. Do not lie on me. That was you who had sex with that white man, not me."

She frowned. "I did, didn't I? His name was Mark. Mark Henderson. I wonder what he's been up to."

"Well, don't call him because I doubt that he'll remember you, especially from that long ago."

Monica's jaw dropped and she twitched her finger from side to side. "Are you crazy? What I put on that man, he'd better remember me. I put in some overtime and he almost cried when I left."

Monica was good at exaggerating. I thanked her again for the gift then snapped my fingers.

"I almost forgot to show you this," I said, thinking about the necklace Roc had purchased for my birthday. I ran to my room to get it. When I returned, I gave the bag to Monica.

"Oooo," she said, reaching in the bag to pull out the box. "Tiffany & Co."

"Craig said Roc purchased that for me for my birthday when they were out of town. Isn't it the prettiest necklace you've ever seen?"

Monica nodded and lightly rubbed her fingers across the diamonds. I could see her eyes well with tears. It took a lot for Monica to show her emotions. She wasn't that kind of person at all. "I know Roc had his flaws, Dez, as most men do. But I have to say, he really loved you, or loved you as best as he knew how."

I swallowed hard, knowing that all too well. I held back a tear that was trying hard to escape from my eye. "Look, put that thing away. I just wanted to show it to you. It's my birthday and I told myself that I was going to celebrate and be thankful for all of the blessings I have."

"Right," Monica said, choking back her tears too. She put the box in the bag, but it dropped to the floor. She hurried to pick up the necklace. "Forgive my clumsiness. I hope I didn't damage the diamonds."

Monica bent down to get the box, and when she stood up she had the box and a receipt in her hand. Her eyes bugged and she made a whistling sound with her lips. "$8,375. Now, that's a lot of money for a necklace."

"Tell me about it. Roc should've known better. He knows that I would never wear anything like that. It's nice, but it's really not for me."

Monica kept squinting as she looked at the receipt. "Di . . . didn't you say Roc bought this for you when he was out of town?"

I nodded. "That's what Craig told me. Why?"

Monica was still engrossed with the receipt. So engrossed that I got up from my chair and walked over to her. "If Roc bought this when they went out of town, why does the date on this receipt show the seventh of March? Today is the twentieth, and Roc was killed in January. A dead man can't buy a necklace, can he?"

I snatched the receipt from Monica's hand. "There has to be some kind of mistake," I said. "Maybe he said . . . said, I don't know, but he told me Roc purchased it."

Monica and I were left scratching our heads. Something didn't add up and I wanted some answers. Something was eating away at me where I thought Roc was still alive. I wanted to believe that he truly was. This thing with the receipt made me wonder. I told Monica about what I had been feeling inside.

"I really and truly can't comment on what you're feeling, but you saw the man, Dez. Didn't you? Wasn't he dead?"

"Yes. He was."

"Then where are those feelings coming from? It all seems very strange, especially that receipt, but I don't want you getting all worked up over this. Do find out what's up with that receipt, because it's obvious that somebody lied to you. Why, is the question?"

I agreed, but my issues with the receipt weren't going to get resolved today. I did my best to enjoy the rest of my birthday with Monica and Chassidy, but the next morning I called Craig.

"Hi, Craig, this is Desa Rae. I was wondering if I could meet you somewhere so we can talk. Will you be at the shop today?"

"I'll be there around four or five. I got some runnin' around to do, but right now I'm gettin' ready to have breakfast."

"Where? Maybe I can join you."

"I'm on my way to Goody Goody on Natural Bridge. Do you know where that's at?"

"Yes, I do. I'll meet you there within the hour."

Doing the norm, I dropped Chassidy off at school and headed to Goody Goody to meet Craig. I just couldn't let this go, and I'd be lying if I said I didn't think I was crazy for having these feelings. I mean, I'd seen Roc lying there, dead. I knew it was him, but the only thing that bothered me was I couldn't find the courage to get closer to him. Maybe these feelings wouldn't exist had I actually touched or moved him. I was so confused, but when I got to Goody Goody, hopefully, Craig would clear things up for me.

Craig was already there when I got there. He waited for me to come, and then the waitress sat us at a booth. All I ordered was orange juice, but Craig ordered pancakes that were supposed to be the best cakes in town.

"So, what do you want to talk about?" he asked while rubbing his ashy hands together.

"I discovered something yesterday and I really need a clear answer. Call me crazy if you want, but there is something inside of me that believes Roc is still here. I don't know why I'm feeling this way, especially since I saw his body with my own eyes. But I can't let this go, not until I'm one hundred percent sure."

Craig scratched his head. "I don't know what to tell you, Desa Rae, but Roc is gone. I know it's hard to let go of the people you care so much about and this shit, man, it's been mo' hard on me than everybody, with the exception of you and his kids. I wish he was alive to help me with all the shit I'm dealin' with at the shop. There was so much stuff he left for me to handle. I do it because I don't want to feel as though I let him down. What I don't get is, you saw him at the morgue. It was him, Desa Rae, nobody else. You got to accept that shit and move on."

I lowered my head, feeling horrible about meeting him here about this. But there was still the pendant/necklace from Tiffany's. "You remember the necklace you gave me from Roc?" I asked, then Craig nodded. "When did he get it?"

"Right before that, uh, shit happened with you at the police station. Remember when we were out of town in Michigan? We stopped in Troy, Michigan and Roc got it for you then."

"Well, that's not what the receipt says."

I gave the receipt to Craig to see his expression when he looked at it.

"Look at the date. It says March seventh. Roc was dead by then."

"There must've been some kind of computer glitch or somethin' because I know when he bought that necklace."

I sighed and touched Craig's fidgety hands, which were on the table. "Craig, all I have to do is call Tiffany's to find out when and where that purchase was made. I may even go to the extent of trying to see who went into the store to make the purchase. Please tell me the truth. This is so serious. I feel as though I'm losing my mind over this."

Right then, his cell phone rang. He pulled it from his pocket and looked at it. He didn't answer, so the person called back again and yet again.

"Answer your phone," I said. "I'll wait, especially since it seems like someone really wants to speak to you."

"It's just my kids, buggin'. They always call back when I don't answer. As for the necklace, here's the truth. The fellas and me felt bad about how shit went down. Real bad. And while we did all we could to save Roc, it wasn't enough. We knew how he felt about you, and . . . and it really troubled me to see you go through like that. So, the fellas and me talked about doin' somethin' special for you on your birthday. I personally went into the store and bought the necklace for you. I said it was from Roc because I knew you'd appreciate it more from him than you would from me. Now, getting to that ring. The real deal is he bought that. He picked that out and he mentioned proposin' to you again. Why ain't you wearin' the ring? He would want you to."

I was saddened that Craig had a legitimate answer for the necklace. After all, I knew Roc would never purchase anything for me like that.

I snapped out of my thoughts and blinked. "I . . . I don't know why I'm not wearin' the ring. Maybe one day I will. As for the necklace, it's nice, but I knew Roc would never buy me anything like that because I wouldn't wear it. Sorry to have bothered you with this."

I eased out of the booth so I could leave, but stopped to ask one more question. "Where is Li'l Roc at? I haven't seen or heard from him. It's not like him not to call me or Chassidy."

"He's takin' this real hard, Desa Rae. You know how tight him and Roc were. Give him time. I'm sure he'll call."

"Okay. If you happen to see him, tell him I love him. If he wants to talk to me or visit he can."

"Not sure when I'll see him, but when I do, I'll be sure to pass on the message."

I left feeling satisfied with Craig's response, and I was more convinced that Roc was actually gone.

Chapter 25
Roc

I stood beyond the sliding glass doors that viewed the blue ocean waters and white sandy beaches. A cool breeze was blowing, and as I glanced up at the dark sky, a storm looked to be rolling in. I walked farther out onto the balcony that stretched around the entire penthouse. I could see several people running for cover because the wind had picked up. The casual white shorts I had on were about to blow off, so that was when I headed back inside. As soon as my bare feet touched the marble floors, the phone rang. Li'l Roc rushed to it before I did.

"Daddy, it's Craig," he said, handing the phone to me. He then ran to the open kitchen and pulled on the stainless-steel refrigerator.

"How did it go?" I asked Craig.

"It was tough. It's hard to see her like that and I almost fucked up."

"Meanin'?"

"Meanin' I left the receipt in the Tiffany's bag."

I eased back on the white contemporary couch that sat solo on the marble floor. "You did what?" I said, raising my voice a notch higher. "And let me guess. She saw the date of purchase."

"Exactly. But I broke it down to her like this. I told her I bought the necklace because I wanted her to have somethin' special and I pretended that it came from you. She said that she should've known better because you would never buy her no bullshit like that."

"She said it was bullshit?"

"No, I mean, she said you wouldn't buy her nothing like that 'cause you knew she wouldn't wear it."

"She got that right, she wouldn't. How is everything else goin'?"

"Accordin' to plan. I'm holdin' it down, but Desa Rae still didn't seem convinced. Sometimes when you got that connection you just know when things don't feel right. I hate to see her because she be questionin' every little thing I say. Even when my phone rang, she was like . . . who dat? I was like, Roc, man, please don't call back. She looked like she wanted to snatch the phone and answer."

"Just keep on doin' what you do. Tell the fellas I said what's up and I'ma send Gage there next week to get some things for Li'l Roc."

"Oh, yeah, speakin' of Li'l Roc, you may need for him to call Desa Rae. She's askin' about him. If she calls Vanessa, you know she may start talkin'."

"Vanessa has been paid well to keep her mouth shut. She ain't gon' say nothin', but I don't want Li'l Roc to talk to Desa Rae. I don't want him involved with this."

"I told her he was takin' it hard and probably needed time. I just hope that time don't run out and she start questionin' more people."

"If she does, work it out and clear it up. Always remind her what she saw at the morgue and be done with it."

"Will do."

We ended the call and I sat back on the couch, thinking about all that had happened. For a man like me to have peace, this was how I had to do it. And the thing is, I saw this day coming years and years ago. What Dre did to me was my wakeup call. There were too many niggas like him who were within my circle or who were trying to get in it. Staying in the same environment that I was in, it only meant my life span would be cut short. My children's lives would always be at risk, and I feared that Desa Rae would get caught in the middle.

When Dre's friend shot me, one bullet grazed my neck and the other went into my shoulder. The rapid loss of blood caused me to weaken and pass out. The fellas drove me to a hospital, where the doctors were able to do their thing. Shortly thereafter, the plot for me to play dead began. There were too many murders that day and they all were connected to me. Even with Dre being dead, those crooked-ass cops still wanted money. I could never pay enough money to make them stay quiet about the killings. They would make my life miserable, showing up whenever and demanding a li'l something to fill their pockets. I got tired of that shit and I didn't want to go back to jail. I didn't want Desa Rae to sit in the courtroom and have to hear a judge give me twenty years to life for murder. If I told her about the plot, I wasn't sure if she would roll with it. So, for now, I had to do what was necessary. I wasn't even sure if I would ever let her know I was still alive, because if I did, she'd probably hate my fucking guts for putting her through this. I believed that things were better left as is, and now sitting on a mountain of cash, she and Chassidy could have anything in life they ever wanted.

The destination of my new penthouse was kept a secret. Gage knew where it was, because he was my running man. No one else knew nothing. Not even Craig, who I trusted, but I didn't trust enough to tell where I was. I hadn't done much at all to the place, but

Chapter 26
Desa Rae

My mind was made up. I decided not to return to work, and if I did, I would find a new job. After what had happened to Roc, I decided to live my life a little differently. Here today, gone tomorrow was stuck in my head and I decided to live every day that I could to the fullest. I had access to an enormous amount of money, but I hadn't used any of it. Not saying that I wouldn't, but for now, it just didn't feel right to me.

"April showers bring May flowers," Monica said as we walked through the Galleria Shopping Mall, doing a little shopping. "By then, we really need to take a trip. I would love to go someplace I've never been and I know you would too."

"Yes, I would, so I think we need to sit down and plan something. But before I do anything, I really want to go see Latrel and Angelique. They're always coming to St. Louis and I want to do something real nice for them, especially for the baby, too. She'll be here in a few months and I'm so happy that they're having a girl."

"I think that's what Angelique wanted. I really like her. Latrel know he lucked up on a jewel."

"She did too. My son is all that and then some."

"Yes, he is."

We headed to Nordstrom and I reached for Chassidy's hand so she wouldn't run off. Monica started telling me about her hooking back up with Shawn, who she originally thought was a lost cause.

"See, I didn't want to tell you because I didn't want you talking about me. But I am seeing him again and I'm a bit more open about things this time around."

"Meaning marriage?" I teased.

"Yes, marriage. I could see us going there, especially since—"

I stopped in my tracks and put my hand on my hip. "Since what, Monica? No, you didn't, did you?"

She nodded. "He proposed and I said yes! I couldn't wait to tell you, but I didn't want to do it over the phone."

I gave her a squeezing hug. "Congratulations. I'm so happy for you and I can't wait to help you plan for this."

"No rush. I'm thinking sometime later this year. It's going to be simple, so don't be running around here making a big de-do about it."

"Weddings are a big de-do and . . . and where is your ring at? Why isn't it on your finger?"

We sat down in the shoe department and Monica reached into her purse. "I put it in here because I didn't want you to see it. To be honest, I hope the talk of marriage doesn't make you uneasy. I know you and Roc were supposed to get married in May and I'm sure it's been on your mind."

"It has been, but I'm okay. I appreciate you thinking about my feelings, but you have your life too, Monica. You've been so supportive, and don't hold back on anything because you think my feelings will be hurt."

Chassidy had run off to look at shoes. She brought a pair of Jimmy Choo shoes over to me and placed them in my lap.

"Mommy, these are so pretty, aren't they?" she said.

I always looked at the prices on everything, before I did anything else. I squinted at the price and frowned. "Nice shoe, but look at this price," I said, showing Monica the $1,095 price tag.

"That is a bit much, but, hey, you got it. Chassidy, tell yo' mama to buy those shoes for you. She can save them for you when you grow up."

Chassidy showed her pearly whites, but she knew better.

"On a serious note," Monica said. "I wouldn't buy those shoes either, but you shouldn't be so uptight about the money Roc left. If he wanted you to have it, then have at it. Be responsible and honor his wishes by taking care of the kids, yourself, and you can take care of your friend, too. I'm just saying."

"Monica, you know you can have anything you want. I've just been skeptical about all that money and I still can't believe I have all of it. Is there something that you need?"

Monica smiled and crossed her legs. "I'm so glad you asked."

We both laughed.

"No, really. All I want is my house paid for and to send my kids some money. That's it, unless you want to buy me a new car, too."

"Let's see. You've talked about one of those Range Rovers for a long, long time, haven't you?"

Monica pouted and nodded. She already knew it was a done deal, but we had to finish shopping first. The car shopping would be planned for another day.

Several hours later, I dropped Monica off and Chassidy and I headed home. I was in my closet hanging up my new outfits when I heard the telephone ring. I yelled for Chassidy to answer it, and a few minutes later, she rushed into my room with the phone in her hand.

"Mommy, Mommy," she said with excitement in her voice. "Li'l Roc is on the phone."

I smiled, eager to finally talk to him. But when I put the phone up to my ear, all I heard was the dial tone.

"What did he say?" I asked Chassidy.

"He said hi and asked what I was doing. I heard my daddy say something in the background, too."

My breathing halted. I felt like cement had been poured over me; I couldn't move. "Sweetie, are . . . are you sure you heard your daddy in the background or someone else?"

Chassidy nodded.

"I know yes, but was it him or could it have been someone else?"

"It was him."

I checked the caller ID that revealed a long-distance number. When I called back it rang three times and went to voicemail.

"Hi, this is Desa Rae. Li'l Roc, call me. Call me back, please."

I quickly called his grandmother's phone number, but when she answered, she told me that Li'l Roc was with Vanessa.

"He's been with her for a while. Try to reach him over there," she said.

"Thanks, Shirlee. I will."

My adrenaline was going. I moved over to the bed to sit down. Could Chassidy have actually heard Roc's voice? She got on the bed with me and laid her head against my arm. When I called Vanessa, she didn't pick up.

I truly hated to go there, but I had to. I left the house with Chassidy and we drove to Vanessa's house to see if Li'l Roc was there. While in the car, I dialed the long-distance number that was on my cordless phone, but this time, the phone went straight to voice mail. I didn't leave a message.

Minutes later, I knocked on the door to a two-story house that looked paid for by Roc. The only time I ever came over here was to pick up Li'l Roc or drop him off. I was never invited inside. Vanessa made it clear a long time ago that she didn't want me there. I hoped her attitude had changed, but when she opened the door, I wasn't so sure.

"Hi, Vanessa," I said, being as polite as I could. "If you got a minute, can we talk?"

She widened the door and let me and Chassidy come inside. Doing exactly what I had taught her, Chassidy said hello to Vanessa as soon as we stepped into her house.

"Hi, cutie," she said. "You know yo' daddy spit you out, girl. You are too cute."

"Thank you," Chassidy said, blushing.

Vanessa turned on a light in the living room and we all stepped farther into the room and took a seat. I was so surprised by how cordial she was. I got right to the point. "Is Li'l Roc here?"

"No, he's not. He's at a friend's house."

"You mother said he was over here."

"That's because my mother doesn't always know his whereabouts."

"Does his friend have a name?"

"Tony."

"Can I call Tony's house to speak to him?"

Vanessa sighed and her nice demeanor was over. "No, you may not. And what's with all the questions? Damn."

"I just want to talk to Li'l Roc. I haven't heard from him since Roc's situation and that seems so odd to me. Chassidy said Li'l Roc called today, but when I got on the phone he hung up. She also said that she heard Roc's voice, but we know that's not possible. Either way, I just want to make sure Li'l Roc is okay."

"I did hear his voice," Chassidy said, pouting. "It is possible."

Vanessa slightly pursed her lips. Now, as much as she still loved Roc, if Chassidy said she heard Roc's voice, Vanessa would question her. She didn't and that left me even more suspicious.

"It is possible, Chassidy," I said, knowing that something wasn't right. "Very possible." I stood up and took her hand. "Thanks for your time, Vanessa. Please tell Roc, I mean, Li'l Roc, to call me."

"Sure."

Chassidy and I left.

If I was crazy, then so be it. And to prove my point that I wasn't, the next day when I called the number, it was disconnected. How did I know that would happen? This was getting deeper and deeper by the day, and I had one last move to make before I would put this to rest.

Craig had just opened the shop and only three other mechanics were there with him. The place wasn't crowded yet, but I was sure that it would be soon. I opened the door and went inside. Troy wasn't at the front counter, so I headed to the back waiting area, taking an opportunity to look at Roc's office. The door was open and the lights were on. I went inside and couldn't believe that I could still smell his scent. His jacket was now gone and his office had been cleaned up. I sat in his chair and pushed the intercom button on the phone.

"Good morning, fellas," I said as my voice could be heard over the intercom. "To Roc's office, or, as he would say it, get the fuck in here now!"

Craig was the first one to rush out of the shop area. Romo followed, then Butch and Gage. Troy must've just gotten there, because he rushed to the office too.

They all stood in the office, glaring at me as if I had gone cuckoo. Maybe so, but at this point, I didn't give a shit what they thought of me.

"You're really not supposed to be in here," Craig said. "But what's goin' on?"

"Craig, you know what's going on better than I do. And why am I not supposed to be in here? Roc would want me in here, or has he ordered you to keep me away from here?"

"Desa Rae, this is . . . it's gettin' kind of hectic, sweetheart," Craig said, trying to show empathy. "You're makin' this real hard on all of us, because we don't know what else to tell you. Roc is gone, Dez. He ain't comin' back."

"Never," Romo added. "I feel Craig on this, 'cause we havin' a hard time dealin' with this shit too. My heart raced comin' in here. I haven't been in his office since . . ." Romo tightened his eyes and swung around to avoid eye contact with me.

"I know Craig has said this before to you," Gage said, adding his two cents. "But if you need anything from us let us know. Somewhere down the road, you gotta accept what has happened. We don't want to keep revistin' that day in our heads, though. Maybe you need some kind of counselin'. I'll go with you, if that's what you need, but just tell me."

The only one who hadn't said anything was Troy. All he did was nod the whole time. I stood up and placed the strap of my purse on my shoulder. I laid the ring Roc had supposedly purchased for me on the desk.

"Whichever one of you purchased that ring, you have horrible taste. I know Roc wouldn't buy me anything like that, just like he wouldn't have purchased that necklace."

"He did purchase that ring!" Craig shouted and tightened his fist, pounding it on Roc's desk. "He's gone, Desa Rae! Accept that shit, ma, and stop makin' us feel guilty because we couldn't save him!"

I raised my cracking voice and was unable to stop the tears from flowing. "He's not gone, Craig, and you know it! Stop lying to me, please! All of you," I said, looking at every last one of them. "Stop lying! Do you all have any idea how much this shit hurts? Huh? I know Roc is somewhere out there because I can feel it in my fucking heart and soul. Why are y'all doing this to me? Making me crazy and telling me things that aren't true! What did I ever do to any of you, but love the hell out of a man who many of you would die for?"

No one responded. All they did was intensely stare at me, even Romo, who had turned around with fake tears in his eyes.

I took a few deep breaths to calm myself. "If I'm wrong about this, God help me. I am so, so sorry. Please forgive me and charge it to my mind and heart that can't let go. But if I'm right, tell Roc that I said you all are in the wrong profession because y'all are damn good actors. Every last one of you has put on quite a show, especially you Craig. You need an Oscar."

I stepped forward to leave, but stopped without turning back around to look at them. "I'm not coming back again. But do me a favor and tell Roc that if or when he wants to talk, I don't know if I'll be able to listen. Either way, he'll know where to find me. "

I left, washing my hands of all of it.

Chapter 27

Roc

Gage leaned over the balcony and sipped from a glass filled to the rim with Patrón. I sat behind him in a lounge chair with my hands placed behind my head.

"All I'ma say is she got some balls," he said to me, referring to Desa Rae. "You wouldn't want to see her like that, and she ain't buyin' what we tryin' to sell her."

"That's because I got Li'l Roc over here usin' my phone to call people, Vanessa and her mom can't stay consistent, and y'all tryin' too hard to convince her. The less said the better. Romo told me Craig over there poundin' on desks, lookin' like a fool. Just stick to the plan. As much I want to see Desa Rae, and tell her why I'm never comin' back, I can't. She's gotta believe that I'm dead and maybe she'll forget about me as time goes on."

"She said she wasn't comin' back and she returned the ring. She also told us to tell you, if you were alive, to kiss her ass, she hates you, and she said her and Chassidy may be better off without you. Even if you did reach out to her, somethin' tells me that you may get your feelings hurt. Desa Rae ain't no joke."

I felt like Gage was bullshitting me, just to get me to make a move. Then again, I knew Desa Rae well. She could have said something to that effect.

"Her words sting, and she damn sure ain't no joke.
That's why I knew I couldn't tell her what I had to do.
She wouldn't have understood why I had to kill Dre,
man, and the last thing I wanted to do was fight with
her. Now, I'm done talkin' about this because it upsets
me. I'm goin' to bed."

I went into my room feeling horrible and could only
imagine what Desa Rae was going through. I saw those
tears before, as well as her anger. But it was nothing
like when I lay in that morgue, pretending to be dead.
The sound of her cries haunted me every night and I
barely got any sleep. I took off my robe and turned the
music up loud. I lay in bed on my back and stared up
at the ceiling. My mind wandered, and I cracked a tiny
smile when I thought about each time we rediscovered
Black Love.

*That day, I was embarrassed to tell Desa Rae my
thoughts and was almost speechless. "You'd better not
laugh at me. And if you do, I'm never doin' this shit
again," I said, holding the paper in my hand.*

*She looked puzzled, and even though she was mad
at me, she listened to what I had to say. "Go ahead,"
she said while sitting on the couch. "Read it."*

*I cleared my throat and began to read from the
paper. "What is Black Love and what does it really
mean to me? For years, I thought that Black Love
represented drama and disrespect. In order to get
somewhere as a black couple, there had to be pain or
no gain. My partner didn't have to show love, 'cause
she didn't know love. And if we ever had to go to blows
with each other, then that just meant we were angry
because we couldn't bear to be without each other.
Yeah, that's what I thought, but for all of these years,
I've been wrong about Black Love. Dead wrong. Now,
I know better, 'cause true Black Love is alive in me.*

I feel love like I have never felt it before and it's so energetic that it takes over my mind, body, and soul. It makes me laugh when I want to cry, it makes me strive harder when I want to give up, it causes me to be real with myself, as that is sometimes so difficult for me to do. Even in my darkest hours when I feel hopeless, or if I don't want to go on, the feeling of Black Love picks me up and lets me know that I must move forward. Yeah, I finally get it, but I hope Black Love don't give up on me, because I will never give up on it."

I folded the paper, kind of embarrassed to look at Desa Rae. But tears were in her eyes and she nodded with approval. "That was nice. I have to ask, but did you write that? I mean, you just don't seem like the type of person who—"

"Yes, I wrote it. I know it was corny and everythang, but I just wanted to share with you my thoughts that I often write on paper. I did a lot of writin' when I was locked up, too, and these are my real thoughts, ma. I wanted to take this opportunity on your B-day to share that with you, even though we got some serious problems in this relationship."

"Thanks for sharing. Your words were beautiful. I really don't know what else to say, but I will never give up on Black Love either."

At least she didn't lie. She hadn't given up on us, I did. I told myself that this was the right thing to do, and if it was, why was I feeling like this? It had been almost four months now and I couldn't shake this shit. Time, though, was everything. In due time those feelings would fade for either her or me. That was what I kept telling myself, every day, every night, and every hour. But then, there she was making her case for Black Love again.

*Desa Rae came to my shop that day to break it
down for me. She looked past Raven, who was sitting
on my lap, and gazed directly at me. "Yes," she said.
"To truthfully answer the question that you asked on
my birthday, yes, I am very jealous of your relationship with Raven. An . . . and right now, all I can do
is take you back to this thing you once referred to as
Black Love. Do you remember Black Love, Roc? If you
don't, I do. Because Black Love makes what others
may see as impossible relationships, possible. Black
Love makes a woman living with too-high standards
jump back to reality. The reality is I love the hell out
of you, Roc, and I am willing to accept who you are.
I will grow to love your family and friends as you do,
because Black Love is about acceptance, not judging.
I will not make you feel like my son; rather, I will
make you feel like my king and not tear you down
anymore. I hope you understand that, sometimes,
Black Love can make you so bitter when you don't get
it right. An . . . and when it shows up again, one may
find themselves unprepared. I was unprepared for
the man who had the courage to show me what Black
Love is really about. That man is you, baby, only you.
If and only if you have ever loved me, I want you to
give us our final chance to get this right. Only if you
can promise me no more heartbreaks and headaches,
and that you can be a faithful man, I want you to take
that ring off her finger and put a new one where it
belongs. If you can't, allow me to shed my tears and
leave me at peace. Keep that ring on her finger and
always be thankful that we at least gave Black Love
a chance. Neither of us can be mad about that." She
paused for a moment to wipe the tears from her, then
walked away, leaving the ball in my court.*

No doubt, I let her down. I broke promises when I placed a new ring on her finger that day. I promised her no more heartbreaks and headaches, and to be a faithful man, yet I failed to come through. The more I thought about it, the more I struggled with what to do, the more I realized that Desa Rae was much better off being without a murderer. That was on a for-real tip and even I couldn't deny that.

Chapter 28
Desa Rae

Monica had sent me a beautiful bouquet of flowers, thanking me for the new car and for paying off her mortgage. I was waiting for her to give me an estimate on how much to send her two kids, but no matter how much it was, it was worth it. Our friendship was priceless.

I was starting to feel better. Mainly because I kept some hope that Roc was alive. I kept wondering if he ever showed up, what would I do? It would be so difficult for me to forgive him for putting me through this, and I couldn't even face a man who caused me so much pain. Then again, I only wished that I were given that opportunity. An opportunity that I had to realize might not ever come. I saw his dead body with my own eyes. He was dead, and maybe it was time for me to release all of this nonsense in my head and face it.

To help ease the situation, Monica and I planned a road trip for the second week in May. Our first stop was to drop Chassidy off with Latrel and Angelique. They were so excited to see us and Angelique greeted us at the door with a growing belly.

"How is she?" I said, bending down to pucker at Angelique's belly.

"She's fine, Mama, but she is so ready to come out."

We hugged and then I reached over to give Latrel a hug. Chassidy was all over him and I was always full of smiles when my children were together.

Latrel carried Chassidy's bags into the guestroom and she followed him. Monica and I followed Angelique as she wobbled into the great room.

"This house is so beautiful," Monica said, looking up at the high, vaulted ceilings. Arched glass windows let in sunlight that lit up the great room. A T-staircase led to the upper level, where there were four bedrooms and a bonus room. The kitchen was made for a chef. The engineering degree Latrel received from Mizzou allowed him to get a job making enough money for him and his family to live comfortably. Of course he always dreamed of being a basketball player, but I know he wasn't disappointed that it didn't pan out. Angelique had a degree in journalism, but she didn't have to use it unless she wanted to. With a baby on the way, her career was on hold.

"Whew, ladies," Angelique said, easing down to sit on the couch. "I sure do be glad when this is over. I don't know how women have two and three kids. One is enough."

"Does Latrel know that?" Monica said, sitting down next to me. "I can't believe all y'all gon' have is one baby."

"Three," Latrel said, coming into the great room with us. He looked like he had gotten even taller. "Three, but I'll settle for two."

"When you get finished talking, I'm the one who has to carry the baby. If I say one, it will be one," Angelique said.

I high-fived Angelique. It was good to see her standing up for herself, because there was a time when I was worried about Latrel running over her with his so-called female friends.

"Don't be high-fiving her," Latrel said. "When you only have one grandkid, I don't want you picking up the phone griping to me about it."

Showing how two-faced I could be, I turned to Angelique. "He's right, Angelique. I at least need two grandkids. Will you reconsider?"

"For you, Mama, yes, I will," she said. "Anything for you."

She playfully cut her eyes at Latrel, but he ignored her and kept playing with Chassidy, who loved attention from her big brother.

"What's that cooking?" Monica sniffed the air. "Something smells good."

"You can be sure that Angelique didn't cook it," Latrel said.

Monica looked at me. "Di . . . did we come at a bad time or something? Maybe we should walk back out the door and try this again."

I agreed. Angelique and Latrel were throwing jabs at each other that left me shocked.

"You're right. I don't cook much, but please pay Latrel no mind. He's just bitter because he hasn't been getting any nookie."

"None," Latrel added. "Not even a kiss."

"Awww, poor baby," I said, getting up to kiss his cheek. "Mama got you. Muah."

Latrel blushed while Monica and Angelique shook their heads. Chassidy got jealous, so I had to give her a kiss too. Afterward, we all went to the kitchen to get our grub on. Latrel made lasagna and garlic cheese bread. I hadn't been eating much at all and had lost almost fifteen pounds.

"Slow down," Monica joked as she saw me gobbling down two pieces of the cheese bread. "Save some for us."

"I'm trying to gain my fifteen pounds back. I love my curves too much to let them go for good."

"I love mine too," she said, handing her plate to Latrel. "Now, give your auntie another piece of that lasagna."

Latrel was pleased that we enjoyed what he cooked. He even baked a chocolate cake that melted in our mouths.

"You need to give up that engineering degree and become a chef," Monica said. "This cake is off the chain."

"I know I can cook," Latrel boasted. "But I'm perfectly fine with the career path I chose."

Not as happy as I am, I thought.

After dinner, we stayed up most of the night talking and laughing. Monica and I were heading out to Vegas in the morning and I was so ready to get our little road trip started. By morning, though, we hadn't had much sleep. We had a long drive ahead of us, but we were definitely up to it.

I gave plenty of hugs and kisses at the door. Chassidy didn't look sad at all, and since she was staying with Latrel until the end of the month, I was the only one frowning about that.

"Have a good time," Latrel said along with Angelique. They waved and watched us get into the SUV Monica had rented. She was driving, but I was sure to watch the road because she was reckless.

No sooner had Monica driven down the street then she was already sending text messages to someone.

"Look," I said, turning in her direction. "If you want to text, let me drive. Please."

"I'm just sending Shawn a message to let him know how much I miss him. I really do, but I would rather be doing this than laid up in a bed somewhere with my legs cocked open. That man knows he loves to have sex."

I crossed my arms and pursed my lips. "Really now. It's him who is sexually active, not you?"

"I'm not sexually active. What makes you think I'm sexually active?"

"Because you are."

"No, I'm not. I have sex once or twice a week with my man. Now, tell me again how many times you and Roc used to have sex?"

I sat quiet and didn't say a word. Monica thought she offended me and reached over to touch my hand.

"I'm sorry for saying that. You know how I am. Sometimes I—"

I threw my hand back at her. "Girl, please. No need to apologize for bringing up his name. You know that doesn't bother me. And to answer your question, I'll just say a whole lot."

We laughed, and when Monica got on the highway she took off.

City after city, state after state, we drove through to get to Vegas. I was tired of getting in and out of the car, eating at the nearest restaurant we could find, and holding on tight as Monica tackled many curves on the road.

"You know what?" she said with potato chips in her hands while driving.

"What?"

"I really don't see how Oprah and Gayle did this mess. My ass is hurting in this seat and I can't get comfortable. All this driving is too much."

I couldn't help but to laugh as I watched Monica squirming around in the seat.

"Watch I get hemorrhoids," she said. "And while you're somewhere gambling, I'll have to be soaking in a tub."

"Your problem, not mine, because I do intend to get my gamble on," I said, snapping my fingers in the air.

Monica playfully rolled her eyes at me and turned on Sirius Radio. Faith Evans had just started to sing "Tears of Joy." I reached for the volume knob and blasted it.

"Oooo, that is my song." I closed my eyes and slowly moved my head as Faith sang about how the man in her life had her so messed up. Like me, she sang about being through the ups and downs, the highs and lows. I was all into it until Monica pushed my shoulder.

"Girl, what you know about that?" she said.

"I know all about that crazy love," I said, still snapping my fingers.

Listening to the song took me there, and when it was over, all I could do was exhale.

"Don't get me wrong," Monica said. "I love that song too. But if you really want to go there, I got a song that will do it."

Yes, while driving, she rummaged through her CDs. She slid one in and we were hit with Curtis Mayfield's "Diamond in the Back."

"Yes, ma'am," Monica said. "Turn it up, turn it up!"

I loved this song too, so I turned it up. We were swaying around in the car, singing the lyrics and snapping our fingers.

"Though you may not drive, a great big Cadillac . . . gangsta white walls . . . but remember brothers and sisters, you can still stand tall . . . just be thankful for what you got."

We sang in unison and pointed at each other. When I said, "running in the back," Monica stopped singing and turned down the volume.

"Running in the back?" she questioned. "Who's running in the back? The song says 'diamond in the back.'"

"I know it, but it also says 'running in the back.'"

"No, no, no! Listen to what it says, Dez."

She turned the volume back up and we carefully listened in. I still heard "running," but she swore the whole song said "diamond."

"Now, why would somebody be running in the back of their own car? They may have diamonds back there, but there is nowhere to run."

We cracked up. I couldn't remember the last time I laughed this hard. We listened to Monica's whole CD that took us way back, until "Pimp Juice" by Nelly came on.

"Isn't that the song with the video where he swiped a credit card through that girl's ass?" I asked with a frown.

"Through her big, round ass, but that's not the song. I know which one you're talking about, but I can't remember it."

We both were fans of Nelly's music, but couldn't remember which song it was. Since we couldn't, Monica changed the subject.

"Since I'm getting old, I'm going to make a bucket list," she said. "You should think about making one too."

I looked over at her with raised brows. "Are you serious? A woman in her forties is not considered an old woman. So I will not be making a bucket list. However, I would like to know what's on yours."

"I'm starting my list off with Barack Obama."

"I wouldn't mind meeting him either. Maybe one day I will."

"Meet him?" Monica said, licking her lips. "Oh, I'm not interested in meeting him. I had something else in mind."

My jaw dropped then I whispered as if the Secret Service were in the car with us. "Are . . . are you talking about, you know . . . wanting to do the wild thing with the president?"

"Dez, I really and truly do not know about you sometimes. You know darn well that's what I'm talking about, so why you over there acting all brand new?"

"Because he's the president, that's why."

"And? He has sex too."

"Duuuuh, with his wife, I hope so."

"Forget you," she said. "He still tops my bucket list. Who would top yours? And don't say Lance Gross because he looks too much like Roc."

I rolled my eyes. "I was kind of thinking him, but I would add someone like . . . like Bill Clinton."

"Bill Clinton?"

"Yes, Bill Clinton, if he weren't married to Hillary. There is something about powerful men that's so attractive to me."

"I feel the same way, but Bill I could not do."

We went on and on about our bucket lists, and when we finally arrived in Vegas and stood at the doors of the Venetian, the hotel of our choice, we were exhausted. I almost crawled on the floor to open the door to our room, but I didn't. Once we got inside of the 1,980-square-foot renaissance suite, I fell back on the couch and Monica hit the floor. The two bellhops who assisted us left our luggage at the door and told us to let them know if we needed anything else. Within minutes after that, we passed out.

For the next few days, Monica and I partied, we ate, shopped, went to the spa, gambled, ate some more; basically, we had the time of our lives. From Vegas, we were supposed to drive to California, but that did not happen. This road trip stuff was not for us, so we decided to ditch the rental car, leaving it in Vegas, and caught a plane back to St. Louis.

I sat in first class, shaking my head at Monica who came up with this bright idea. "Seven days was enough for me," she said. "My bed is calling me and I'm not going to call Shawn to tell him I made it back home. I need at least another week to recuperate."

All I could say was, "Me too."

Chapter 29

Desa Rae

Home is where the heart is—yes, it was. I enjoyed myself with Monica, but no luxury hotel room in the world could satisfy me more than my own bedroom. Ever since we had gotten back from our half-assed road trip, all I had been doing was sleeping. Trying to play catch up, but hadn't caught up yet. The phone had been ringing off the hook. The kids were calling, Reggie had called twice, and I was surprised to get a call from Mr. Anderson. He asked if I would stop by on Friday to see him, and said that he needed to speak to me about something urgent. I called his office, just to see what he wanted.

"I'd rather we talk in person," he said. "Please. It's important. Around noon, if you don't mind."

"Sure, Mr. Anderson. I'll see you Friday."

Even though I had been upset with Mr. Anderson, I didn't want to play him off. There was a time when he came through for me; plus, I wanted to be nosey to see how he'd been managing without me. I wanted to see what Shawna had been up to, or if she had been fired.

The answer to those questions came on Friday, when I sat in front of Mr. Anderson's desk and he shared with me a little personal problem that he had with her.

"She's been stalking my wife and is threatening to go to the other executives and tell them what's been going on with us. Things have not been the same since you left, Desa Rae, and I'm asking if you'll come back. I will fire Shawna and deal with the repercussions later."

"Stalking your wife," I said, displaying shock and disgust. "That's awful. I'm surprised that a smart man like you, Mr. Anderson, didn't see this coming."

"I did, but then again I didn't. Shawna came off as an ambitious woman, looking for an opportunity to learn something around here. I thought she could benefit from learning a lot from you, and you know how I'm always looking out for women, especially African American women around here."

"The opportunity Shawna was looking for was with you. She didn't care about anything else, but getting an invitation to your bedroom. I appreciate you looking out for African American women, but the one you should be looking out for is your wife."

It was funny how it was easier to say how I felt about my boss, especially when I didn't work for him anymore.

Mr. Anderson lowered his head, putting on the same sob look that he did the last time he was in this predicament. I bought it last time, this time I couldn't.

"I feel so embarrassed by this," he said. "I knew I could talk to you about it, and I hear you loud and clear about my wife. There are just a lot of things that you don't know about us, but I have been wrong on so many different levels."

I thought I'd heard enough. I stood up, asking Mr. Anderson if there was anything else.

"Nothing else, but can I count on you to return? The other executives are on my back about firing you. I really do need you around here."

Some men were something else. Slap a woman in her face, and hope like hell she'll come back. For me, no, not this time. Mr. Anderson was on his own with this mess.

"Mr. Anderson, I can't. If you had asked me a month ago, maybe I would have said yes, but today is a new day. I'm tired of the foolishness, and you made your choice when you fired me. I will never understand why your wife just doesn't divorce you, and when you mentioned those things that I don't know, the truth is, I don't want to know. It's none of my business. All I care about right now is me and my family. Work on getting yours together, because I'm sure they're sick of it. Good luck and I appreciate the opportunity that you gave me."

I left Mr. Anderson's office thinking about the no-good men like him, including my father. Reggie too. *Running from one woman to the next, searching for something from different women and never finding it. Many kids being born in the process and then the men do what they know best and run.* I could go on and on, but in my case, I was doing exactly what my mother did when my father was in my life one minute and out the next, or when he supposedly had died. That was do my best to take care of mine, especially pertaining to Chassidy. Roc wasn't here anymore, so I had to stop complaining and step up. It was my duty. I wanted Chassidy to feel special like my mother made me feel. Daddy or not, I was my mother's number one priority.

There were plenty of times when I watched my mother put me before herself. Like when we didn't have much food in the house. We would sit at the table together and she would watch me eat, while she ate nothing. In the winter time, she wouldn't have a winter coat, but I did. I would look up at her as we stood in the frigid cold waiting for a bus to come, and wonder why Mama didn't have on a coat. Time and time again, she sacrificed so much for me. I intended to do the same for Chassidy, and I had to be honest with her about Roc's death. She needed to know the truth. I didn't want her to grow up hating me because I fabricated a lie about him coming back. I believed the only lie my mother ever told me was that Daddy was dead. I wished she would have told me that he was alive and he just didn't give a damn.

When I got home, I called Latrel and Chassidy to see what they were up to. I smiled when he answered the phone laughing.

"What's so funny?" I asked.

"What's funny is this face over here your daughter is making. Am I supposed to be scared or what?"

I knew exactly what face Latrel was talking about and I told him to put Chassidy on the phone.

"Hello," she said in a sweet, timid voice.

"Uh, what are you doing? Didn't I tell you about making those faces?"

"What faces?"

"Chassidy, you know what faces I'm talking about. That ugly face that your daddy told you was cute."

"Those faces are cute," I could hear Roc say in my mind.

"I don't think it's cute," Chassidy said. "I'm only trying to scare Latrel."

"Why are you trying to scare him? What did he do?"

"He farted and it stinks. Angelique had to spray something and we all choked on it."

I could hear Latrel saying something in the background.

"I'm going to tell Latrel to knock it off, but this is my last time telling you about those faces. If you continue to make them, I'm going to put you on punishment. Are you ready to come home?"

"Not yet, because I don't want to get on punishment."

"Then no more scary faces, all right?"

"Okay. Here's Latrel."

Latrel got back on the phone, laughing. "She's hilarious."

"Yes, she is, but mind your manners. That's awful."

"What's awful are those faces she be making. She must've gotten that from Roc. I could've seen him teaching her something like that."

"Bingo. She surely didn't get it from me."

"She gets a whole lot of other things from you, but I'll keep my mouth shut about that. "

"Please do, if you don't want to find yourself in trouble."

"Big, huge, gigantic trouble," Roc would always say. I could hear him now.

"I don't get in trouble anymore," Latrel said. "Not by you anyway. Angelique? That's a different story."

"Well, tell her I said to be nice to you. I'm getting ready to cook something to eat and I'll call you back later."

"Make it sweet, ma," Roc would've replied. *"Real sweet."*

"All right, Mama. Love you."

"Love you too."

"Not as much as I do," Roc confirmed in my head.

I hung up with Latrel, not knowing what was going on with me. As our official wedding day was tomorrow, I had been thinking more and more about Roc. I kept what I was feeling inside and had stopped talking about him so much. Every once in a while I would say his name. I was trying to forget about him and live with the fact that he was never coming back. I had gotten somewhat used to being by myself and sleeping alone. Some nights I lay awake all night thinking about him, and then there were other nights that I could go straight to bed with no problem. This was a process, no doubt, but I was proud of myself for doing my best to pull it together.

On Saturday, May 19, I had to keep myself busy so I wouldn't go crazy. I kept thinking about what I would be doing right now if Roc were still alive. I visualized myself running around in my bedroom, trying to get ready, Monica helping me and Chassidy complaining about something that she didn't like. Latrel and Angelique would be here too, celebrating the day that was supposed to be one of the best days of my life. I pictured Roc waiting at the altar for me, inside of New Northside Baptist. He said only a few people would show, but I visualized many of his friends being there. I couldn't even get mad at him, because today was supposed to be our day.

Unfortunately, it wasn't, so I found myself at the grocery store, picking through some grapes and trying to find the best bundle.

"That one right there, ma. Those look real sweet. Taste them."

Hearing Roc's voice in my head was starting to drive me nuts. I had been thinking about going to see a psychiatrist, because I still had so much inside of me that needed to come out. I chose the grapes that I had my hand on and continued to go shopping. Minutes later, I found myself in the baby aisle, thinking about the day that I told Roc I was pregnant.

I stood with my hand on my hip, scanning over the numerous rows of baby food, formula, and Pampers.

"Let's see," I said as if I were in deep thought. "What kind of formula do I—"

"What you drinkin' baby formula or somethin'? Or you tryin' to hook up one of yo' friends?"

"No, nothing like that." I picked up a can of formula, turning it to read the label on the back. *"Yep, this would be for newborns,"* I said, putting the can into the cart.

I looked at Roc and smiled, but he seemed clueless. *"What?"* he said. *"What's wrong?"*

"Nothing."

I picked up a bag of newborn Pampers and whistled as I tossed them into the cart. *"Do you think those will work? If anything, I just hope they're affordable,"* I teased.

Roc shrugged his shoulders. *"Shit, I guess they'll work. And affordable for who? You?"*

"No, not me. You."

I looked into Roc's eyes again, but this time he stared back. His hands went up to the back of his head and he turned around.

"Ohhh, shit! How could I be so stupid!" He swung around to face me. *"Earlier you said that you got somethin' you can't get rid of. You fuckin' with me in this baby aisle and shit—Dez, baby, please tell me. You pregnant?"*

Roc was so loud. I now figured this was a pretty bad idea to tell him I was pregnant while in a grocery store. It was too late to change my mind, so I slowly nodded.

He tightened his fists and turned back around. *"Hell, yes!"* he shouted as if he were Tiger Woods putting the ball in at the eighteenth hole for the win. *"Fuck yeah, ma!"* He swung back around to face me. *"Why . . . when, why you fuck with me like that? Ma, I've been goin' through some shit all day, and this the kind of shit that brings happiness to a nigga! Yes!"*

I hadn't gotten a chance to say anything, and it was interesting to watch Roc express himself. He picked up several bags of Pampers, throwing them into the cart. "Hell yeah, I can afford this shit. And then some. I ain't gon' argue with you 'bout this either and my li'l nig . . . kid will have nothin' but the best."

What a memorable day that was. Roc had run around the same store that I stood in today, telling several people that he would be a father. I just shook my head, thinking about how unfair life could sometimes be.

After I went through the checkout line, I piled the groceries in my trunk, but didn't feel like going home just yet. I drove around, listening to soft music and thinking. Before I knew it, I was near Roc's shop on purpose. I turned the corner and slowly drove by to see what was up.

"*Come in,*" I heard his voice say. "*You scared?*"

My eyes began to water, and for whatever reason, I pulled my car over to the curb. Dressed in blue jean shorts, white Nike tennis shoes, and a Black Girls Rock T-shirt, I got out of the car. I saw Troy outside smoking a cigarette and he was conversing with three other men I hadn't seen before. I stopped to speak, then asked Troy where Craig was, just to make it like I had business to discuss.

"He inside," Troy said. "G'on in there."

There was a time when I couldn't get past the front counter. I guessed they were trying to protect Roc, and now it was easy access. I walked inside and waved back at a little girl sitting with her mother as they waited for their car. As I neared Roc's office, I could hear his voice again.

"*Just don't slap me. Remember the last time you saw me alive, you slapped me.*"

I whispered, "I'm sorry," and paced myself to the back waiting area. When I got there, I slowly turned to look at Roc's office. The lights were on and someone was sitting at his desk with his back turned. I couldn't see who it was, but the beat of my heart had already picked up speed. I felt something inside that gave me chills. And right when I got to the doorway, the chair swung around and it was Craig. His eyes widened and he looked surprised to see me.

"Aye, let me hit you back. Desa Rae just walked through the door." He paused and then repeated my name. "Desa Rae. Roc's woman." Somebody kept him on the phone and he looked unnerved by what was being said. As I moved farther into the room that was when Craig hung up.

"Gage told me to tell you what's up," he said.

"Tell him I said hi."

"Have a seat," he said. "What can I get for you?"

I sat in one of the chairs and crossed my legs. "I just stopped by to see how business was going."

"You should know by lookin' at the bank statements. Aren't you gettin' them by now?"

"Yes, but I don't open them when they come in the mail."

"You should because business is boomin'. I pay the fellas, then divvy up the rest between Li'l Roc and Chassidy."

"It's what Roc wanted, so thanks for taking care of that."

"No problem."

Silence soaked the room for a minute, as I took time to look around. "I sure do miss him, Craig. Today was supposed to be our wedding day and I just came down here because I wanted to feel close to him. For whatever reason, I thought he would be here."

"I'm sorry. And I ain't never felt that close to nobody to experience what it is that you're talkin' about. I wish he were here, though. Wish we were at y'all weddin', celebratin' right now."

I swallowed the baseball-sized lump in my throat and stood up. "This was ridiculous and I shouldn't have come here. I'm not going to take up any more of your time, Craig. I got places to go and people to see." I spoke with a forced smile, trying to hide my hurt.

"Okay, Desa Rae. Good seein' you and tell Chassidy that she'd better get down here and see me and the fellas. We were just talkin' about her the other day. Roc damn sure loved his pretty girl. Ain't that what he used to call her?"

I was in a daze, thinking about Roc saying that to Chassidy. "Yeah, he did. I'll be sure to tell her to come see you, and you be sure to tell Li'l Roc that I'm anxious to see him. Has he been here?"

"A few times. Vanessa been trippin' since Roc's departure and she's been MIA."

I had nothing to say about that, so I said good-bye to Craig again and left. I sat in my car thinking for a few minutes. When I started talking to myself that made me feel as though something could really be wrong with me.

"You told me to go inside, but for what?" I said out loud, waiting to hear Roc respond.

Nothing in return. I drove off, and to keep busy, I stopped at a flea market on Chambers Road to look around. I bought two purses, some jewelry, and a few more books from a book vendor inside. I put the items in my trunk and when I got back into my car, I heard the voice again.

"Damn, ma, you didn't buy me nothin'? That's cold."

I drove off, and at each stoplight, I paged through my iPhone, trying to find a psychiatrist's phone number I could contact early Monday morning. I found one and sent the information to my inbox.

"I need to talk to somebody about you," I said, out loud again. "Because you are not going to drive me crazy. Sorry."

I headed down New Halls Ferry Road, deciding to go see what was happening at New Northside Baptist today. I was curious to see if someone else was getting married, if there was a funeral, or if the church was closed. From the outside, it looked as if no one was there. There were a few cars parked on one side, but that was it.

"Didn't you say I'd know where to find you? Come inside."

"You said that at the shop. Fool me once, shame on you. Fool me twice, shame on me."

"That ain't how George Bush said it."

I couldn't help but to laugh, and then shortly thereafter I began to feel awkward. I was in my car, talking out loud to a dead man, and was trying to find him. Prayer was what I needed, so I parked my car and went inside of the church. As soon as I opened the double doors that led to the sanctuary, I saw a young man playing a piano, and another one was standing next to him. A lady was sitting in the first pew, all by herself. She looked to be praying.

Both of the young men spoke, inviting me to come in and have a seat.

"Pay us no mind," one of the men said. "We're just practicing."

"Pay me no mind, either," I said. "I just need to pray."

Before I closed my eyes, I gazed around at the beautiful sanctuary that would've been perfect. There were plenty of pews, all covered in a burgundy cloth. Two baby grand pianos sat on both sides of the church and several rows in front of the church were reserved for the choir. A balcony sat from high above and a stained-glass window with Jesus on it was up front. I closed my eyes and bowed my head, praying for my sanity, my family, and others. I asked that God help me heal from the loss of Roc and to give me the strength to go forward. I also thanked Him for all that He had done for me and thanked Him for whatever was to come.

After ending my prayer in "amen" I stayed sitting on the pew. The woman to my right had gotten up to leave, but the two young men were still doing their thing. As one of them beautifully sang the song "Father, I Stretch My Hands to Thee," I could see goose bumps on my arms. The spirit was working me, so I covered my face with both hands and released my emotions. I sobbed uncontrollably, regretful that May 19 had come to this.

"Lord, why?" I cried, still shielding my face and trying hard not to embarrass myself in front of the two young men. He stopped singing and the sound of the piano went silent, too.

"It's gon' be okay," I heard one of them say.

He touched my hands, trying to remove them from my face

"No, it's not going to be okay," I said, choked up. "It's never going to be okay."

"Yes, it is. Trust me, we'll be fine."

I recognized the voice again and lowered my hands from my face. I blinked several times, then scooted away from a vision of Roc that stood right before me. My heart was racing so fast that I grabbed my chest and squeezed it.

He touched my shoulders and looked directly into my eyes. "Just, calm down," he said in a soft tone. "Sit up and let me explain this to you."

For a few seconds, I couldn't move. I didn't breathe, nor did I blink. I couldn't believe it was him, until I reached out my shaky fingers to touch his face. I could feel it and a flood of emotions took over. I was happy, yet mad at the same time. My facial expressions were all over the place and the knot in my stomach kept tightening. Roc hurried to sit next to me on the pew, trying to hold me, but I wouldn't let him.

"Why did you do this to me?" I cried out. "Why, Roc? There is no explanation . . ."

I couldn't get my thoughts together to finish the sentence.

"Yeah, there is an explanation, but I can't spend a lot of time here explainin' it to you. I want you to—"

"No, no, no! Hell no. You just can't come in here and do this, Roc!" Saying his name and seeing him like this was too much. I reached over and touched him again, mainly his tattoos that were visible by the wife beater he wore. I looked at his baggy jeans, which were held up by a Polo belt, and touched the waves in his hair just to be sure he was actually there. If I thought I was losing my mind before, now I really felt that I was. I couldn't get the right words to come out and I felt like I was having an anxiety attack since I was so fidgety. Him being close made me nervous.

"Are you gon' make me sit here and explain all of this to you?" he said. "Please, Desa Rae, come with me."

I shook my head again and closed my eyes, trying to fight this feeling of hate, anger, yet so much love and happiness at the same time. I raked my fingers through my hair, pulling it and knowing that I was about to lose it. "Please . . . please tell me how you could do this to me. I don't under . . . understand, Roc, how could you?"

Roc kneeled on one knee in front of me. He rubbed up and down my legs, trying to calm me, but it was not working. "Desa Rae, please," he said. "Let's go. I'm gon' tell you everything. I promise I will tell you every single thing."

"Promise. Really?" I said with confusion on my face. How dare he talk about a promise? I wanted to slap the shit out of him, again. I could've punched his chest and pushed him away from me. I wanted to do all of that, but couldn't.

"I know I'm in no position to be makin' you promises, but listen to me, okay? I did what I had to do. There was no other way, ma, and I had to cut ties. If I didn't, there was goin' to be a lot of heat swingin' my way and things would've gotten real ugly for all of us."

I lowered my head and squeezed my forehead. "So, instead of telling me, you decided to play dead? You thought it was best that I thought you were killed? Is that what you're telling me, Roc? How many times are you going to do this to me? You pulled this shit on me when you went to jail. Then you turned around and left me when it came to that situation with Ronnie. Then you were going to run off with Raven and get married. Now this? Roc, this is too much. It's hurts too much and I can't take it anymore. I can't," I cried.

He leaned forward and put his arms around me. "I know, ma, I know. I'm so sorry and you have my word that I will never, ever leave you again. I swear I won't."

I felt like I was throwing a tantrum, trying to make sense of this as I pounded my leg and backed away from him. "But you said that before. You said that you would never leave me and Chassidy again, but you did. You keep doing it over and over and this time you went too far."

Roc nodded and remained calm as ever. "I agree. I did. I regret that I didn't tell you sooner, but I couldn't. If I could have, I would have. But I had to get out of here, so I wouldn't be arrested. I killed Dre, Desa Rae. I murdered my cousin for setting me up. I didn't know what the consequences would be and I didn't want you and Chassidy caught up in that shit. God, please forgive me for sayin' and doin' all of this, but, Desa Rae, you gotta understand what I was dealin' with."

I felt like a balloon that had just deflated. "I know exactly what you're dealin' with: a bunch of liars who will say and do whatever to protect you. At this point, I don't know what you want or expect from me. I'm so happy that you're alive, but what do you want from me? I have nothing to give because I've already given so much that I'm drained."

Much frustration was on Roc's face too. He sucked in his bottom lip then let out a deep sigh. "What I want is for you to marry me. I want you to go home, get Chassidy, pack your things, and leave with me. I gotta get out of here, ma, and I don't want to go alone."

Of course I felt better knowing that Roc was alive and well, but this was too much for me to deal with in one day. In one year, for that matter, and I still had concerns about so many other things. I was trying to talk myself out of this, but it was very hard to do.

"We've had some serious problems, Roc, and I don't—"

"Every relationship has problems. Why stand here, right now, after all that's happened, and go through the bullshit again? Please stop holdin' on to the negative and let go. There comes a time when you gotta squash some shit and allow things to get better. Neither of us has been perfect and you know this. Be willin' to meet me halfway, and once and for all, let's call a truce."

I couldn't understand how Roc thought this was so easy. "I can't talk about us right now," I said. "I know you didn't expect to come up in here and think that we could just patch this up and ride off into the sunset like nothing ever happened, did you? Please tell me that you didn't think that."

He held out his hands. "Call me a fool . . . a damn fool, but I did think that you would understand why I did what I had to do."

"You didn't have to do anything, Roc, but tell me exactly what you just told me. If you had, this outcome would have been so different."

I picked up my purse from the pew and walked away. As I proceeded down the aisle, Roc yelled after me.

"How many times, Desa Rae? How many times are we gon' do this, before we get it right? I walk away, you walk away, and we have yet to make the decision to do the right thing. Look, up until now, you kept your word about Black Love and said that you would never give up on us. I'm here to prove to you that I kept my word too. I came here today to marry you. Stop fightin' this and let's do this shit, ma."

After seeing Gage sitting on the back pew, obviously, I'd have to put up a fight if I wanted to leave. He wasn't going to make it easy. I turned around with a frown on my face. I wanted to tell Roc what I thought about his idea to get married and about his lying-ass friends, who would pay a price for this. But no words would leave my mouth.

"Don't leave me," Roc said with sorrow in his eyes. His voice switched to a higher pitch and he darted his finger at me. "'Cause if you leave, this is a wrap. I am not comin' back, I'm tellin' you now that I'm never, ever comin' back! You can never say that I didn't tell you because I'm tellin' you now, right now that this is our last muthafuckin' chance, so please do not walk out that door!"

My chest heaved in and out, as I glanced at the piano player and singer who stood in awe. I charged toward Roc, standing in front of him again.

"To hell with Black Love, Roc. This is more like a crazy love that I don't want no part of. To me, you were dead anyway so why don't you—"

Roc grabbed my face, lightly squeezing it in his hands and speaking in a calm manner. "But I'm not dead. I'll settle for crazy love. Stop all this madness and be with me. Didn't you learn anything durin' our time away from each other? I know I did. With each passin' day, I wound up lovin' you more. Let go of what you're feelin' inside. Show me some love. I need some love. I want to know that you're happy to see me. All I've heard so far is the disappointment. Look at me and tell yourself that I'm alive. I'm here with you, right now, and I'm alive."

More tears rushed to the brims of my eyes, before spilling over. I stared into Roc's eyes, telling myself that he was really alive. My wish had come true. All that I'd been feeling for the past five months was real. The real Roc stood before me, but I didn't know how to respond.

Helping me get there, he pulled my face to his, so our lips could touch. He pecked my lips twice, waiting for me to reciprocate.

"I, Roc Dawson," he said with another kiss, "take you, Desa Rae Jenkins"—he kissed me again—"to have as my fine-ass wife, to hold, honor, cherish, treasure, and to be faithful to you." Another kiss. "To be at your side always, in sorrow and in joy, in the good times, even troubled." Kiss. "To never betray you again and to always be there for you, especially when you need me." Roc paused and pecked my nose. "I promise you all of this from my heart, ma, and for as long as we are blessed enough to live."

Roc went all in with the next kiss, still holding my face and not letting go. Something took over me. I slowly opened my mouth and allowed my hands to creep up his back and touch him. After five long months, I secured my arms around the man who made my life feel so worthy of living. The one I could never do without and the one I was so happy had made it back to me.

Roc let go of my face, allowing my tongue to willingly dance with his. He wrapped his arms around me and we both could feel the thumping of our hearts.

He backed away from our kiss and turned to the piano man and singer. "Would one of y'all please do me a favor? Go get the minister, before she changes her mind. Please."

One of them jetted to go get the minister, but before the minister even made it into the sanctuary, I stared up at Roc, touching his handsome face again.

"I, Desa Rae Jenkins, take you, Rocky Dawson, to be my lawfully wedded husband. Before this one witness who probably thinks we have lost our everlasting minds, I vow to love and care for you as long as we both shall live. I take you with all your faults and your strengths, and I offer myself to you with my faults and strengths as well. I will turn only to you for all of my needs, wants, and desires, and as your wife, I know you will always turn to me for the same. Where we go from here, I trust that you will lead us down the right path. I love you so much, Roc, and I'm happy that you found your way back to Black Love."

Minutes later, the minister entered the sanctuary and shook our hands. He invited us to come into his office for a private talk, and thirty minutes later, Roc and I stood in front of the sanctuary and got married. Afterward, we took off.

***

Never in my wildest dreams could I have predicted any of this. I never would have thought that me, Roc, Chassidy, and Li'l Roc would be living happily together in a secured, private location where nobody . . . nobody would ever find us. That was, of course, with the exception of my dear friend, Monica, and my loving son, Latrel. Oh, and Gage, too. I couldn't get rid of him if I tried, because he was still, and would always be, Roc's right-hand man. I, on the other hand, would always be the woman who helped Roc discover the true meaning of Black Love. It wasn't always easy, but in many cases, the fight, the struggle, and the sacrifice to keep Black Love alive was worth it.

ORDER FORM
URBAN BOOKS, LLC
78 E. Industry Ct
Deer Park, NY 11729

Name:(please print):_____

Address: _____

City/State: _____

Zip: _____

QTY	TITLES	PRICE
	16 On The Block	$14.95
	A Girl From Flint	$14.95
	A Pimp's Life	$14.95
	Baltimore Chronicles	$14.95
	Baltimore Chronicles 2	$14.95
	Betrayal	$14.95
	Black Diamond	$14.95
	Black Diamond 2	$14.95
	Black Friday	$14.95
	Both Sides Of The Fence	$14.95
	Both Sides Of The Fence 2	$14.95
	California Connection	$14.95

Shipping and handling-add $3.50 for 1st book, then $1.75 for each additional book.
Please send a check payable to:
Urban Books, LLC
Please allow 4–6 weeks for delivery

ORDER FORM
URBAN BOOKS, LLC
78 E. Industry Ct
Deer Park, NY 11729

Name:(please print):_____

Address: _____

City/State: _____

Zip: _____

QTY	TITLES	PRICE
	California Connection 2	$14.95
	Cheesecake And Teardrops	$14.95
	Congratulations	$14.95
	Crazy In Love	$14.95
	Cyber Case	$14.95
	Denim Diaries	$14.95
	Diary Of A Mad First Lady	$14.95
	Diary Of A Stalker	$14.95
	Diary Of A Street Diva	$14.95
	Diary Of A Young Girl	$14.95
	Dirty Money	$14.95
	Dirty To The Grave	$14.95

Shipping and handling-add $3.50 for 1st book, then $1.75 for each additional book.
Please send a check payable to:
Urban Books, LLC
Please allow 4-6 weeks for delivery

ORDER FORM
URBAN BOOKS, LLC
78 E. Industry Ct
Deer Park, NY 11729

Name:(please print):_____

Address: _____

City/State: _____

Zip: _____

QTY	TITLES	PRICE
	Gunz And Roses	$14.95
	Happily Ever Now	$14.95
	Hell Has No Fury	$14.95
	Hush	$14.95
	If It Isn't love	$14.95
	Kiss Kiss Bang Bang	$14.95
	Last Breath	$14.95
	Little Black Girl Lost	$14.95
	Little Black Girl Lost 2	$14.95
	Little Black Girl Lost 3	$14.95
	Little Black Girl Lost 4	$14.95
	Little Black Girl Lost 5	$14.95

Shipping and handling-add $3.50 for 1st book, then $1.75 for each additional book.

Please send a check payable to:

Urban Books, LLC

Please allow 4-6 weeks for delivery

ORDER FORM
URBAN BOOKS, LLC
78 E. Industry Ct
Deer Park, NY 11729

Name: (please print): _____

Address: _____

City/State: _____

Zip: _____

QTY	TITLES	PRICE
	Loving Dasia	$14.95
	Material Girl	$14.95
	Moth To A Flame	$14.95
	Mr. High Maintenance	$14.95
	My Little Secret	$14.95
	Naughty	$14.95
	Naughty 2	$14.95
	Naughty 3	$14.95
	Queen Bee	$14.95
	Say It Ain't So	$14.95
	Snapped	$14.95
	Snow White	$14.95

Shipping and handling-add $3.50 for 1st book, then $1.75 for each additional book.

Please send a check payable to:

Urban Books, LLC

Please allow 4-6 weeks for delivery

ORDER FORM
URBAN BOOKS, LLC
78 E. Industry Ct
Deer Park, NY 11729

Name: (please print): _____

Address: _____

City/State: _____

Zip: _____

QTY	TITLES	PRICE
	Spoil Rotten	$14.95
	Supreme Clientele	$14.95
	The Cartel	$14.95
	The Cartel 2	$14.95
	The Cartel 3	$14.95
	The Dopefiend	$14.95
	The Dopeman Wife	$14.95
	The Prada Plan	$14.95
	The Prada Plan 2	$14.95
	Where There Is Smoke	$14.95
	Where There Is Smoke 2	$14.95

Shipping and handling-add $3.50 for 1st book, then $1.75 for each additional book.
Please send a check payable to:
Urban Books, LLC
Please allow 4–6 weeks for delivery